Author Vanessa Wrixon

CW00458049

Book Title Temptation

Vanessa Wrixon

© 2021

Self-published

(devilvness@yahoo.co.uk)

Thank you for buying my book

Hope you enjoy reading it

Vanessa

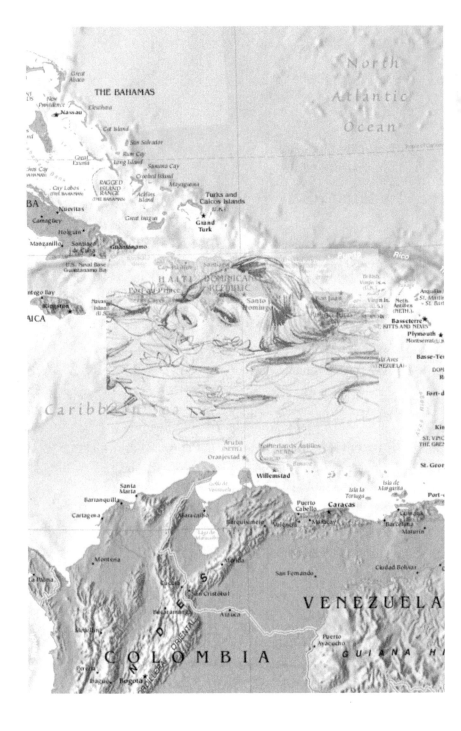

Chapter 1

Since taking over the running of the Alise local newspaper, I have made sure we remain the best paper by reporting on some amazing stories. I am also quite proud that I have managed to set up some international links as well, so we can now collaborate with the BBC and CNN. We have even signed a new contract with a mobile network.

Television news viewing and printed newspaper circulations have declined somewhat over the last few years, as our younger generation, have shifted more to downloading and viewing on social media and apps via their phone, so by working together, it ensures the jobs for my staff are safe. I know I have achieved a lot and should be content, but there is something still gnawing away at me, I am hungry for more, restless, I need something else, something different in my life, but what, poses the question?

It's not a personal relationship that's for sure, Goldie had taken it upon herself to set me up on a few dates, apparently I needed a boyfriend, however, none of them suited what I wanted in a man, they were either handsome with absolutely zero personality or they had fantastic personality but looked like the back end of a bus. Anyway I'm proud to be a strong single woman, I'm steadier in my emotions and more confident than I have ever felt. I have learnt lots of skills along the way to help me to develop a stronger psychology, including resilience and independence. I can take care of myself, so I'll be just fine without a man in my life for now.

What I needed was a different job. I am fed up of being an open-minded editor who understands the importance of democracy in our region, in particular, where dictatorships can dominate due to the social structure of our fragile democratic system. My good instincts and dealings over the years with the Caribbean people and their sometimes, negative bad-minded culture, made it easy for me to know how to handle them. I also made sure I kept in contact with my contributing writers and prided myself on excellent communication skills, I was always there to assist them should they need it, and help guide them in the right directions.

I tried to be a role model like my old boss from my very first job on the newspaper in Sussex. Dennis Markey, I will always remember him, he was a larger than life, jovial character, an expert on how to write clear and concisely, he made it look so easy. He was amazing, helping and supporting reporters and people in the community from different diversities and ethnic backgrounds, he viewed everyone as individuals and helped them accordingly. He was an effective editor with strong personal communication skills, investing as much time as was needed in his reporters, talking through story ideas and flushing out unique story angles.

However, since starting my journalistic career in those early days, things have changed in the media profession. I am fully aware that we all have to move with the times and adapt to changes over the years, but it just isn't journalism anymore, it's more like a puppet show. At times it feels like all we seem to do is pull strings in order to gobble up the worst of the worst, the more violent or shocking the stories are, the better. If we can report on smarter stories than other papers, it will keep us the best and most lucrative newspaper on the Island. The whole journalism, media industry have become far too greedy and unfor⁺unately I am a part of it.

We don't seem to have an 'off-switch,' only the most immoral and those without any scruples amongst us are victors and so it goes on. Morality is for losers and the winners, are the ones constantly pushing the bar to the extreme. The journalists of days gone by used to collaborate together, they were seen as heroes, reporting news whilst putting themselves in dangerous situations. But nowadays, we no longer need to play by any rules, step on the wrong toes and it isn't a matter of bribery or negotiation anymore, you are taken down a dark side street, roughed up or maybe even end up with a bullet in your back.

Besides, here in the Caribbean, the new breed of journalists are 'Barbie and Ken dolls,' it's all about their image, they have very little substance between their ears. Oh how it's changed, what once was the shining age of journalism, one that rooted out the corruption, had now become a corrupt industry itself.

Perhaps it was obvious where it was all leading, turning society's watchdog into a guard dog for the powerful.

At the Alise we see the news as it's happening instead of getting recaps the next day with the rise of the internet and the 24/7 news channels directly at our fingertips. We try to be the first to break any story, leaving little time to fact check first. The rush to be first often leads to misinformation being published, causing confusion and sometimes outrage. What used to be a cardinal sin is now less of an issue, because being the first to hit publish is such a priority.

The one thing I do miss most about the 'good old days' of journalism is time. We have to be fast, there is simply no time to become deeply engrossed or to develop and ponder on our stories. True investigative journalism is an art that is slowly fading. One of the main reasons is that the money isn't there for it anymore, doing a real investigative piece takes a lot of time, which in turn takes a lot of money. So I have decided that I don't want this type of superficial existence for me or for the Alise anymore.

Chapter 2

I was sat staring out of my office, listening to the noises that are a sort of fabric that weave into the matter of this place, into my matter too, they get into my soul and become part of me, it was market day you see.

Outside, the market had a heart, a rhythm and a beat, like music, that brought it alive. The crowds have a life of their own, their vibrant clothes shining and shimmering in the morning light, lots of people moving like enchanting shoals of fish. There is loud chatter between sellers and buyers, old friends catching up and others just propping up a lamp post, idling the day away. It's busy that's for sure, but the hustle and bustle brings a life to this market which I wouldn't want to be without, its the good heartbeat of the town.

I continued to watch and reminisce about old times, my pencil balanced firmly in my mouth like a rolled cigarette when Goldie strolled in. "an envelope special delivery fah yuh" she uttered in her loud Caribbean accent "What, how weird!" I took the brown envelope from her and looked at the outside, post marked BVI. I couldn't think who I knew in the British Virgin Islands or why I would get post addressed to me here. For the most part it was usually an email that pinged its way to the Alise 'for the attention of' so normally, the only post to actually be delivered to the office were bills or junk mail.

Goldie stood facing me as I ripped open the envelope and extracted a typed note. I looked up pensively, "Wah a in empress" Goldie asked seeing me slightly unnerved. "Not sure, it seems to be from a BVI paper inviting me and one of my reporters to take a trip to Anegada all expenses paid." "Eh ah con" Goldie replied. "Mek wi investigate more, Nuh worry yuhself" with that and before I could digest it all, she snatched the letter and its envelope from my hand and disappeared back to her desk.

I followed her to my door stunned by this flash of energy. I stood watching her for a minute, mesmerised as she went into tornado mode tapping away on her keyboard shifting in her chair like she had 'St vitas dance," a whirling dervish. I smiled to myself as I returned to my desk, looking at the half organised clutter that I needed to address staring back at me, willing me on. Trouble was, where on earth do I start?

My trusty mahogany desk consisted of three drawers on the right hand side which I kept reasonably tidy, there wasn't much room to stash anything away in them and on the top, sat my MacBook Pro along with my mobile, ok so tidy so far. On the left of my desk sat a pile of neat paperwork next to a tin half full of chewed pens and pencils. That could easily be sorted too. However it was the cabinet that need most of my attention and energy. It was piled high with paperwork stacked into a higgledy-pigedly mess that could topple over at any given moment and send my office into absolute disarray.

If my mother was here now, she would be appalled, she would tell me that tackling this mess isn't just about clearing up, its about the ability to take control of my life with a steady consistency. Once tidiness is mastered it can be transferred to many areas of life, emotionally, practically and academically. I smiled to myself once again, good old mum!

I glanced back at the door, still no Goldie, she must be doing some in depth research. My eyes suddenly caught the attention of my water dispenser standing alone in the corner almost empty, a lonely jam jar placed underneath its tap kept it company. I was so lazy, I could actually go and get some paper cups from the storeroom, but I hate that room, I can never find anything so try not to go there, usually the office junior is more than happy to help the editor, i.e., me! If not Goldie will go, she loves it, she says its her Shangri-La, a place to forget the world and become absorbed in the chance of discovery. Note to self, I must ask Goldie to get cups, for now my jam jar will suffice. I had found the jar in my bag one day, no idea why it was there or how it got there, but it worked well as a cup, I just need to remember to wash it out.

A few hours later, having still not tackled the paperwork stack, I was engrossed in reading the days final edits before they went to print, when Goldie swung round my door. "Jaz" she screamed, I jumped. "Get ih, ah real local paper

confirmed ih paid fi by an anonymous person ahuu waah wi tuh write ah story bout dem an di BVI, Mi spoke tuh di mon deh." "And this would be who exactly," I asked finishing of one of the edits, "BVI Beacon Newspaper" she replied.
She sat down opposite me and continued, "Apparently eh a an invitation by one addi most prestigious an luxurious travel consortia dat write fah di BVI. Di newspaper hav joined forces wid di British Virgin Islands Tourist Board." She paused momentarily to take a breath, "Wi will collaborate wid di BVI an tug help market di destination by a duh ah spread an help lure travellers tuh unique an exclusive bespoke holidays eena Anegada. Di BVI newspaper si dis as ah huge accomplishment fi fi dem Island an a very enthusiastic bout wi a go Dem tink will bring tourists tuh waan unique experiential travel tuh Anegada inna fucha."

So for those who have absolutely no idea what she has just said and for me to be absolutely sure. It is an invitation by one of the most prestigious and luxurious travel consortia that write for the BVI. The newspaper has decided to join forces with the British Virgin Islands Tourist Board. Our main aim at the Alise would be to collaborate with the BVI and them help market the destination by doing an article for social media and a travel app, in order to help lure travellers to unique and bespoke holidays in Anegada and in the process gain ideas for unique travel experiences within the BVI in the future. The BVI newspaper view this as a huge accomplishment for their Island if it comes off and are very enthusiastic about us helping them, they have picked the best newspaper in the Caribbean allegedly!

I was completely at a loss for words, so shifted awkwardly in my chair, Mmhm, how very strange, it somehow didn't have a good ring to it. Brilliant, just when I thought I was the master of my thoughts, fate is taking on a new turn. I felt afraid again, triggered by what could be a real threat and by all those memories of threats. Hopefully I managed to remain in control on the outside and hide it from Goldie as I regained some composure.

However in my head, my thoughts decided to go on a car journey, taking me to different places, trying to figure out what was going on. Each destination may have been beautiful, bewitching even, but because my mind was in a complete whirl with many different perspectives, all I actually managed to say was, "Ok, thanks Goldie, you have certainly done your research, do we have a contact name?" She shook her head, "Just let me do a bit more digging and let me sleep on it before we take this any further, I just need to be 100% sure on this." Goldie sighed and shrugged, allowing her response to have the benefit of both empathic and logical thought. "Ah course Yuh haffi bi sure Jaz, Buh ih appears tuh bi legitimate."

She was right, it did seem legitimate on the surface, but it suddenly brought back all the memories of when I was sent to the press reception at Iberville, a huge mansion in St Kitts, to do a piece for the Alise on its owners Lord and Lady Wrexham. The estate was of historical value, being in her family and involved in the sugar cane industry for years, but Lord Edward Wrexham had wanted to turn it into a resort to make money from the local tourism industry. Lady Amélie Wrexham was absent from the press launch reception but around the same time, a woman's body had been washed up on the beach and there was a huge cover up operation involving the local police. I began asking too many questions and was kidnapped and held hostage, so you can understand my hesitation with this out of the blue trip to Anegada.

Two of my dear friends, one a colleague from the paper at the time, Winston and Candice, my friend from the morgue tried to help me escape, but in doing so they lost their lives. Eventually, I found out that Lord Wrexham and Tilly, also my old boss from the newspaper had murdered Lady Amélie Wrexham as well as Winston and Candice once they had served their purpose and the black mail options had run out. Tilly put me through hell to try to ensure my silence, however I still managed to report the both of them to the High Commission and Police Federation, there was even a big spread in the Alise featuring my story.

They were both arrested and following the court case, were imprisoned for life. However with the assistance of some corrupt officials and lawyers, they managed to escape and end up in a fight with a local fisherman in a bar, they then fled for their lives and have not been sighted since.

Luckily I had just finished the edits and wanted to call it a day, I wasn't going to be able to concentrate for too much longer. My best option was to retreat to my shack for a well earned glass of wine and some food, which I must remember to buy from the mini mart on my way home. My journey home and evening alone would give me more time to think straight. "Goldie, can you take this to print for me, do you want a lift home?" I yelled from my office, "Nah get ah date at Ziggy's Waah fi cum?" She replied as she wandered in to collect the edits. "I'll give it a miss if it's ok with you, see you in the morning."

With that she blew me a kiss and disappeared off to Colby's print room. I tided my desk as best I could, closed down the office laptop and picked up my bag and mobile before strolling outside to the heat of my car.

Goldie was my perfect employee, she put everyone at ease and drew them into liking her, she could get us the sweetest deals, taking over our competitors for a song while they grinned and hung on her every word. Since Petra, my old boss had left and returned to England, we had become even closer, you could say we were best friends as well as work colleagues, we just clicked.

She was similar to Candice in a way, I looked up at the sky, a single cloud floating like a white wispy ribbon in the blue sky, delicately forming a half-spiral, an angel force of artistic creative genius in the atmosphere. Here I digress for a moment. Oh, poor Candice, she and I were such good friends, she died too soon, her life brought to an abrupt end whilst trying to protect me from the perils of Ed Wrexham and Tilly Colspur. She could be anywhere in the universe, yet my bonds of love for her will always remain. Gosh, had it really been three years since those strange events at Iberville!

Despite being similar to Candice, Goldie was her own person, she had a kind of brutal honesty that could test most friendships, but I appreciated it. I always knew where I stood with her, she was generous to a fault, both with her time and her possessions. She had very few friends so her loyalty to those who stuck with her was really fierce. There is a saying here in the Caribbean. "Some friends are for a reason, some are for a season and some are for life." She was for life and I loved her.

Chapter 3

A short drive later, I reached the mini-mart, it was quite odd in looks, wedged between two tall dilapidated buildings, it looked squashed in. The sign outside read, 'Bobby's Mart' it was old and some of letters were becoming illegible, when where the paint was peeling off from the constant exposure to the sun and salt, but at least the owner kept his windows spotlessly clean so you could see inside and his hand drawn sales posters always enticed you in.

Once inside the mart, it almost resembled a corridor, far longer than it was wide with shelving spanning both sides stocked full of goodies. There was no theme or organisation to the layout, it was all just crammed together rather than artistically placed. Rows upon rows of mixed tinned and boxed goods, fruit, veg and snorkel masks sandwiched between alcoholic beverages that ranged from a variety of rum to Carib beer to wine with household and personal sundries hidden amongst them. Bobby's Mart had everything you could ever want all under one roof which was good for the Caribbean, usually you had to go to three or four shops to get what you needed and even then you are extremely lucky if you get everything on your shopping list.

Bobby's Mart was the best, luckily for me it was on route to my shack and is well known by us locals. It has been in the Edness family for generations, Agwe the present owner, is third generation. He knows all of his customers by name, which gives his shop that little bit of 'je ne sais quoi.' Sometimes people just pop in to chat and pass the time of day, he doesn't seem to mind, he often describes his little store as the heart of the community and he runs it with great pride and joy.

Unfortunately the place is a mecca for petty thieves, because of the way the shop is arranged it is difficult for Agwe to see anything from the cash desk. So often kids enter in pairs, then one will buy some candy from the counter and keep Agwe busy, whilst the other stuffs their backpack full of more expensive goods from the back of the shop that they can then flog by the roadside later. By the time Agwe has noticed anything untoward, coupled with the slow speed at which he travels, means they are long gone, along with his produce.

Nothing ever gets done about it, it just accepted as the norm. Having said that, when it gets too bad and the mart owners complain to the Crime Prevention Officer, Inspector Shole Danner, who to be honest has tried to implement a variety of crime prevention programmes here on St Kitts, which have included improving community relations, unfortunately it has all just been met with resistance. At present he has resorted to enlisting us here at the Alise. We publish a statement in our paper on an adhoc basis, well as and when he emails me one, it doesn't really do anything, I doubt people even read it. It is more a word of caution or advice.

The last one was short and sweet we printed read.
A word of caution from your Crime Prevention Officer.
I urge all of you not to shoplift, you will be prosecuted if caught.
Please can everyone be vigilant throughout our stores especially when they are crowded.
To any persons who are attempting to shoplift. I urge you,Do not shoplift. Be honest.
Inspector Shole Danner.

If you ask me, it lacks punch and I should stop putting it in the paper, but it fills any small space left over.

I finished my shopping and stayed for the obligatory chat with Agwe before making my excuses to leave and drive back home laden with bags of food and red label wine of course. I was much improved these days, although I still drank probably more than I should, but nowadays I cooked more meals from scratch rather than buying ready made ones, I felt much better for it. It was Goldie's inspiration that sparked me into cooking, she told me it gives you the chance to relax, become healthy and be in a different mode from work. A few lessons from her and I was hooked, she made me feel at ease when mess happened or things went wrong, we just laughed and made jokes and generally had a good time.

At first I wasn't very good, but the more I paid attention to her details and tips, the better I got and the more fun it was. I learned not only how to cook but how to grease my pans properly and measure my ingredients correctly. Now I am free to make up my own recipes and change things around, I love that. It's just as with anything I guess, you have to learn the rules before you can break them in your own artistic way. I still don't try anything too adventurous at the moment unless Goldie is with me, but it's a start and I have impressed my mother with my new culinary skills, which is always a Bertie bonus in my books.

Chapter 4

Reaching home, I checked my postbox and retrieved yet another brown envelope postmarked BVI, identical to the one that came to the Alise. I placed it on the table as I unpacked the shopping bags, took out a bottle of wine from the fridge and poured myself a rather large glass before strolling outside with the envelope in my hand. I sat on my deck where the sun was just beginning to think about cooling itself down for the day, took a couple of sips from the glass, then ripped open the envelope which, rather oddly, was in pristine condition. It was as if it had travelled in some sort of steampress rather than in the hand of a local mailman, they were never particularly careful and most mail was mangled or torn on arrival.

I pulled out a typed card invitation and read it:
I am delighted to invite you plus a reporter from the Alise to enjoy an all expenses paid trip to Anegada. You will both travel business class, stay in a beach front villa and there will be $1000 to spend. You deserve a break, come and visit the Island and use this opportunity to promote Anegada to your readers.

There was an editor contact from the BVI Beacon, who had also included details of our assignment, along with two open ended airline tickets to Tortola, ferry tickets to Anegada, airline and ferry schedules and who we would be met by at the ferry dock on our arrival. It was very precise, all we had to do was contact them with dates. This was all very sudden and strange! Lots of questions begin to spun around my head, annoyingly no answers accompanied them. Why the Alise, why me, why now, how do they know where I live, am I being stalked what is going on? Normally I would have some sort of pre warning from our media network at some story that was going to break or a tentative email to test the waters first.

I suppose one saving grace was that there were at least contact details so maybe I should get in touch and check this out further. But to send plane tickets, even if they were open ended, surely there should have been be some sort of contact before paying the air fare of people you didn't know, what if we refused to come, had work commitments or had no valid passports? Probably not the latter in the world of media!

I was frustrated, I had no answers, none of this made any sense. I sipped more wine in the hope that it would energise my brain function and shed some light on the situation. My heart skipped a beat as the porch door banged, I had forgotten to close it properly, thank goodness that's all it was. I was scared again, actually quite scared. I felt the fear in my chest once more waiting to take over, sitting like an angry bull propelling me towards an anxiety attack as the memories of three years ago at Iberville started to emerge. No, no, I was not going to let this happen.

From a recent book I had been reading, funnily enough, called 'The Confusion' it states that confusion is when fear scatters the higher thoughts to promote the chance of a subconscious solution finding its way through. Change to a place of loving support and calmness and the confusion goes because logical thought and empathy are now the survival advantage. If the brain believes one has time to think in safety, it will begin to think, to focus.

So I need to put the book into practice and take my mind off my immediate thoughts, I looked out to sea there were pelicans diving in groups of three, funny creatures, large and clumsy, enjoying themselves diving and splatting in the water, sometimes claiming a fish other times just having fun. I took a deep breath, there's something about being at one with nature, it helps my fear evaporate, maybe the scent of fresh air reminds me of freedom, maybe I just made that up. However, what I do know is every sense of nature converges into an energised joy, a bond that is tangible and blended and it helps me to relax.

I took another sip of wine and heard my mothers voice echo in my head, "Jasmine yesterday is history, tomorrow is a mystery and today? Well, today is the present! Think about the future that awaits you and go get it." I still felt somewhat unnerved despite sipping more wine from my glass. Why is life such a rollercoaster, astounding me one minute with its sudden feeling of wonder and achievement, but then in the next breath, leaving me feeling despondent and in a complete state of melancholy? Despite everything, I still sit here anticipating the possibility of a thrilling adventure or a deep dark mystery depending on which way I decide to look at it.

I decided the best thing to do was to video call mum. It was late afternoon here so evening where she was, I added five hours and decided she would still be awake. Mum was great, she was always ready to offer up sound advice and put my mind at ease. She was a reliable and safe place for me always to go to, she was the strongest and softest person I have ever known. I pulled up her number from my favourites list and waited patiently as it rang.

After a couple of minutes she was connected and appeared on screen wearing her favourite apron, she was cooking dad's supper as he had arrived home from the pub later than usual. Anyway, this apron was a staple of my childhood, patterned with all things British, from teapots, bull dogs to the palace guards, I smiled, apart from the garish apron, on this particular occasion she seemed to also resemble a disco ball.

She had overdone the red lipstick and her lovely platinum hair looked as if it had just had a shock, no comb had been near it on this particular day. Beneath her apron, she wore a blue cotton dress covered in yellow primroses styled in a way that resembled the 1950s. She took great pride in removing her apron and showing me, twirling unsteadily around, apparently she had made it out of old curtain material she had found in a box when she had tidied out the loft!

She was always one for surprises, each day a multitude of tiny things that made me smile and laugh from my lips to my toes, I loved that about her. Anyway despite her particular quirky attire, she was still wearing her warming smile and her kind eyes still gleamed making me feel instantly at ease. It made me remember the aromas and warmth she brought me when I lived at home, my memories of my mother's love, those small moments of affection that built the foundation of who I am today.

After the usual conversation about what was happening in Henfield she told me about the odd new neighbour called Mrs Pollock who had moved in next door. She grew strange tall plants that smelt, local gossip said it was cannabis although there was no concrete evidence of this. Apparently there was an altercation when the village policeman went around to investigate and Mrs Pollock would not let him in. Despite being in uniform she thought he was a murderer and hit him over the head with a rolled up newspaper.

My humour started to bubble around me as I laughed, "What a loonie," I said giggling. There was a little rise in the corner of mums mouth and her eyes gleamed as she replied. "Jasmine Tormolis, it is not funny, she's not a loonie, just creative, free spirited and a bit barking mad. Your father won't even talk to her, he is afraid of being hit, she is quite strong you know." We laughed even more, it was like she was sitting right next to me.

I explained what was happening here with work, how I wanted something different and no, I still didn't have a boyfriend, etc. Eventually I brought up the subject of the strange invitation to Anegada from the BVI Beacon newspaper, she listened intently taking everything on board.

I told her about how it had arrived in the post at work and here at the shack, rather than in an email format from the prestigious and luxurious travel consortia that promote the BVI. Goldie and I would collaborate with the newspaper and help market the destination by doing a spread in the hope we could lure more travellers to holiday in Anegada. Mum listened whilst she made odd facial expressions, when I remarked how off putting it was, she explained it was just exercises to keep her face muscles tight, she did it daily!

Despite appearances, she had actually been inwardly digesting what I was telling her, ready with a strategy that was several moves ahead of what I was ever capable of. Her words had a kindness and a slight concern too them, but that's natural I suppose. "Jaz, I have to admit it does all sound a bit strange. But you said you have details of a contact and Goldie had investigated the paper. I have had a quick look on my pad," (course she had). "It all seems above board, there is a BVI Beacon paper and they are looking to improve tourism in Anegada, working with the tourist industry."

She was so funny, trying to keep up with technology, but she coped well and seemed to be able to work most things even if it was a phone call to me to help her if she got stuck. Dad, on the other hand still used paper and pen, he liked snail mail. "Technology has accelerated the world to the brink of catastrophe," he would say looking up from his newspaper each morning. Mum would just sigh and reply, "Move with the times, you silly man, look how far we've come from apes figuring out hammer and rock." I remember we all used to just fall about laughing, it's true what they say, laughter is infectious. They do get on well, as long as dad obeys and respects his curfew, they have a steady quiet lifetime of mutual affection and dedication.

As much as I appreciated mum's advice, there was always a sermon lurking. "Jaz, my darling girl, never be like a flag dependant on the capricious breeze for its' direction. Be the captain of your own ship, chart a course and navigate with determination through any choppy waters. You alone are the master of your own destiny and responsible for the keeping of your humanity in the harshness of life. Do that and, no matter what happens, dad and I will always be proud of who you are." I was completely lost after that, no idea what she was trying to say. "Thanks mum, duly noted but what on earth are you are on about, do you think it would be safe to go?"

The facial expressions stopped as she looked quizzically at the phone screen. "what I mean my darling is, be brave in any storm, push your fears aside and walk past it with nonchalant ease." "Mum please stop with the speeches, are you reading these from your iPad?" No darling, from the big book of quotes, I borrowed from the library, it's very interesting, look." With that she held up a big red thick book, I peered at it trying to look interested. "Lovely mum, but do you think it is safe to go?" She yawned, smiled and turned off the oven at the same time as dad pottered through with a wave of his hand, he knew better than interrupt women chatting.

Chapter 5

We must have been on the phone for over an hour, how time flies when you have a conversation that flows easily with listening, intelligent responses and laughter from both parties, that's what happens when mothers and daughters connect. Eventually a decision was reached, I should go, it would do me good to have a break after everything that had happened in the past. Despite my reservations that there may be more to this trip than I had been told, she assured me that I could look after myself and I would have Goldie with me. The life-changing traumas at Iberville were a one off, nothing like that would happen again. This offer was, after all, a free return trip with tickets, I might even find a boyfriend, oh mum, stop please!

After we had reached a conclusion about the trip, we spent a further half an hour or so as I watched the sun go down and she saw the moon rise over Henfield as she handed dad his meal. I then took her inside to my kitchen as she wanted to see the contents of my fridge and cupboards. You know what mothers are like, rather than take my word that I was stocked up and eating well, she had to be sure for herself. Thankfully my fridge and cupboards were full, otherwise money would be transferred into my account, non perishable food parcels would arrive and another lecture would begin.

As we ended the video call, it was really getting quite dark, where mum was and her supper would need reheating. She wanted to stay online and watch the sunset go down with me, but it would be another couple of hours before it revealed its red-velvet sky of fire, which then would become an orange ball replaced with a special kind of warm blackness, holding the stars and helping them shine brighter. So we agreed to do that another time.

I wandered into the dining room and switched on my laptop. I had once owned a computer but it suddenly died a very inconvenient death, right in the middle of an article I was writing at the time. Luckily for me, Colby managed to extract all the information for me and backed everything up on a drive he happened to have lying around. I was really grateful, however it meant that I had to invest in a brand new and much sleeker, shiny laptop. That was about a year ago now, then top-of-the-range, now hardly worth its weight in bricks but still it serves its purpose and I can't afford to keep updating to newer models.

A flashing white arrow appeared on an otherwise blank screen awaiting its next instruction, I typed in BVI Beacon newspaper. Their website contained lots of information, I scanned through its various menu options, it was defiantly legitimate.

I read; The BVI Beacon is a weekly newspaper founded in 1984 and published on the island of Tortola in the British

Virgin Islands. In 1991, the paper expanded and moved into a traditional West Indian style house on Russell Hill Road, it soon became the best weekly paper for the whole of the British Virgin Islands. In recent months the BVI Beacon has been working with the local tourism industry and the creative industries, newspapers and magazines and social media to boost tourism. The plans are to run a series of features on the individual Islands, including promoting Anegada's cultural heritage.

Ok, so this was the real deal, but it still didn't really explain why the Alise, myself and one of my reporters had been chosen. I know we were the best newspaper on the Island and our recent deals with the BBC and CNN had raised our profile, but St Kitts is not exactly local to the British Virgin Islands so we are not an obvious choice. I decided I would email them from work tomorrow to clarify a few things.

I wandered into the kitchen and took a bowl of soup out of the fridge, reheating it in the microwave, I had made a batch of soup as my bowl of tomatoes was looking a bit squelchy and they needed using up. I took the heated bowl back to my desk and between mouthfuls, found myself looking at travel guides. There are loads of them, the best two were Fodors Guide and the Lonely planet, I found myself immersed.

According to the Fodors travel guide, Anegada is a coral Island in the British Virgin Islands, its name is derived from Spanish origins meaning drowned Island. It is the only coral

Island in the Virgin Islands' volcanic chain and hosts the most striking coral reefs with clear springs bubbling up from the coral beds rich in needle fish, bonefish, stingrays, parrot fish and other marine life. The Island is a snorkelers and scuba divers paradise, taking in all the reef's mazes, tunnels and drops and Horseshoe Reef is renowned for its numerous shipwrecks. Fantastic, I loved to dive and snorkel, but hadn't had any opportunities recently. I may even be able to kite surf, I have always wanted to do that and already had one lesson.

The Lonely Planet guide suggests that this is a beachgoers delight with calm and quiet shores, including Cow Wreck Beach, Flash of Beauty, Bones Bight and Loblolly Bay, all of which boast secluded white sandy beaches. There are waterside restaurants whose speciality is seafood, especially the local Spiny Lobster. On the wildlife front, the Island is home to flamingos, rock iguanas and rare sea lavender, whatever that is. Looking at the photos on the websites, it did look like a beautiful and inviting place. I couldn't believe how flat and low lying it was. The coral atoll in the British Virgin Islands is only about twenty-eight feet above sea level, so a complete contrast to the hills here in St Kitts.

There is something about the pure and warm Caribbean in general that has a magic to it. Most of the people here have expanding smiles, igniting music and invite the gift of dance, a great vibe. I guess that's why tourists say they fall in love with the Caribbean. I certainly love St Kitts and Nevis and I am sure I will love Anegada.

I closed down the laptop and sat back in my chair, there was an explosion of excitement in my brain. More possibilities than I was conscious of, but I had hundreds of ideas in my buzz of electricity. It was the calling card of adventure, of paths awaiting my feet. Whatever was ahead could be a great challenge, but it was my adventure to take, I smiled, we just had to go!

Chapter 6

The following day at work, I had a video conference call first thing, with various editors from all over the globe. A halo of holograms organised about a computer, sitting there as if by some astral projection. Luckily it only happened once a quarter, it enabled all the papers to get together and talk about new technology, stories, etc and how best it could suit their papers. We also had to produce financial forecasts and audit results, all of which we made up, quite mundane really.

The only excitement it brings, is watching everybody's expressions and body language as everyone tries to speak at once, each one with the best to offer, it makes it entertaining and more bearable. Their voices get louder and louder in order to make themselves heard, then comes the arguing about nothing, for nothing, to gain nothing. The impersonal nature of these link-ups makes us forget who we are and what we are to one another as full on "Hulk-mode" engages with fists banging on tables and tempers rising. I smirked, I feel like doing something mischievous, I know that sounds childish I grant you, but I need to break up this monotony.

I was bored stiff and didn't wish to interrupt the flow of Julian Wade, an editor of the 'Oklahoma' which was the "Worst Newspaper in America." The paper only focused on right-wing political views and he was no exception. He sat there, his over-indulged form squeezed into his aristocratic Power Suit, trying to make himself imposing. During his rant I could feel myself drifting off thinking about the trip to Anegada and making notes for my email to the BVI Beacon.

As I re-entered reality after putting the world on hold, I found the topic had moved on, but luckily there still wasn't any actual 'conferring' going on. That would imply that everyone would have to listen at some point and take into consideration each others perspectives but to be honest, no one was doing that. Could we really integrate new information and 'live edit' our own brains or were we all going to leave the call with the same bias and static opinions we entered with? Sadly, despite us being intelligent adults I feel the latter is an appropriate assessment.

As the conference call had now descended into arm waving and rude gesticulations, Goldie began to make silly, distorted, humorous facial expressions at me from my doorway. Desperately trying not to laugh, I shooed her away with a really weird hand gesture, as if my hand had gone into some form of spasm. I managed to make my excuses and abruptly end the call.

What a complete waste of a couple of hours out of my life, which I would never get back. Now for some real work, I read the days' edits so far and was impressed with the output from my team. I also plucked up courage and started to tackle the mammoth task of clearing the stack of paperwork on the filing cabinet. Well, to be honest, some of it had toppled over in the night as the cleaner had left my window slightly ajar, I couldn't leave it lying on the floor, what would that look like to the others, not a great example of an organised boss!

I prided myself on high standards and strived for efficient organisation as far as the paper was concerned. As Editor, I needed to be a good leader, one who walks to the beat of a steady drum, however at this present time there was so much disorganisation and untidiness in my role as the boss, how on earth could I expect my employees to attain high standards.

Don't get me wrong, I am all for fun, I can be funny too, we are all complex and simple. Different needs arise at different times, we all wear different hats for different roles and switch gears when we need to. I remain my most ridiculous self in private, but the commander in public.

I didn't see Goldie again until late morning when she flew into my office at breakneck speed plonking a glass of lemongrass lemonade and a large piece of ginger cake she had made the previous day on my desk. She startled me as she arrived to the point where the pile of papers I had picked up off of the floor and were now held in my hand flew off and spread themselves into more disarray. "Goldie, for goodness sake, I have picked them up once already". "Hush tap a di tap," she replied, we both laughed as she helped me gather them back up and place them in a neat pile on my desk.

"Did yuh fine anyting out bout trip? Wah did yuh decide? Did yuh email dem" she asked as she stood munching through her own piece of ginger cake in front of me. "Too many questions Goldie." She smiled and dropped a piece of ginger cake on the floor, as she picked it up and put it in her mouth she said, "Mi tink deh a more tuh dis trip buh nuh sure wah. Will wi bi eena danger?" "That crumb could have anything on it now it's been on the floor." I giggled, "Cleaners bin nuh she? ah bit ah dirt nah guy hat yuh Jaz." The sound of our laughter became so loud that I could see through my open door the rest of the office stop and look, smiles appeared on their faces, we had a soul elevator moment for all those that heard it.

I gained back my self control and uttered. "I think you're right Goldie, there is more to this trip, I have a strange feeling that someone from past events is trying to catch up with me, but I don't understand why, I thought it was all laid to rest." "Yuh tink eh cud bi Tilly or Ed?" "Possibly, but why, why the BVI Beacon, Why would they contact a newspaper? They were supposed to be in hiding." Gosh now I have all the unanswered questions.

I pulled out the card invitation and plane tickets from my bag, "These came to my shack yesterday." I told her. "Yuh stalking yuh." She said spraying a mouthful of cake crumbs over the tickets as she held them in her hand. "Thank you Goldie, that is not helpful." I replied retrieving the tickets and brushing the crumbs into the bin. It was a conundrum I must admit.

Neither Ed (formerly Lord Wrexham of Iberville fame) nor Tilly, his runaway lover had been heard of since they disappeared from Ziggy's bar after the fight with Mogsey and that was three and a half years ago. They went into hiding and there had been no further sightings of them since, well none that I am aware of. Local gossip, if it is to be believed, says that they fled the Island and were now living overseas somewhere protected by a piracy gang.

I am not entirely convinced that this is true unless they have completely managed to change their looks and names. Since the Commissioner and Police Federation had joined forces with the Ministry for National Security, the Caribbean police force have had to up their game. Corruption in the force is being tackled and crime rates have decreased, there is also more transparency and openness with the media.

One of the major improvements since the union of authorities is to ensure that all entrances to the Caribbean; airports, ferry docks and marinas, are now closely monitored and manned twenty-four seven by the police or security agencies to cut down on drug trafficking, which has become rife here.

I sat down in my chair, I could no longer resist the aroma from my desk, a perfect blend of spicy and sweet, a delicious and moist auric brown dark ginger cake still stared back at me. Goldie pushed it nearer to me announcing that it was criminally easy to make, even I could make it, that was all very well but eating it would be a crime for my waistline. My tastebuds went into overdrive, telling me it will taste heavenly, so eat it! A brief battle with my conscience, willpower caved and then one bite was all I needed, I knew instantly that this cake will be added to my growing list of indulgences.

I followed it down with a large slug of chilled lemonade. Drinking in this heat feels like the greatest luxury on earth, I felt a chill run down my throat, followed by a numbness creeping in to my brain, I coughed, Goldie laughed. "That's wah hap'n wen yuh drinkz too much fizz too faas." I raised my eyebrows as I composed myself and finished off the ginger cake and lemonade, licking my fingers to remove the last remnants of sweet stickiness. "Goldie, let's go, if we stick together like limpets we should be fine and if by some madness Ed and Tilly are involved, I think I want to find out what they want from me and what is going on!" Goldie's facial expression showed an agreed satisfaction, she smiled in a way that told me I had accomplished a much needed task, even if I have used up all my thought energies in the process.

I can read her like a book, the slight curve from the corner of her mouth and her youthful confidence which she wore with a light raise of her eyebrows coupled with a quizzical but joyful look in her eyes gave her thoughts away. Now she appeared relaxed and at ease as she no longer had to keep on at me to make a decision. However, there was still a gnawing at the back of my head telling me something was not right with all this, we could be in danger if we went, fear of the unknown I suppose.

Being brave meant being afraid, or at least it did for me, so I must go. Nowadays I try to face my fears and conquer them, how else am I ever going to make any true progress in my life if I keep letting fear rule over me? I refuse to be moulded by those who want me to be conveniently placated, or expect me to shy away from the battlefields they create. If I keep telling myself I am a warrior and when faced with adversity I have the ability to think calmly and rationally, then I can conquer all!

Goldie continued to babble away at me in her own made up language, her way of encouraging and reassuring me to see all that I was capable of, she saw my strengths and could always make them stronger. So with that in mind, I got to it and pinged an email to our contact at the BVI Beacon newspaper, Mr T Meyers, with some questions that needed answers as well as agreeing to the trip, but just needed him to confirm some dates. Goldie moved behind me, leaning in, she put her hand on my shoulder as I pressed the send button and the message flew off into the great digital ether.

As it disappeared I noticed the email address I used, was different from that of the contact details cited on the BVI Beacon website, it almost seemed like a personal email address, tm947@beaconuse.com. Goldie must have noticed the concern that was taking over my facial expression, "Nut worry Jaz, Ih ok tuh bi anxious Eh ah protective mechanism Dem a deh ask yuh tuh check fi traffic before yuh cross di road." I smiled she was right. "Betta git shopping den." She squealed. Shopping, yes now that was a good idea.

Chapter 7

The rest of the day saw a return to normal operations. I tried hard to concentrate on the rest of the edits and then tackled more of the paperwork on top of the filing cabinet. Unfortunately, my mind kept wandering off in different directions, I found myself every now and again looking at websites and making lists of all I needed to do to prepare for the trip, including shopping for new clothes, so everything took me twice as long.

Just as I managed to get myself focused on work properly and not think about the trip, an email flew into my inbox. It was from the BVI Beacon, Mr T Meyers confirming details of the trip to Anegada.

Hi Jasmine, I have set the wheels in motion for you and Goldie to arrive with us on the 16th March, three weeks from now. Air tickets booked with SKB airlines from Robert L.Bradshaw International Airport St Kitts to Terrance B. Lettsome International Airport Beef Island Tortola. From there your connection to Anegada is via Tortola Fast Ferry aka, Smiths ferry. I will meet you at Anegada ferry dock and accompany you to your Cow Wreck Beach villa. I will bring you both up to speed then.
Regards, T. Meyers.

I won't bore you with all the email details, but suffice to say the rest of his email was cleverly worded in order to avoid answering any of my questions. That was ok by me as he couldn't worm his way out of it when we were face to face. It does seem slightly strange that it is still all so secretive. I would at least expect some sort of brief, in order for us to plan our article, we would normally try to do some of the research in advance, it's easier that way and makes us look more professional. I forwarded the email to Goldie and looked up the BVI Beacon again on the laptop. For some reason they seemed to have updated their website, which meant I couldn't get in to all of the menu I did previously. Mr T Meyer's name was on there as Executive Editor. I searched his profile on LinkedIn and found out quite a lot about him, no photos mind, but I did conjure up a mental image, suffice to say, I was looking forward to meeting him in more ways than one.

I'm not quite sure how it happened but when I looked up from my laptop at my office, it seemed to resemble complete carnage once more, I summoned Goldie. Immediately she was at the door, "Yuh shouted tap a di tap." I laughed "sorry didn't mean to be that loud, look at this mess, can you help me?" She nodded and quickly turned into her whirling dervish mode. "Si BVI ave changed fi dem website Duh yuh tink dem ave si ours an did tink dem did hav tuh upgrade it?" She said as she patted the neat pile of paperwork on my desk. So she had been looking to, her smirk that followed brought a look of mischief, innocent fun. We burst into fits of giggles like children, goodness knows what they thought was happening in the other office.

Finally the day came to an end, Goldie grinned, "Yuh a ah messy tap a di tap Buh mi luv yuh." I replied, "Yes, I know, I just can't seem to get through this mess." A text message sounded on my phone, she peered over as I looked. It was from my mother, reminding me that holidays and the run up to them should be about having fun and relaxing and she had sent me an email.

All very good but in this instance what she fails to understand is that there are a thousand invisible hoops to jump through before I even set off, both personally and professionally, fail to jump through any one of them and someone is bound to get angry, usually me!

I opened the email from my mother, for once Goldie was speechless, as was I. There it was staring at us both, a bikini she saw online, the top contained two small triangles of pink and purple swirl material, the bottoms much the same, two triangles held together with tassel ties. There was a written correspondence that went with the dreadful image:
Jaz shall I buy this for your trip? It is tan-through which means you don't get tan lines and it is a little see-through when it is wet. Might catch you a nice boyfriend!

I almost choked, "Mother," I said out loud, Goldie chuckled, "A yuh gwine guh fi eh den Yuh mon trapper." Without any thought I replied "No way." I texted her back immediately, just incase she had any ideas of purchasing the thing. I didn't want to offend her, so elaborated on the truth and told her I had recently bought a new one, so no need for another. "Cum pan lets guh yaad." Goldie announced and that exactly what we did.

Once indoors, I immediately plonked myself in front of my laptop with a family size packet of crisps and a large glass of wine for the second night in a row, this time I was going to surf the web for holiday clothes, or at least that was my excuse and I was sticking to it.

I didn't need to do much housework anymore, as I had employed a cleaning lady twice a week. My little shack doesn't get very dirty as it is only me here, but it always feels lighter and brighter when she has been. If I was here, working from home, she would evoke a calmness in me as I heard the furniture glide over the wooden floor and the soft sound of my broom as it sweeps. She does frequently tell me I am messy and have too much clutter to dust, I am aware of that, but time always seems to run away with me.

I will digress for a moment, my cleaning lady is called Benita, she is of a large build but confident and sassy, she's "got it going on" that's for sure. She is loud, always laughing as if she were still a child, it is who she truly is, that joy, that sound tickles everyone near her. Her dark skin has a deep richness, wrinkles showing the map of her soul. Her hair, you could sculpt, a natural God-given bounce, born to be worn loud and proud. She always sings a 'tidy time song' when she cleans, it is a homely vibe, I like it. Benita is built from love and wisdom, she has written the story of her life with the sweetest of hands.

Anyway, back to trawling the web. Online shopping is my mecca, make-up, clothes, perfume, shoes, etc, they are all my guilty pleasures. Given the opportunity, I can surf for hours taking inspiration from different sites and usually spend a lot of money which I don't always have, good job for credit cards. The down side to this magical currency is that I can't see the money so I tend to spend more and I have to find the money to pay it all back. Unfortunately there are no friendly bank managers with benefits here.

It's a good job I live in the age of online shopping, as here in the Caribbean, there aren't any what I call proper clothes shops. That is unless I want to look like a walking rainbow made from lycra or tent fabric. The Caribbean people as a whole like to express their culture by using vibrant colours, patterns and shapes. It is said that they feel a joy within and a connection to Mother Earth, the Caribbean women's fashion is designed so that they feel a part of nature, connected and cradled. They are quite proud of their (to me) dreadful fashion sense, but as I am not a true native I can get away with just wanting to look elegant in simple stylish clothes, usually blue or black from amazon.com.

By now I have perused many sites and seemed to have filled a considerable amount of shopping carts, some with junk that I don't really need but like, whilst others sit piled high with new outfits necessary to impress. My problem now is that I have to stop. I forced myself to empty and delete the junk carts and paid for the ones that I did need, well want. Brilliant all purchases should be with me in about a week, move over Paris Hilton, I will look fabulous but not stand out in a crowd, just the job!

I finished the last dregs of my wine and munched up the rest of the crisps, great nutritional intake tonight I thought to myself. I closed down the laptop and decided to retire for the night, not sure I was going to be able to sleep. I felt a lot of nervous excitement, telling my brain I wanted to sleep is like trying to tell a fire not to burn. My eyes are alight, every muscle wants to move, to dance, to jump and there are more ideas queuing up in my mind ready to explode. Coupled with the fact that I have just drunk a whole bottle of wine and a salty bag of crisps, I was wired for sound, so I decided to read for a while.

Chapter 8

I was half way through a murder mystery book by Robin Stevens called 'The Case of the Drowned Pearl.' A brief synopsis as far as I have read is; It is about two girls, Daisy Wells and Hazel Wong, who have become friends since a chance meeting in a whiskey bar in France, 'La Maison du Whisky'. Daisy was shy whilst Hazel was quite wild given the chance. Daisy was at a crossroads in her life, between adventure and shyness. Hazel convinces her that alcohol is a sensible choice to give her adventurous self a boost. After that they travel together and wherever they went a mystery or murder seemed to find them. They tried to turn their hands at being amateur 'Sherlock Homes'.

Whilst on holiday in Los Angeles, they went to Malibu beach with two men they met whilst travelling and who then tagged along with them, George and Alexander. Whilst swimming they discovered a body, which they reported. However after doing some investigative work, they find out that she was Antonia Braithwaite: a famous swimmer, nicknamed The Pearl, she was due to compete in the Olympics. Initially it appears she accidentally drowned in the sea, but it's odd that this should happen to such a strong swimmer, even more mysterious is that when the two friends pull her onto the beach, she smells strongly of Pears soap and has pearls sewn into her skin.

The book is an easy read for me, a bit of light hearted fun and reminds me of my childhood 'Famous Five' books in a way, with stories you can always walk away from, then return and pick up exactly where you left off. I find it fascinating how books are the legacy of their author's thoughts, preserving ideas in ink on papery leaves that will always stay for centuries to come.

With a stretch and a yawn, I snuggled down under my duvet as happy as a cat in the sunlight. I know it sounds sad, but for me, falling asleep was one of the best parts of the day. Hidden under my cozy hug, snug and safe, letting the world of dreams come to me in its dancing way, I must have gone out like a light.

I awoke the following morning to the steady patter of rain on my window, scattering the nascent rays of rising sun. The sound brought a calmness to me, my soothing melody. I lazed in bed a bit longer listening to the sounds until my alarm chimed, the opening curtain call for my day.

I got up and opened the shutters, the rain had passed and the air was warm, a rainbow hung in the sky reflected into the sea by the now up and coming sun. Above it is a perfect daydream blue, decorated with wisps of brilliant cloud. I stared at it for a moment, the rainbow has such bold colours arching across the sky, mother natures perfection at its best.

Today I did not have to rush into work, there are no meetings or conference calls first thing so I decided to run myself a bath, in the world's most tiny swimming pool as I call it. I made myself some breakfast and climbed into the bath. Passing time, soaking in the heated water, feeling it hug every inch of my skin so gently, I breathed in the aroma of the bubble bath, mango, lime and coconut, it was my heaven, my energiser.

This moment of inner peace was short lived as part of my breakfast that was fit for a king fell into the water. I really needed to stop eating in the bath, scrambled eggs piled high on a bread bun, never tasty when soggy. As I scooped as much of the bread out as I could and flicked off the bubbles, I finished eating it with some apple juice and then climbed out of my egg infested bath.

Most of my mornings are spent doing the necessary preparation on autopilot while my brain prepares for every possible scenario it can, finding solutions to problems that don't yet exist, just in case. If I think back, this time last year I went to work with an enthusiasm, now it's more of a function more than anything else.

Over the next couple of weeks reporting on some scandalous news features kept us busy. One was about Caribbean cocaine trafficking. We managed to be in the thick of it, reporting in real time as five British men were arrested after a tonne of cocaine was discovered on their yacht as they were leaving the Caribbean to sail to Europe. It was linked to an ongoing investigation into international drug trafficking. The other scandal we picked up was about Chinese exports to Cuba. China is one of Cuba's top supporters and political allies, I suspect, in part to annoy the Americans. However their exports to Cuba fell to their lowest level in a decade. This was not good news, as Cuba is dependent on imports for much of its consumption, but it began to fall behind on payments, so the flow of Chinese goods was ebbing away from them.

We also managed to create a bit of a stir with one of our other stories about our sister Island, Nevis. Since 2008, there had been a global crackdown on offshore finance, but Nevis had continued to offer a secret haven to the super-rich. Nevis had been implicated in some of the most sordid financial scams, from Britain's biggest-ever tax fraud, to the fleecing of six hundred and twenty-thousand vulnerable Americans in a $220m payday loan scam.

The stance we took revealed the difficulties the world faces in trying to put an end to tax evasion, fraud and kleptocracy. Goldie managed to get a great angle from a lawyer who had extensive experience of the Island and had what he called 'a working knowledge' of how the scams worked to exploit tax-systems and peoples greed. In return for his offer to help us dig into the facts, we had to give him our assurance that he was not to be identified in any way as he was currently still working with Nevisian officials and didn't want to risk his job or to become a target for criminals. We even managed to get an obscure comment from Donald Trump, we suspected not entirely honest, and if we had run it mayhem would have been created, so we didn't. You see what I mean about 'we gobble up the worst of the worst, the more violent the stories the better, anything to keep us the best and most lucrative newspaper on the Island.'

We also had to cover an election piece. Our Mayor called a general election a year ahead of schedule to catch both the opposition off guard and to win a new mandate before the Island's economic situation worsened. He changed the Island's legislature over the weekend, paving the way for a short campaign period, so at the drop of a hat, authorities opened several voter registration centres as the elections commission ramped up preparations. I think The Alise, other newspapers, locals and dignitaries alike were all in a complete spin to try and get everything ready. Still it meant time flew by very quickly.

My evenings are just as busy, video calls with mum, showing her my holiday attire, where I was staying, how work was, did I want to come home this year for Christmas, and the rest. She also brought me up to speed with her gossip, I must say Henfield has become quite the hub for unusual activity.

The village green had held a neighbourhood barbecue, for better or worse everyone knew one another. Apparently whilst Gary was playing his cello and Lorna was playing her guitar, dad paraded around with his ten tonnes of cinnamon buns he had made for dessert. All was well until Mrs Pollock turned up, mum said that she looked as if she was already dead and wore clothes that looked like they were cast-offs, but they knew she was alive as she breathed and shouted obscenities at everyone.

Anyway a squabble broke out between the Reverend Duff, (vicar) and Mrs Pollock during some face painting, the argument grew from nowhere and quickly turned into a tornado. The vicar by all accounts looked shell shocked as dad's cinnamon buns were commandeered and began to fly in all directions, knocking some people to the ground. I was in absolute stitches as she told me this, tears bursting from my eyes to join in the laughter.

Mum continued that it was eventually brought under control by several police officers who were as inspiring as damp lettuce on a dirty plate, they needed some speed. Mrs Pollock was caught, but only after she had to be coaxed off the roof of the cricket pavilion, which she had climbed to escape arrest. Anyway she was whisked off in the police car and has not been seen since. I was in even more hysterics by the time she ended the call and continued to titter to myself for a while after that, picturing the scene.

Goldie also came over for more cooking revelations, general chit-chat and trip planning, we even had our own bizarre evening, as we tried on our holiday clothes and pranced around in front of each other as if we were on a catwalk. Goldie in her 'glamorous' shopping bargains, well I use the term glamorous very loosely indeed. Most of her clothes were loose, flowing dresses and skirts, with the odd shorts thrown in, all with differing prints, pink with baby blue flowers, big red roses and orange dahlias, she looked like an expanse of wallpaper, even her leggings and swimwear were just as garish but it did suit her personality. In complete contrast, mine was elegant but inconspicuous, dull even, sticking to neutral and pastel shades in dress, tops and trousers, shorts and swimwear.

We did have some laughs trying it all on, swapping outfits as we pretend to be models walking back and forth on the deck with our dead eyes, dead emotions and fallen faces, just like the fashion models. So much fun, our giggles rolled about the air in fits and bursts, loud, soft and back to loud again. Clowning around is so underrated, we should all do it on a regular basis, letting it take us away from our worries.

As the day of departure drew ever closer, I packed and unpacked my suitcase several times. It is always such a daunting task for me, I have a habit of packing far too much and then when I take out some of my clothes to travel 'more lightly,' I end up repacking them again as they are a necessity. It drives me mad as no matter how many different ways I pack, there is never any room left for essential items such as toiletries.

Exasperated, I decided I would fix this once and for all, so fired up my laptop and punched in, 'how to pack a suitcase properly'. I ended up on a website called 'Smarter Travel,' which doesn't really show you how to pack less items, but just maximise the space, for example rolling clothes up and putting things inside shoes and hats. What a fantastic revelation, not only did this provide me with more space but it means I can pack more stuff!

Not the correct way to look at this as I find out, after several re-packs the only way this lid is going to close is by my sitting on it. I lifted the suitcase, as it had to be a certain weight and to make sure I could actually carry it. Well, I just about managed it, but my twenty kilogram weight limit was exceeded, the scales read, twenty-six kilograms. What a waste of time, the website was of no help to me at all, I have to unpack yet again.

Staring at the pile of clothes on my bed, I really need to sort this out, my only dilemma was what do I not need to take. I video called mum but she was out playing bridge with Mrs Barton, so dad answered instead. Before I could say anything he peered right up to the screen and said. "Jasmine are you donating to Oxfam, you have a lot of stuff? "Dad this is my holiday stuff," I replied little annoyed. "Ahh, then you'd best speak to your mother, she'll be back later, wearing apparel is not my area, bye darling." With that he was gone. Dad was old before his time, I loved him but he never came alive unless he was with his huge train set he had build in the garage. I think he did it to seek solace from mum. Otherwise he would do as he was told and just say, "Whatever your mother says, Jaz."

Several hours and a lot of sighs later, I manage to get my packing down to a fine art and even more impressive manage to scale everything down. I retrieved my backpack from the back of the wardrobe, I loved it, many a time it had sat comfortably on my back whilst out and about. It was given to me by my parents when I announced at the age of fifteen that I wanted to leave home and see the world. I laughed to myself, "Teenagers eh." It has that well-loved look, it's pattern of spring flowers made it feel like home, although they were slightly faded, showing signs of being washed too many times. I packed in all essentials necessary to be got at quickly, such as my passport, mobile phone, tickets, money, notebook, pen and camera. I then found a few snacks in the kitchen, so added them. To be honest, by the time I had finished even my back pack was full to overflowing.

Chapter 9

The day of our trip finally arrived. I made sure everything was up to date and had briefed Pia about certain things that may come her way. Not sure if it was a good idea leaving Pia in charge, but I had given her strict instructions, Colby would keep an eye on her and I would remain in contact, so what could possibly go wrong!

Pia was one of our sub editors and worked well with Goldie, she was a newcomer to the paper. She had experience and fitted in well with the rest of the team, although she did have the loudest voice in the room and could be heard wherever she was, even more so than Goldie and that took some doing. On every subject she was opinionated but if you didn't agree with her she never got angry, she just pitied you for not understanding the 'correct' way to think about it.

Whenever a work colleague, friend, or even an acquaintance, was in trouble she was right there with both boots on. Calmly she would take charge, steer the most efficient course through the problem but never stick around for any appreciation. You could forget to call her for a month or three and still she'd be happy to talk to you, she never seemed to harbour a grudge. She often says grudges are for small brains, it takes creative intelligence to see things differently.

Anyway she is a safe pair of hands and I'm sure she will rise to the challenge, if not take over my office.

As I was hauling my suitcase out of the door, my trusty backpack slung over my shoulder our airport taxi arrived. I was going through the lists in my head ensuring I had everything and done everything I needed to do, when a holler reverberated in my ears like a clap of thunder, it was Goldie, climbing out the cab dressed as what can only be described as a traffic light, red t-shirt, orange jeans and a pair of green trainers, her hair wrapped in a green scarf which matched her shoes. I smiled, what a sight to behold. I looked at what I was wearing, quite plain in comparison, blue t-shirt, jeans and my comfy white sketchers. "Yo empress,Yah suh," she screeched.

I made my way to the waiting cab driven by one of our locals, Bragi. He was obese, grey-haired and shaggy-faced resembling an unshorn sheep, his body was trying to escape from his shirt, which was tenuously buttoned across his bulging chest. His personality was equally as big. "Jasmine, Cum pan baby love Eh holiday time Git unnu luk gud arse inna cyar.' Lovely, how dare he make reference to my derrière. He ushered us both into the cab and slung my luggage into the boot of the car like it was some hammer throw, good job it was a solid case.

As I climbed in beside Goldie, thunder began to rumble in the distance, a bolt of lightning cracked the blue sky in two followed by a few splashes of water. For the last couple of days, I have been hoping I'd wake up to the gentle patter of rain on my window, a welcome escape from the scorching heat, and now, here it was, beginning to cascade in diagonal sheets in its full glory. Brilliant, and on the day we are flying too!

As we set off, the inception of the storm began to arrive. The rhythm of the downpour beginning to unleash a torrent of its own, the building winds rousing the trees into a vortex of dance as the rain began to fall even more, sounding like prairie hailstones on the roof of our mobile metal shelter.

The cab rocked us from side to side as Bragi concentrated on steering through the growing puddles as we travelled the familiar road to the airport. Seats and windows shook with every small bump, the air conditioning whistling with extreme pressure as it was pumped through the one filter that was working. But we didn't care, it was the first day of our adventure, we continued to chatter non stop, our voices rising and blending together in the sweet ritual of best friends.

A twenty minute ride later and we arrived at the airport, clambered out of the cab and stretched. Bragi unpacked our luggage, plonked it on the pavement before holding out his hand ready to be paid, "two dalla tuh yuh sistren," he said. Goldie winked, "Half price a nuh it? bikaaz enuh wi." Bragi smiled and nodded as we handed him the money, with a wave he climbed back into his cab and was gone.

It was about nine o'clock in the morning, the worst time to arrive, it was humid, we could feel the heat already beginning to reflect off the tarmac as the rain continued to lash against the concrete breeze blocks which encased the airport. A woman with striking translucent skin walked passed us, she had a locket hung around her neck like a gold medallion, her emotional amour. She smiled and commented, "Better not get these wet," as she removed her fashionable high heeled boots before wading barefoot through a rather large puddle. Great idea, but not the type of shoes to wear in an airport or for travelling.

Robert L. Bradshaw International Airport terminal building was more like a large shed than a modern airport building. The walls were a drab olive green colour, decorated with faded posters of the Island which served to hide the peeling paintwork. It looked tired and about twenty years out of date, but it served its purpose connecting all the Islands together and flying to Antigua in order to connect with worldwide flights.

We made our way to the top of the steps to the arrivals lounge and the SKB check-in desk. I felt myself perspiring, it was humid outside but inside, the terminal offered absolutely no relief, in fact I would go as far as to say it was even hotter. Signs flashed in front us, stating that the air-conditioning was being adjusted. Mmhm, I have learnt over the years that signs in the Caribbean do not always mean what they say, for example, air-conditioning is being adjusted probably means that the air conditioning is in fact not working! Wonderful, we are trapped in a confined space, hot and bothered with quite a few other hopeful travellers but at least we aren't getting wet, so that is a Bertie bonus.

We stood in the check-in queue, chatting to each other and watching the people who had made it past the check-in desks and were now flowing through the security gate, all moving like chaotic rainbows, so many brilliant colours, each one heading for a destination of their own making. It is fascinating to see, every colour that can tumble from a box of paints is all together in this building.

We checked in with the usual coldness and mumbling from the airport staff, smiling and politeness is not part of their job description. But the worst is yet to come, immigration and airport security, this encounter is horrific here in the Caribbean. There are many reviews on Trip Advisor from travellers that say it is the worst experience ever and spoils their holiday. Despite the abundance of complaints, nothing ever changes.

The rude, no sense of humour immigration staff seem to have the sole aim of discouraging people from ever using the airport again. Whilst the airport security who are rough and built like brick houses give the impression that they don't want to be there and its your fault they have to come to work.

Unfortunately for me, a very obese security lady felt the need to pull me out of line for additional screening, no reasons given, as per usual. Her gait was very awkward, her Afro hairstyle was gathered in a hairband and stood up on her head like a toilet brush, she was perspiring badly and I felt myself edge away from her body odour as if she has something contagious. She did not have the mantra, "Eat less, exercise more," I know that sounds rude and I am sorry, I have nothing against larger people but she was rude and very rough as she patted me down and made me remove my shoes, all probably because we had an altercation as I profusely refused to obey her order, when she asked me to drop my trousers.

It took us nearly an hour to clear immigration and security, due to their disorganisation skills. There was the obligatory pushing, shoving and a free for all to collect our belongings from the conveyer belt. Goldie spoke to a tall uniformed gentleman who was stood to the side of the conveyor belt and told him how bad this experience was and that there was absolutely no leadership, as she was a reporter, she was going to write an article in the Alise about it. He did blink and nodded gently, but there was no change in his facial expression, it was almost as if he was practising being a mannequin.

Just as we thought we could now start to relax and had accomplished the biggest feat, an announcement was made that our flight was to be delayed. Great, that's all we needed! A exasperating piece of news, equally as frustrating as the storm which was now howling outside. The large screen displaying our departure times showed our flight would be delayed by at least two hours, this meant we would miss our ferry connection.

A sea of irritated and annoyed faces lurched towards the departure desks, whining with an equal premise of complaints. Much like everyone else we wanted to get on the plane and fly off. We wanted the storm to end, but it was no use complaining about it, the airport staff could do nothing about the weather at this moment in time and the storm outside could easily pull any impatient plane out of the sky, we just had to sit it out knowing we were probably safer on the ground at least.

We sat down in the plastic seats, brushing away the debris from the last person who sat there. We were still chattering away to each other listening and replying, only pausing to take sips of our airport decaffeinated, should be disgusting, coffee. Our conversation was so much more than words, it had smiles, gentle shrugs and lights in our eyes, both elevated by each other's presence, even our silences are comfortable. These are moments to savour, the company of each other, a sense of peace that comes from feeling loved and protected, within the arms of our true friendship.

During a pause in our conversation, I took a sip of coffee and sent Pia a text from my mobile, she replied almost immediately informing me that all was okay and as I had only been gone a few hours it hadn't given her sufficient time to cause any chaos. Ok noted! Goldie smiled as she put her head on my shoulder and read it. "Nuh flies pan har den," she laughed.

I replaced the mobile into my backpack and pulled out a brown paper bag full of my favourite sweets, chocolate pralines in their purple wrappers. I offered them to Goldie, who of course took a few, "Dees a tasty," she replied as she took a few more for luck, I giggled "make sure there is some left for me." As I replaced the sweets back into my bag I felt a sudden wave of apprehension, I shivered, when I did feel any anxiety or fear, I tried not to panic anymore, I've been there before and I know the feeling well, which makes it a little less scary. If I am honest I think I am actually stronger for my battle scars, instead of letting my fear hold me back and stop me from reaching my dreams, I conquer it, making it a little easier each time. I felt Goldie's hand grip mine. "A yuh ok empress." She asked. "Yes, yes, sorry just worried about the trip, I suppose" I answered. We stared at each other for a moment, smiling as she gripped my hand tighter "Nuh bi Mi wi mek sure wi tan safe." At that moment I believed her, she would actually, make sure we were safe.

Chapter 10

Waiting for our delayed flight seemed to turn into eternity, but eventually the wind and rain had blown away the cobwebs and it stopped as fast as it had arrived, letting all flights resume again. The screen above went blank and then displayed every flight as fast as it could, causing a sea of faces to lurch forward in unseen currents, flowing like water to their destinations, ignoring the flight numbers that were being called. I have to say Goldie and I followed suit, negotiating the way ahead as small groups stopped now and again causing small eddies. The rest of us flowed around the outside to reach the departure desks ready to be herded onto the tarmac and led in single file to board the planes, the odd person taking their chances with the officials and stepping outside the cones, only to be herded back to the pack very quickly indeed.

I hated flying, but it was a means to an end if I wanted to see different countries. I tried not to travel overseas too much with work, sending Goldie or Pia in my place. Ah yes Pia, I must text her again before we take off.

It didn't matter how salubrious the furnishings inside an airplane were, to me it is just a flying metal tube, a tin can with wings where people cough and sneeze, children scream and the toilet is nearly always occupied. I crossed my heart as we stepped over the threshold and smiled stiffly at the sexy sassy flight attendants who ushered us to our seats, backpacks colliding with the cabin interior. I looked at Goldie as she pushed me forward, we smiled at the heavily made up flight attendants, they portrayed an image of the good, the bad and the downright naughty tales of life in the air.

We found our seats quickly as we had been treated to first class. The curtained-off section had about twenty recliner seats at the front of the aircraft, so there was space, comfort and privacy. The service was going to be good too, according to our in flight guide, we will get complimentary snacks and meals with free alcoholic drinks.

Our flight was direct with no stop over in St Maarten. As we took off and climbed into the air, I relaxed into the seat listening to the hum of the engine, Goldie leaned across me to see out the window. Every red roofed home appeared like an autumn leaf lying gently on the earth, surround by little green trees and roads shining like silvery stems on an English frosted morning. The patchwork world below looked so enchanting, even the sea glimmered and the atolls became weirdly transparent.

An attendant arrived next to us beaming with the enthusiasm of someone new to the job. She asked if we would like any hot drinks as she placed a wrapped sandwich, a small square of cake and a bottle of water in front of us. We declined and instead both went for a small bottle of red wine each. She handed us the customary green bottle, deeper in colour where the red wine sat within. Goldie nudged me and giggled, "Pree dis." She proceeded to send the poor attendant into disarray as she asked for a wine bottle shaped more like an hour-glass so that her hand could fit around the middle more comfortably.

The attendants had been taught to serve whatever the customer wanted, but on this occasion she will fail, as far as I am aware they is no such thing. I felt quite sorry for her so said, "Ignore Goldie, she is just teasing you." The attendant smiled, nervously grasped her trolley and moved forward. "Goldie, we will never be able to travel first class again, our page has been marked," I told her. A senior male attendant arrived by our seats, "Is there anything I can do for you ladies?" he asked, I nearly sputtered my wine out of my mouth as Goldie replied. "Yuh waan tuh sidung pan fi mi lap lover bwoy?" Poor man, he was suitably embarrassed, although I doubt it was the first time he had been asked to sit on someones lap, he was quite handsome in an odd type of way. Goldie had gone too far, but she knew how to apologise, yep, blame it on the wine! "Suh hush fi mi fren Nuh sure wah cum ova mi Mussi di wine." He smiled and disappeared further down the plane, without uttering another word.

As we started to tuck in to our food, the female flight attendant reappeared wanting to collect up the trays as we were about to land at Terrance B. Lettsome International

Airport, Tortola. We quickly crammed in the food and gulped back the wine, retrieving the cake and water bottles to put in our backpacks for later, as she arrived once more and clanged our trays into her trolley. With that the announcement came to take our seats and buckle up as the plane started its descent until eventually its wheels kissed the earth once more with a small and joyous bounce.

After collecting our luggage from the baggage carousel and clearing immigration and customs in record time, we walked out of the airport into the heat of the sun. It was still very hot but with no signs of the rain storm we had left behind.

We stood outside the airport terminal as the heat licked at our faces and coiled around our limbs like some great hot blooded serpent, a clamminess soaked my t-shirt forming a map of some foreign land. Beads of water trickled down my face into my eyes, stinging them with a mixture of salty sweat and running mascara, a glistening mess. We both mopped our foreheads with our hands at the same time and giggled.

We made our way to the shuttle stop, dragging our suitcases behind us. As we waited for the shuttle bus to take us to the ferry we watched the ground smoulder sending up a disorientating haze, the grass stood still as if too hot to move, even the birds were silent, there was no shade to help us cool down.

It wasn't long before the shuttle bus veered around the corner, an old model bobbing and creaking along, with worse suspension than a homemade pram, my heart sank. It came to a halt in front of us and the driver pulled the doors open, then stood ready to take everyones money in any form they liked, crinkled notes or coins. I caught sight of the tyres, bald! The paintwork showed barely a hint of yellow under the thick red dust of the region, the windscreen had only a small clear section for the driver to see through, the rest was covered with baked on dirt.

Not wishing to sound rude, the driver also looked like he was living on borrowed time. We boarded, with some trepidation, time to take our life in our hands amid differing cultures and characters, English, Chinese, American. Some considered themselves extremely knowledgeable, trying to educate everyone on the bus about the Caribbean whilst others sat quietly, trying to peer out of the dirty windows or just buried themselves in their guides, memorising the most idyllic places to visit. One thing was for sure, we were all crammed in like sardines.

On arriving at the ferry port we all bundled out and retrieved our luggage, thankfully we didn't have to queue for the tickets as Mr Meyers had sent all these in advance. Unfortunately as we walked onto the dock we were told that we had missed our ferry due to the delay in our flights. A porter approached us pulling a cart laden with toilet rolls. His wizened face peered out from under a wedge of blue hat, his eyes were so heavily lidded and weighed down with wrinkled folds that it was almost like talking to someone who was asleep, yet he was quite alert, informing us that there was not another ferry until the following morning at six.

We did not particularly want to stay in Tortola, we had nothing booked here and anyway Mr Meyers would be expecting us and we were already late, so I took a punt and called him on a contact number he had given us in case there were any difficulties such as this. He was very pleasant and understanding as I apologised for our delay and its reason. He told us not to worry, he would organise a private plane to collect us from Terrance B. Lettsome International Airport, we just had to make our way back there and go the Charter flight check-in desk, he would sort it, how very efficient!

We sat on the ferry dock waiting for the next bus to arrive about twenty minutes from now, this gave us time to savour the delights of the dock and to people watch which was quite amusing. I also sent another message to Pia as I had forgotten to do it before we took off. There was no reply, oh well no news is good news I thought to myself.

The next ferry in was the day tripper to Virgin Gorda, it was called 'Sea Nymph'. Goldie looked it up on her phone, it had originally been built for Island trade, however since the bottom had dropped out of the sugar market it had been converted into a speed boat come ferry. By now it was about three o'clock in the afternoon, but the day tourists still came, wearing wild floral prints and gold medallions, cameras at the ready as they filed onto the boat. The ferry's engine chugged a little before roaring into life and took off with all the smoothness of a go-cart over speed bumps, we laughed knowing that the tourists were in for a white knuckle ride.

Chapter 11

The small airport bus arrived, this time there were only a few of us that were returning to the airport, so we had ample space. Thank goodness the uncomfortable journey was short, as the seats and windows rattled with every small bump in the pot holed road and we jostled back and forth. There was a strong aroma of petrol as the dodgy air conditioning coughed and spluttered.

A woman shifted in her seat, as she sneezed, then came a courtesy 'bless you' coughed out by the man sat next to her. I dread to think what we were inhaling. The brakes squeaked suddenly and we all lurched forward, grabbing hold of the seat in front as the bus came to a halt at the traffic lights. The shuttle bus then continued to trundle on to its destination ignoring the fact that the traffic lights had not yet turned green. It was one of the worst bus rides I have ever had as it repeats its eternal pattern of stops and go's, its erratic driver failing to avoid any of the potholes. In fact it would not surprise me if we had become stuck in one, some of them were mighty deep it felt like the bus was going to tip over, anyway someone was looking down on us that day as we eventually pulled up outside the airport terminal once again.

We walked to the Charter check-in desk and were greeted by a very polite lady who took our luggage and escorted us into a small sparse room to await our plane, we had just sat down and were attempting to extract some cake from my backpack, when we were called to the door by a tall man in a grey suit.

He looked far too tall for his build, maybe he had stopped growing and had to be stretched on one of those medieval racks. His face was mostly obscured by a red scraggly beard that clung to his skin, he met our gaze with confidence and escorted us across the tarmac handing us complimentary juice cartons, which we drank as we walked to our waiting plane.

Both Goldie and I felt like celebrities, royalty even, as we were greeted by a handsome French pilot. "Bonjour ladies, my name is Maxim and I will be flying you on your short journey to Anegada." Oooh, we drooled, he had a smooth resonating sexy accent that captivated us entirely, we were infatuated. He had it all, the sexy voice, good looks, those serious kissable lips and muscles to die for, he looked as if he had just strolled off the set from 'Top Gun,' and both of us have just reinvented him in our minds as an impromptu porn star!

I could have stood there all day simply listening and smiling at him, but he was way out of my league. I felt myself blush as he took each of our arms and guided us up the steps of the aircraft one by one. Goldie found it hilarious, making a noise which was a cross between a snort and a drunken laugh, she never did know when to breathe between giggles, poor Maxim looked quite embarrassed possibly shocked by our antics.

From the outside it just looked like a small six seater plane, but Mr Meyers had arranged for us to fly in Air One. This plane was well known for transferring Caribbean dignitaries, how on earth did an executive newspaper editor of a small Island manage to accomplish this, even I couldn't pull strings to fly in Air One. I must remember to ask him, but today at least I wasn't going to question too much, just sit back and enjoy the ride. It was our own private charter, and we could indulge ourselves for the short journey.

Inside it resembled a billionaire's toy. It had the scent of opulence without being ostentatious, it felt spacious with plush top of the line fabrics and was spotlessly clean. There were no rows of seats, just six elegant leather loungers and a coffee table with ornate cabriole legs. The windows had plush grey curtains and there was a decent sized flat screen set to one side. Maxim handed us a glass of champagne and closed the plane door. He made sure we had our belts secured, which Goldie took delight in, before going through to the cockpit. We could hear him talking to traffic control and once he had the all clear, we rose smoothly into the sky like a bird.

Goldie and I reclined the seats, I stretched out my hand to the window and felt the coolness of the glass. "Wi a film stars fram Hollywood." Goldie remarked, yep she was right, all we needed now was the red carpet treatment when we got off the plane. I pushed a button on the side of the seat and a tray popped out with more drinks and nibbles, Goldie did the same, we both smiled and then our smile turned into an auditory firework, fits of laughter firing off. Goldie put some of the nibbles and alcohol in her bag for later, well why not, this is the only time it's ever going to happen.

The short flight passed too quickly, the airplane rode through the sky as if it were on sleek and perfect tracks, but to be honest at that moment in time, we probably would have said the same about any form of transport, too much excitement and champagne you see, we weren't drunk just high on life and slightly merry!

As we flew in to Anegada, I felt bewitched. Looking out of the window at the completely flat landscape with sherbet coloured houses, that stood proudly with their flat red roofs clustered together like old friends, reassured by their closeness. A beautiful expanse of emerald green dotted with tiny atolls in a sea glistening with the sun's rays, it looked so beautiful. The runway appeared ahead on its green of the land, the airport looked tiny and there was a busy harbour running alongside it. Maxim came onto the speaker. "Ladies please ensure your seatbelt is on and your seats are adjusted for landing, the runway is only 762 metres which makes landing a bit tricky." Did he need to say the last bit

Goldie and I put our seats up and stared at each other, we clutched hands and gripped them tight, as if we were going to die. Maxim, our Tom Cruise look alike, managed it with supremacy and with a slight bounce the plane wheels reconnected with the runway. He braked hard bringing the plane to a gentle trundle on the small runway before coming to a halt in front of the Captain Auguste George airport building.

As we stepped off the plane and onto Anegada soil, we looked around, on one side of the runway was a row of coloured houses, on the other, a shallow turquoise hue with utterly clear water, every fish and rock could be seen, I took a deep breath in, so here we are, the start of things to come.

Maxim escorted us through passport control to the entrance of the airport, he placed our luggage next to us and shook our hands. "Thank you for a wonderful flight." We both said together, he was so handsome, a true gentleman, polite strong, confident kind, oh need I go on. He makes me want to feel how his lips move in a kiss, how his hands would follow the curves of my body. My lusting was cut short as he said, "Its my absolute pleasure ladies, enjoy your stay in Anegada, Au Revoir." With that our adonis strolled back to the plane and our celebrity status trip ended.

Despite the email assurances, Mr Timothy Meyers was not there to meet us, we asked some people at the bike hire place, but nobody seemed to know him. A man approached us and offered to take us to the villa in his cab, we thanked him and took up his offer, if I knew what I know now I wish we hadn't done that.

The cab was from some budget company on the Island, it had a dent in the fender, a cracked windscreen and one of its headlights was broken with the outer casing hanging off. We had to plead with the driver to help us put our luggage in the boot. He was about forty or so, dressed in jeans, his face was tanned and perfectly symmetrical, he was muscular but not overly so, but had no personality whatsoever. Goldie was about to kick up a stink when he sauntered round and threw the luggage into the boot then opened the door for us. We giggled and sat in the back.

Inside was a distinct aroma of stale beer, we perched forwards on the back seat trying to make conversation with our driver on the way to the villa, but we were ignored, instead he spent most of the journey fiddling with his mobile phone and radio. He was not going to get ruffled by us at all, his idea of hurrying was probably to bend his head forward. The engine continued to growl as it ambled towards our destination, a small plume of black smoke spat out behind us every now and again.

We decided to sit back and look out the window at the Island's virescent beauty. The scenery here is very different although it is still the Caribbean, there are small pine trees and sand dunes reminiscent of the French Atlantic coast. We passed some salt ponds and lots of what looked like white/ pink powdery soft sand beaches. The guide books were right, although it is a small Island, longer than it is wide, it is definitely the place to relax, a beautiful hidden gem.

Eventually, hot and exhausted from our journey, we arrived at the beach villa. First impressions, it was very welcoming with its bright orange exterior, it looked freshly painted, as if it had only been finished last week, almost too new, it seemed slightly out of place in some strange way, as if it had just rolled off a production line.

We were met by a middle aged woman who had been sat on the balcony waiting for our arrival. She introduced herself as Lourdes, apparently it is a Spanish name deriving from the Virgin Mary. She was casual, but smartly dressed in red shorts, a hipster jacket and a neck scarf. Her face was made up, but not over done and her long black hair was woven into a braid, nothing fancy, just enough to keep it out of her eyes. She rose from the chair to help us with the luggage that we had been dragging behind us, a look of serenity put us at ease, she escorted us inside and placed our bags on the chair, the perfect hostess.

Chapter 12

Stepping into the air conditioning villa was like walking out of the oppressive heat and into an English April afternoon, the air was perfumed like spring flowers. The villa was designed with a diamond-shaped roof, housing two bedrooms, two bathrooms and an open plan living, dining, kitchen area. All surfaces were a white glossy colour which had been iced over the breeze block outer walls. We knew this because there was another villa next to us still in the process of being built.

The villa was a liveable, modern mausoleum, with a porch and verandah that commanded spectacular views of a saltwater pond and the beach, which I have to say looked like pure paradise. According to Lourdes the Island boasted thirty-six miles of unspoilt white sand and turquoise blue waters, if we felt like it we could walk some of it in the evenings. From what we had seen so far, I think we both felt like we could set up camp here forever. I could feel all the tensions being unleashed already, this would be our sanctuary, a cocoon, complete relaxation and rest, although I did need to check in with Pia each day, but I wasn't about to let work ruffle me.

After a whistle stop tour of the facilities, Lourdes left us to our own devices. She had put some food and milk in the fridge for supper and tomorrows breakfast accompanied by two jugs, one consisting of homemade lemongrass lemonade and the other with rum punch. It didn't take us long to decide a rum punch was the order of the day as we unpacked and made ourselves at home.

In the midst of all the unpacking, drinking and chattering, we were startled by a dull ringing noise, we looked at each other in wonderment, until I realised it was my mobile phone muffled from inside my backpack. I dived in and managed to catch it before whoever it was rang off. It was Mr Timothy Meyers, his voice was deep with a rich silky sexy tone, as if he controlled the world, well if his voice was anything to go by, he could control me any day! Everything else could melt into oblivion if you listened to him for too long. A worldly experience seeped through as he spoke, there was more to this guy than meets the eye, I was sure of it.

I put him on speaker so we could both hear what he was saying. "Hello" I said rather cautiously, "Ladies, sorry about not meeting you, got delayed, welcome to Anegada. Are you ok, do you need anything?" "Er, no we are all good thankyou." I replied. "Fantastic, I have booked for us to meet up at The Lobster Trap for supper, is it ok if I send a cab for you, shall we say eight?" I smiled and nodded, not sure why as he couldn't see me, but he must have sensed what I was doing. "Good, I look forward to meeting you both there."

The smooth baritone of his voice reverberated through me, its low rumble was comforting and managed to carry me off into another fantasy world. Luckily Goldie took charge of the situation, stepping forward, peering over the phone she shouted, "Yeh mon dat will bi cool." Then she raised her eyebrows at me and a broad smile appeared across her face as she tapped the off button. I just giggled girlishly.

A few more rum punches later and it was already seven, we needed to shower and get ready. I tugged on my matchstick blue trousers and ballet flats, wrapped a blue silk scarf around my waist, up over my torso, then tied the ends behind my neck to fashion a halter-style blouse, then I piled my hair up on my head with a few soft spirals left to dangle about my face. Goldie on the other hand was quite the contrast. She appeared in a greenish-blue dress with red flowers, made of soft, satiny fabric, knee length but loose like a sack, her hair resembled a mop. I wondered if she had actually looked in the mirror, if a cat had eaten her hair and puked it back out, then let it dry in the sun, it would have looked better. Never mind, the tangle would take hours to brush out and we didn't have that much time.

The cab arrived at the villa as planned and drove us the short distance to the Lobster Trap. Mr Timothy Meyers was waiting by the entrance for us and may I say, what a sight to behold, well in my opinion anyway, even better than Maxim, our French pilot. My eyes were instantly drawn to him, he had light brown skin and his dark shining eyes made me feel a little weak at the knees. He was a fair few inches taller than me, which I like, slim, but muscular, with a body any girl would fall for. I could easily become smitten with this man in an instant, but knowing my luck on the relationship front, he was probably married or homosexual or both!

I had stared for far too long as he introduced himself and showed us both to our seats, what a gentleman, he was chivalrous, warm and kind, all of which are strengths and virtues I like in a man, he could be my gallant protector any day. Goldie, on the other hand, seemed completely oblivious to his handsomeness, if there is such a word and instead was taking in the ambience of the restaurant, the happy chatter, fragrances and colours, or at least I think she was.

The restaurant did have a calming feel to it. It's deck and terrace overlooked the ocean as far as your eye could see and tonight, it was as still as a mill pond. A slumbering giant, powers untapped, muscles un-flexed, dozing, dreaming and caressing the shoreline with its scattered sequins catching the lights strung around the pontoon.

The restaurant wasn't particularly busy, which was good news, it meant we didn't have long to wait for our meal. We needed something fairly soon to soak up all the rum we had drunk. The nibbles from Goldie's bag hadn't done the trick and we had to throw away the cake from the airplane as it had become a sticky ball of gloop in the heat. The waiter arrived with a menu, "Just Carib all round for now, thank you." Mr Meyers ordered. "I have pre ordered three lobsters with rice, salad and black beans, I called Irvine, the chef earlier." Divine, nothing like fresh seafood, he must have quite a status here on the Island, being able to click his fingers and it all falls into place. I listened as he spoke, trying to work out his accent, it was smooth but playful and entirely captivating. Goldie kicked me under the table to get a grip of myself, but I ignored her.

The cool beer and appetisers of Hot Pepper Shrimp arrived quickly and were very tasty but I could have done with a glass of wine instead, on the whole the Caribbean is not the place for wine. Rum, and rum-based cocktails, of course, beer, certainly but wine is a no go. It all has to do with the hot humid climate and not being able to grow good wine grapes, it's hard to develop a tradition for wine drinking without local winemaking and the imported wines are just too expensive.

As we waited for the lobster to arrive, the conversation flowed easily between us, every now and again Goldie would fidget, adjusting the strap of her dress and applying another coat to her already red lips. I moved in my chair trying to inconspicuously invade Mr Timothy Meyers personal space with just the right look of heat in my eyes, to let him know the desire to play was there if he wanted to.

The chef arrived with our lobsters and had a short dialogue with Mr Meyers, the food looked delicious and the aroma was even more enticing. A whole spiny lobster sat on a bed of rice and colourful beans, its red armour and pincers aloft but no longer ready for combat. It was quite large, so probably had been leading a happy life in the depths of our oceans for some years before it met its demise. Our salads arrived with one of the waiters who also brought more beer. The rice and salad was just as inviting to the eye, rocket and lambs lettuce sprinkled with a rainbow of peppers, chillis and pomegranate seeds, topped off with sesame seeds, a salad to savour.

As we tucked into our meals, our conversation continued about the Island and what we can do here, but nothing about the expected article for the newspaper, still early days, we had only just arrived. We soaked up everything, helped by the ambient music now filling the air. Some people reacted to the beat by getting up and dancing near their tables, whilst others continued to chatter, but the lively tempo lifted us all, moving us to swaying, legs kicking and feet tapping.

We listened to what he was telling us about Anegada as if his words were golden, I felt like we already knew each other, it was so natural, but in reality we had never met, heard of each other, or corresponded through the newspaper before. His attentiveness to what Goldie and I had to say was fantastic, if I'm honest, the most attractive feature I've seen in a man for quite some time, normally what all men hear is white noise and you end up repeating what you have said when they decide to re-enter the conversation.

As the evening went on, it was the best food, drink and atmosphere I have had in a long time with a man. I know Goldie was there, but we always have fun, no matter where we are. Was this guy for real? He was just a bit too perfect. I decided to see if I could find a weakness, so I fixed him a look that would make any person other than him shrivel, he met my gaze with a smile from one who knows he has the upper hand. He lit up a cigarette, I folded one leg over the other and adjusted my halter neck scarf top trying to stay focused on my task. It's a film noir "stand off" of immense sexual power. I knew in my heart that despite not really knowing Mr Timothy Meyers, I had met the man of my dreams and fate has dealt me a dangerous hand.

As the evening came to a close, Mr Meyers escorted us from the restaurant to a waiting cab he had arranged to take us back to the villa. He would be in contact the following day.

Chapter 13

The following day was a beach day, we didn't have to walk far from our villa before the soft white powdery sand engulfed our feet. The sun that was orange only an hour ago, was now shining warmly, turning itself into a bright yellow inferno, a celestial fireball blinding us as it climbed higher in the azure sky. I put my sunglasses on, allowing my eyes to fully open and help a more confident self to emerge. Through my glasses, topaz sunbursts of light smashed against the calming blue of the ocean, lighting up the sea into cylinders of flax gold light, the untouched white sand covered the land as far as our eyes could see. I fell in love with this beach instantly, sheer paradise.

I looked at Goldie as we laid our towels next to each other, what did she look like! She had on a swimsuit in white with pink birds all over it and her sunglasses looked like something an astronaut would wear. They were very shiny, dark silver and so seamless, they simply wrapped around her face from side to side, I was quite the opposite in a plain blue bikini, I smiled, it takes all sorts I thought to myself.

The sand had just the right comforting warmth to rest on, it felt like a cosy hug, matched by the sunshine that filled the sky. We doused ourselves in expensive sun creams, then stretched out our arms and legs to resemble starfish, but really it was to maximise tan coverage. I hoped my skin would pass through the delicate shades of brown darkening as the days went on. Why do we all feel the need to be brown? It looks good but wrecks your skin in later years, oh well what the hell! Today, the only marker of time was the sun above and the moments savoured by the waves that washed the sand in a white lace.

I felt myself drifting off under my wide brimmed hat, as Goldie sipped some water from the cool box we had brought with us, iced drinks were captain's orders for today in this heat. I wriggled my toes, letting the pure sand run between them, it felt soothing. I peered up through my sunglasses at the sun which continued to glisten elegantly in the blue sky. Now and again, a single wispy cloud gracefully floated to and fro, a puff of white magic in acres of blue.

Goldie rose from sunbathing and plunged into the sea, splashing as she went. "Common" she screeched. "A suh fabulous." I heaved myself onto my elbows and gazed at her and a bit more of our surroundings, the graceful arc of sand, glittering under the sun, the waves gently rolling in with a soothing sound and then gently causing a brief flurry on the sand. A few shells were left alone, rolling in and out with the ebb and flow of the tide, treasures of the aquatic world, just slightly out of reach.

My mind wandered in the heat, I felt so good, I removed my hat and shook my hair as a brief soothing breeze hurried past me. I sat up further, curled my legs underneath me and wiggled my fingers through the sand, it was like warm lava flowing onto the beach. Goldie's shouts of fun were becoming louder and louder and she was not going to stop until I joined her in the water.

I stood up and took a few steps to the waters edge, letting the warm water lap around my feet, fizzing and bubbling as it took a shine to me. I smiled to myself, it felt hotter now I was standing, so I ran further in to the sea with an awkward gait and plunged in, immersing myself in the clear water. "Dis a suh cool Di bess." Goldie yelled as she swam over to me, rolling onto her back and then back onto her front like a demented dolphin. I have to agree with her, this Island was different from the paradise of St Kitts and Nevis, there was more beauty here than we could absorb in any amount of words.

Goldie, pushed me and my head bobbed under the surface for a second before I bobbed back up again, "Time fi bikkle an rum." Until she said that, I didn't even realise that I was hungry or needed more to drink, we had completely lost all track of time. Refreshed, we made our way out of the water and towel dried before taking the short meander to the beach bar, we had left the rest of our stuff on the beach, there was no one here to steal it.

The bar was called 'The Conch Bar,' the best way to describe it, is as a little bit of heaven. It was just a couple of metres from the sea, constructed entirely out of driftwood, sea shells, and wrecked boats. T-shirt's hung limply from wooden pegs up above our heads, I expect they swayed brilliantly in any breeze. Steel drum music filled the air without any effort, there was something about the vibrations from the drums that made you feel energised. Locals and day visitors were just lazing away beachside for a no-frills affair, I could definitely knock back a rum punch or two here, and that's exactly what we did do, accompanied by Chicken Roti, plantain and a garden salad, pure bliss.

Goldie leaned on the bar, her black hair touching one shoulder, she lolled her head to one side, pushing out her lips a little. She wasn't drunk yet but she liked to give the impression that she was. The guy at the bar was there to take our next drinks order in a flash, his eyes dropping to her low-cut swimwear. She twiddled her hair with her fingers in a seemingly absent minded way and giggled girlishly before ordering two more rum punches. We watched the bartender as he poured our drinks and stuck a glacé cherry on the side of the glass, he definitely had muscles under his shirt, he was dark skinned with light brown eyes. "Perhaps mi wi cum bac fah him latah." she said loud enough for him to hear. "Goldie, Shhh" I replied trying to get her to turn her volume button down.

It was at that moment, I noticed him. Mr Timothy Meyers was standing at the other end of the bar, with his flawless tanned skin, my attraction was instant, there is something about him that excites and calms me all at once.

A combination of features make him so handsome, but at the same time there was a curious side to him that makes me want to know more. As I look at him, his eyes show an intensity, an honesty, a gentleness, perhaps this is what is meant by the term a gentleman? Not one of weakness or trite politeness, but one of great spirit and noble ways, I really want to get close to him. I bit my lip, my skin tingled and my heart rate began to flutter erratically, I have to admit it, I like him a lot and despite not knowing anything about him, I have this overwhelming desire to be with him. Mum was right, maybe if I don't stuff it up, he might be the man for me and I might find love?

As I sit at the bar, my sex drive and my imagination are at it again, he is already naked behind the bar, he is pulling at the optics as he reaches for me. He grabs me and pulls me towards him with a fierceness as we proceed to our intimate moment, we even have our own dialog. I do have it bad, I have become the director of my own mental porn. Goldie nudged me and at exactly the same time Mr Meyers made eye contact with me. Before I could look away and pretend I hadn't seen him, a genuine grin spread across his face, turning him from handsome to divine. I felt my body flush warm, what was wrong with me? I had never felt like this before about a guy. He started to stroll over, I could feel myself begin to panic, I felt emotionally vulnerable, insecure even. Goldie gripped my hand and giggled, "Yuh a drooling Jaz." I felt my cheeks turn a shade of Champagne pink, you can always rely on Goldie to embarrass you just that little bit more.

Suddenly, there he was, standing right in front of us, a small suggestive smile still playing on his lips, I am sure he would be appalled if he knew what was going through my head right now, hopefully he wasn't aware he was my sex-muse, my present obsession. "Hello lovely ladies," he said, his words sounding like vanilla pudding, sweet in their ordinary sort of way, but with a luxurious warmth to his tone. "Fancy dining with me tonight, I know a great place with fantastic music?" Goldie gripped my hand tighter and giggled, "Sure ting Lover bwoy." She replied before I could even speak, she knows it will take me ages to reply and even then it will be an incomprehensible mutter, as my heart will still be in the process of melting. Funny how well we know each other, he smiled again, just enough to allow a gleam of white from his teeth to break through, it was then I noticed a slight but cute dimple on his cheek, even more attractive.

Goldie turned to the barman, had I missed something here? She was on first name terms with him already. "Leroy fancy a cum fah ah grill an muzik tonite?" she asked. "Where?" He instantly replied, Goldie winked at me "Ritmo y Sabor del

Caribe" Mr Timothy Meyers answered, loosely translated it means rhythm and flavours from Caribbean.

Leroy sneered and winked at Goldie, "Give me a hot girl for a night and I don't care where I eat, I like my women like my coffee cups, tempting and disposable." Goldie stood up on the bar stool and leaned in towards him, "Hell yeh, mi wi show yuh ah out a road type ah coffee, waah fi try ih." With that Leroy also leaned over the bar and grabbed her by the waist. His hand then gently glided through her hair and onto her neck, looking at her in a way that he was definitely keen to find out more.

Goldie's eyes became candles, their light a spark of passion, desire even, a teasing smile crept over her face, goosebumps lined her skin, not the kind that you get in the cold, but the excited kind you get when nothing else matters except right here, right now. I laughed, "Goldie we are just like two silly teenagers, lust will get the better of us," she nodded as the men just looked bewildered.

After managing to haul Goldie away from her exploits, we agreed to meet both men for supper around seven thirty. We then left the bar, a little worse for wear for a spot more sunbathing and swimming and clear our heads before our date night. The two men seemed well acquainted, as we left them behind discussing which car was to be used to pick us up later, did they know each other already?

We were full of excited banter as we both laid down on the fine grains of sand once more, I looked up at the flamboyant yet soothing streaks of colour that had filled the canvas of the sky, breathing in the briny aroma. I wriggled to get comfortable and closed my eyes trying to relax, but we both couldn't settle, nervous excitement I think. A shiver cascaded down my spine as my eyes burst open, my lips curved upwards, in that eureka moment came a cheshire grin, as a rush of realisation hit me. "Goldie what just happened?" Goldie propped herself up on her elbow, squinted from the sun and leaned towards me, "Wi ave dates an eh gwine bi fun, dat a wah." We looked at each other, giggled like two little school girls then got up and ran into the sea, splashing and waving our arms like we were completely insane.

The water was warm and pure, an unbroken calm, speckled by a million fragments of light, each one so tiny but clustered together, utterly beautiful and so soothing. I wanted to dive in cleanly leaving no splashes and cleave the water with powerful rhythmic strokes until I reached the deeper part. However what happened in my mind never turned out that way. I belly flopped unceremoniously into the water, spray flying outwards several feet before I started to swim. Goldie was also writhing around from front to back, diving in and out. If there were any fish watching us, they will be laughing at our swimming antics. We larked around for what seemed ages, no concept of time until the voice of reason came. "An eh gwine bi funout to dry off." Good old Goldie, its quite nice not having to take charge for once.

We lay back down on the sand again to dry off, I put my sunglasses back on, rolled onto my stomach and faced the sea, arms folded in front of me. I was soon lost, gazing at the forever stretching sea masked with an apricot colour from the sun, a beautiful umber flowing into turquoise. I watched as each wave overlapped one another, sending tiny white bubbling crests to the shoreline then retreating with transparent fading water and a gentle shhh.

Goldie rolled onto her front too and poked me."Time guh an git ready" she announced, it was late afternoon and starting to get slightly breezy. We got up, tucked our towels under our arms, picked up the cool box and took the short stroll back to our villa. I stole another look at the beach as we left in order to commit it to my memory I don't just want the photographs I want to bottle the scent and have seashells to touch, I want to recall the feel of the sand between my toes and the clarity of the ocean, I want to be able to come here in my dreams and relax.

Chapter 14

Amid the clowning around and laughter we got ourselves ready for our 'date night,' I was on the edge of my seat as the saying goes, excitement taking over, butterflies in my stomach, I felt slightly nauseated with all this nervous energy. Goldie was first to venture into her shower, put on make up then get dressed in her usual brightly chaotic coloured clothes, but it did suit her, she would never be able to hide.

I got ready in my own bathroom and dressed in more classically restrained clothes in differing shades of blue, they weren't the most sensible for the climate but they would last me decades. When I walked out of the closet to ask Goldie if I looked ok, I had obviously spent far too long getting ready as she had developed the munchies and was sat on my bed, cheese puffs going into her mouth at a beat steady enough to impress any drummer. "What do you think" I asked. "Luk ok Cud bi ah bit more sexy" came her reply as she adjusted my top to reveal more cleavage and made me change my trousers and sketchers for a short skirt and heels. She did my hair in a sort of care free style with curls, freedom of expression via my hair, "Bring pan di art," she said smiling.

She stood staring at me, admiring her work, "Beautiful" she commented as she kissed me on the cheek and bounced back onto the bed, continuing to devour more cheese puffs, she looked positively chipmunk-like. I giggled, she giggled, I don't know why, but we then found ourselves laughing so hard, tears formed and cheese puff crumbs flew everywhere, we just couldn't stop. We laughed until our ribs hurt, then as quickly as it came, the brief outburst of laughter was brought under control as there was a knock at the door. Goldie answered whilst I swept the crumbs off the bed and back into the bowl. Voices alerted me to the arrival of our respective dates, as I looked up, the men were now stood on what was left of the cheese puffs on the bedroom floor turning them into flattened crumb pieces, oh well cleaning could wait until tomorrow, I was on holiday after all!

We all walked into the kitchen, the topic of conversation was that Leroy and Mr Timothy Meyers couldn't agree as to who was to pick us up, so they both arrived in their own cars but followed each other in convoy arriving together, but separate, if you catch my drift, gosh that was a bit convoluted!

Leroy was sporting a pair of khaki shorts and a very Caribbean shirt, he turned up in an old beaten up brown Ford Mustang which made almost as much noise as Goldie. Mr Timothy Meyers meanwhile, was dressed in a pair of linen trousers and a white shirt and drove a shiny black Audi Q7. Funny how they were similar to us, anyway as we both clambered into our respective cars, Goldie turned and looked at me, the corners of her lips fighting a smile, her eyebrows slightly raised. I had to look away before that mischievous look of hers spread and we would start laughing again, we followed each other in unison to the restaurant, Mr Timothy Meyers leading.

The restaurant, or grill as it was known was situated next to a quayside and was already quite full when we arrived. I looked around, there was a lot of noise and smoke too, but it didn't bother me, I loved to soak up the atmosphere wherever I happened to be. There were motor and sailing boats moored all around the quayside, bright yellow-and-green water taxis nipped back and forth between the moored boats, bringing people for their dining experience. As we waited to be seated, I started to people watch, there was an older couple sat side by side, glass of wine each, studiously bent over their meals, savouring the taste. A group of young women probably in their thirties were collapsing with helpless hysterics, as a stern woman sat nearby dining alone, looking on and frowning at their antics. Nearby was a family and their teenage children, their table alive with the usual family dynamics.

Soon we were being escorted through the grill to our reserved table outside. I spied the buffet counter on one side, laden with everything you could think of to eat, along with some foods I have never eaten. Whole fish, spit roasted goat and wild boar, platters of conch, fruits and nuts. Other ocean creatures drizzled in sauces, all begging to be dipped into spicy concoctions, countless numbers of cheeses, breads, vegetables, desserts.

The bar sat to the side of the buffet and was adorned with bottles of different types of rum and beers, I never knew there were so many varieties. As we were seated, the waiter informed us that it was all you can eat and take back to your table as many times as you wanted. "Fi mi type ah bikkle, lets git stuck eena" Goldie commented. Loosely translated it means, my type of food, lets get stuck in, or words to that effect. I was mesmerised by this place, so her comment fell on deaf ears. Every table was covered with wipeable checked tablecloths, upon them sat condiments in plastic bottles and a tube of kitchen roll, no expense spared! It didn't matter though, this was going to be a fun night.

The band was strategically placed on a mock up stage made from wooden pallets, topped with planks of wood for extra support. As strategically placed themselves and their music began to dance out of the instruments, my feet began to tap and my head bobbed to the swinging Caribbean reggae rhythm. Man I loved this sound, deep soul, soothing, sweet as honey pie music. It surged through me, a musical language straight to my soul, the strumming sound had a hypnotic quality, I could easily loose myself to its melody, this was my idea of a heavenly evening, great food, great atmosphere and great company, what more could a girl want.

Mr Timothy Meyers, pulled my chair away as I stood up and we made our way to the buffet, what a gentleman. I think Leroy tried to do the same, but Goldie was up and out of her chair before he had chance. We strolled over to choose our meals, Leroy waved at the barman, ordering water, rum punch and Carib to be delivered to our table.

We sat back down, plates piled high, table laden with drinks. Leroy sat himself next to Goldie, they already seemed more than acquaintances in a such a short time, lovers even, their body language seemed full of desire and the pain of having to wait to get their hands on one another. Mr Timothy Meyers sat next to me, we chatted freely but there was also a heavy awkwardness, it appeared we were on the sensible side of the table.

I began to daydream, taking in his cheekbones, full lips and tanned skin, there was something so sexy in the way he looked. I was definitely falling in love. I became aware of a silence as I drifted back to reality, I knew he had been talking as his lips had been moving, but now he's waiting for a response, unfortunately I didn't have clue as to what he had been saying. I blushed as his look of bafflement became a shy smile, Goldie giggled, "I'm so very sorry" I said, he laughed, "Don't worry, it wasn't important, are you ok? You were miles away." I nodded, embarrassed, he smiled again, before winking at me. I'm sure this was his way of trying to put me at ease, but I had made myself look stupid, why do I put myself through this? We all continued to sit and chat, helping each other find ways to make our stay enjoyable, we were each other's best doctor and medicine combined. The freedom, the music and the smiles from people who care, it's a fragment of heaven, a chance to enjoy their company and start to want more.

I wanted to ask about the real reason we were here, when we would start our article and did he have a plan for it, but now wasn't the time, I didn't want to ruin our evening and anyway every time I thought of a question to ask, the conversation had moved in another direction. There will be plenty of time for the Alise report, which reminds me, I must text Pia before I go to bed and find out what is happening back at the office.

The evening came to a close all to soon, Goldie gave me a hug, announcing she was going back to Leroy's place and would see me later. I waited with Mr Timothy Meyers, as he insisted he was settling the bill before we headed outside to his car. I sat in the passenger seat still with the thought that at no point in the last two days had he brought up the reason why we were summoned here. It keeps playing on my mind, I must ask him, what have I got to loose.

He climbed into the drivers seat, fired up the ignition and turned to face me, as he leant forward my pulse began to race, a small lock of hair tumbled in front of my face resting just on my cheek for a moment until with one gentle slide of his thumb he brushed it aside. I bit my lip, eyes everywhere except trying not to make eye contact with him. He moved closer, his eyes looking deeply into my own, I could not avoid contact anymore. My breathing heightened, but my pensive look melted into a soft smile, my body squirming a little as my muscles tried to relax.

If it were anyone else I would drop my gaze, but with him I'm drawn in to his power, wanting more. His lips touched my cheek and suddenly time stopped still, my heart came to a halt and my breath caught in my throat. Without speaking, our fingers locked together similar to puzzle pieces, as the soft skin of his mouth left the side of my face. My cheeks felt like they had painted themselves a rosy red colour, as a hot blazing fire pulsed through me. He pulled away still not speaking, but our eyes remained locked, they were having a private conversation of their own.

He leant forward again and placed his arms around me, this time I leaned closer into him. The softness and gentle touch of his arm against my neck made me tingle. At the touch of a button his sunroof glided open and we tilted our heads upwards, looking at the stars and trying to spot constellations. This was romantic, it was weird, we didn't need to speak because in our own way, we were already communicating.

He kissed my cheek again, I felt a warmth spread through my limbs and my mind felt a pleasant buzz. This is it, I know I've found what I've been looking for, someone to show me what it means to be happy from the inside out, so my smile can be real and not a mask. Suddenly, my sensible side appeared and I pulled away. "Mr Meyers, this is too fast, we have only just met" I said. "It's ok Jaz and please call me Tim," he laughed and then whispered. I stared at him, why on earth had I just said that? Luckily for me, he ignored my sensible side and resumed play, pulling me towards him, covering my mouth with his hungry kiss. As our lips crushed together, I felt like I was walking on air.

It was pure magic, the way his lips connected with mine, his mouth was so warm, the caress of his lips even softer than I could have imagined, I let out a low groan. Tim held me gently, cupping my face with one hand, he leaned down and softly kissed the tender area at the base of my neck. My body went rigid with surprise, I trembled as a euphoric warmth blossomed within me, I became breathless with delight as he showered me with gentle, soft kisses, each with its own flicker of warmth. He drew back again and spent a moment studying my face, his eyes softening with tenderness before sparking with something else. He tightened his grip again, before crushing my body into his once more, he was so gentle yet firm. I felt a smouldering heat deep within me, I felt completely helpless and I loved it.

I didn't want this moment to end but it had to as we couldn't sit in the car park all night. Tim gently pulled away, closed the sunroof then kissed me again, "Lets get you home." He said as he restarted the engine. We drove back to the villa in silence, I was smouldering, he was unbelievably hot and hopefully if I played my cards right, was going to be mine forever

Chapter 15

After a late night both Goldie and I slept in. Slowly and reluctantly I uncovered my face, letting a warm ball of light filter through my eyelids, waking me to another day of our vacation. I opened my eyes a little more, seeing the rays of brightness casting shapes onto the glossy stone floor and reflecting onto several objects in the room. I blinked a few times, in an attempt to help my eyes adjust to the illumination before sitting up and stretching my legs over the side of the bed. I rubbed my knuckles onto my eyes and stretching my arms above my head I let out a yawn which resembled the sound of a cow.

I meandered into Goldie's room, she was still fast asleep, and alone I might add. I prodded her, she awoke to her soft sheets and the morning light trickling in through the blinds. Shedding herself from the remaining glimpses of a dream, her eyes opened then shut, as she soaked in the warmth of her covers before letting her eyes see the sun's rays flooding her room as I opened her blinds. She let out an exasperated sigh, groaning as she rolled out of bed. "Wah time a it?" She muttered, yawning and stretching at the same time. I laughed, "Does it matter we are on holiday."

I strolled into the kitchen to fix us both a bowl of cereal whilst Goldie got herself up. I sat at the kitchen table staring at the colourful wheels of cereal floating around in the bowl of milk as slivers of light peeped through the half closed blinds, casting thin golden stripes onto the cereal. I opened the blinds and grinned at the morning sun that sat in the sky like a perfect unspoiled egg yolk, it was already hot and made my skin glisten, the nape of my neck felt slightly damp from its heat, I sat back down and lifted a cold glass of sweet tea to my mouth.

Goldie joined me for breakfast eventually and the secrets of the previous night were openly discussed. Our conversation was like a kid's rubber ball bouncing back and forward as we compared notes and bared all about what happened. My night turned out to have been quite tame compared to Goldie's revelations. We began to titter which turned into ripples of laughter and very quickly became great waves of hilarity, we even laughed as Goldie spilt the milk over the floor. Now we had that to clean up as well as the cheese puff crumbs in my bedroom, which by now resembled sand.

My mobile burst into life, surprise! It was Tim, at the same time Leroy appeared at the door to our villa with an armful of Johnny cakes. Were these two telepathic or what! Whilst Goldie babbled away to Leroy, I continued my conversation with Tim. Out of the blue, he had phoned about us doing our article for the Alise. Apparently the person who had initially got in contact with his paper, had been in contact again early this morning and wanted to meet in order for us to do an interview for the Alise. I paused, I had wanted to ask him about this last night, but had been too shy and also got carried away.

I took a deep breath, as I felt a soft panic that I knew could grow or fade depending on what I did or said next. Tim must have sensed my hesitation, "Jaz, don't worry, I will be there as well, it's not just you and Goldie getting the story," "Oh, ok" I replied. "When and where?" "This afternoon three o'clock at Barefoot Buddha, its a little cafe," he answered very exacting. By now I had put my mobile on speaker and Goldie's babble had turned into silence, her head was nodding as she was listening. "I can drive you both there," Leroy interrupted. "Looks like its on then" I answered back. "Ok I will see you there," Tim replied and then continued with, "Jaz, I just wanted you to know that last night, well it's as if space and time became the finest point imaginable, as if time collapsed into one tiny speck and exploded at light speed, my universe wants to begin and end with you, I know that sounds corny, but its true."

Before I answered, I caught sight of Goldie doing some odd gesticulation with her hands and Leroy was grinning from ear to ear. It was then I realised that Tim was still on speaker phone. Embarrassed I clicked off the speaker button but accidentally cut him off, oops, he rang back, "Sorry, I um, accidentally cut you off, yes we will see you at three." I said and with that the phone fell silent. As I grabbed a Johnny cake, both Goldie and Leroy spluttered and then let out a huge guffaw of laughter, "What?" I said trying to cover up my own embarrassment, it made them laugh even more.

I went to my room, slightly exasperated by them, got changed and went to the beach, leaving Goldie and Leroy messing about in the hammock amid straying Jonny cakes which were being scattered on the porch floor. I felt sure he was supposed to be at work, but when in the heat of the moment and all that, they seemed inseparable, how had this happened so quickly?

Once on the beach, I decided to take a stroll along the waters edge, it was so breathtaking, I could walk for miles if I wanted, alone with just my thoughts. Ahead the celestial fireball tried to blind me through my sunglasses as it continued to rise in the sky like a glowing medallion, not a cloud to be seen. Topaz sunbursts of light smashed against the calming blue of the ocean, lighting up the sea, whilst the waves carelessly dribbled onto the untouched golden sand as far as my eyes can see. This is paradise in every sense of the word, my eyes became a digital camera, catching every corner of the landscape and every movement, little crabs, diving pelicans, and the distant white ribbon of the reef.

With every step I took the powdery sand shifted under foot, warm from the sun's rays. This Island was so pure and warm, it had engulfed my soul and made itself at home for life. I guess that is why all traveller reviews say they fall in love with this place instantly, I felt on top of the world.

I paddled for a while, the tide gently dribbling in and out, drawn to the horizon. I couldn't get Tim out of my mind, I knew I was falling in love with him, for me that was the easy part, it's admitting to myself that its happening that's hard. I've had very efficient defences for so long, I was not sure if I was ready for them to come tumbling down just yet. On the one hand I was happy to have met him, but I'm scared too, I've never wanted any form of happy-ever-after until now. I really needed to take control, this was a working holiday, a bit of fun, I would never see him again once our stay was over.

My stomach growled, I patted it, hoping to silence the rumbling, I glanced at my phone, twelve thirty already, I had walked for miles without knowing it. I turned and headed back to the villa at a faster pace, aware of the three o'clock appointment that I could easily miss if I dilly dallied.

I arrived at the villa in record time, perspiring badly from walking too fast in the heat, I was thirsty and hungry. I meandered into the kitchen, there was complete silence, no one was about only the sound of my stomach echoed around the room. I opened the fridge, made myself a sandwich and a drink all whist trying to text Goldie to see where she was. Who knows where or what she was up to but it would be something mischievous and involving Leroy that was for sure.

I finished my sandwich and was tucking into a piece of watermelon before she even messaged back in some undecipherable code. It read 'Mi an Leroy bashy fi each odda eena bar cum ova' which for the English amongst us means "me and Leroy are hot for each other, we are in bar, come over." What is it about a holiday romance that's so beautiful, exotic, exhilarating and so far away from reality that it is usually bound for disaster? A flood of endorphins I guess is all part of it. A few moments of sexual imagination and we all release the troubles of our upper brain and let the space where pleasure is king take over. I texted back "Both of you need to come back here we are supposed to be meeting Tim at Barefoot Buddha in half an hour, preferably sober." Hopefully that would bring them back to planet earth.

I had just finished my third slice of watermelon when she strolled in, Leroy still attached to her arm like an oversized limpet. "Hello lovely" he uttered as Goldie smirked. "Suh much fun wi hav did hav." She managed to utter. "For goodness sake Leroy, put her down," I laughed as I said it, slightly jealous but also a little bit nauseated, Goldie saw the funny side of it too and brushed his arm away commenting, "Shoo, Shoo."

We both showered and dressed in cool but appropriate working attire as Leroy sat at the kitchen table a 'Carib' in his grasp resembling someone from the jungle, wild and unruly, hopefully the offer of a lift was the only part he was to play this afternoon.

His jaw dropped as we both reappeared "Lack unnu mout
Leroy, wi a nah codfish cum alang spit spot" Goldie
announced in a Caribbean Mary Poppins accent. Leroy
immediately jumped to attention and escorted us to his car
which was now covered in sand and dirt. Great, this does not
give a good impression of the Alise, not only were we going
to arrive in a dirty beaten up car but our chauffeur resembled
Tarzan, hopefully we can persuade him to park around the
back somewhere out of site.

Chapter 16

The car journey was, well, all I can say is it was memorable but for all the wrong reasons. Goldie sat in the front whilst I was relegated to the back seat. Leroy's hands almost continually stroked Goldie's knees and possibly further up, the only time they were removed was for gear changes. Slightly embarrassed, I looked out of the window for the majority of the journey, so as not to feel nauseated by the sexual chemistry in the front. If that wasn't bad enough, the radio was on filling our ears with the latest popular but mostly dreadful Caribbean tunes. I must be getting old to think that this music was from the pop idols of the future, God help us!

The car hurtled at a reasonable speed towards our destination, veering now and again to avoid rogue chickens and goats. I rested my hands on the torn fabric of the backseat to steady myself as a half-empty bottle of single malt rolled towards me. To take my mind off of the cars contents and our journey I tried to think about the questions we had planned to ask and what type of angle we should take for the story. I know Goldie was used to 'winging it' and she did a good job but I was the boss and I wanted us to look and act the part and to do a good job with the story. After all, who knows, this could open up new avenues for the Alise.

Thankfully we arrived in one piece and before we got out the car I prepped Goldie with a few details. Leroy got out of the car and was talking to Tim who had just pulled in, both men shook hands. I am still convinced that there is more to these two and that they both know one another. Goldie got out of the car and pulled the seat forward for me. Tim and Leroy smirked as I clambered uncomfortably out of the death-trap trying to look sophisticated.

Barefoot Buddha is a cafe on the other side of the Island, it has lots of square glass-topped tables scattered about in no particular pattern. Small yellow vases of purple lilies adorned each table, and the menus were housed safely under the glass tops. The ceiling fans whirled frantically above a terracotta rustic tiled floor, cracked in a few places, whilst large open windows let the outside in and vice versa.

Outside was a grey stone tiled patio and yet more tables, each one shaded by its own green sun umbrella and arranged to overlook the expanse of ocean. The aromas started to inhabit my nostrils, the smell, more delicious than I could imagine, it captured everything Caribbean, the filter coffee, the various cakes and pastries, the spices, the coconut, the blend was perfection.

We grabbed a table and ordered coffee and pastries, Tim informed Goldie and I that Leroy would be staying as an extra pair of hands as he arrived back from paying. When we asked Tim about this further, he became very dismissive and changed the conversation abruptly. I must remember to ask him more about Leroy's unexpected involvement later, what was he going to do as an extra pair of hands? It really does look more like these two are in collusion with each other.

We all sat at a table next to an open window, chatting and waiting patiently. I looked around still listening to Tim who was talking about the BVI paper, I loved these cute places, each one was vibrant and the locals were always really friendly. I took my phone from my pocket and raised it ready to take a photo of the cafe, just a holiday snap, when Tim lowered it and whispered. "No photos Jaz, owner doesn't like it." I smiled and sighed but obeyed and replaced my phone in my pocket, how strange!

As I turned, I caught a glimpse of a man sitting alone at a corner table near the door. I think he was there when we came in, but couldn't be totally sure, not unusual in a cafe I hear you say. Initially I could only view him as a brownish blur to the left of me. I turned my head slightly more to look at him as he shifted in the chair, crossing and uncrossing his legs, he was wearing a brown topcoat, unusual in this heat and a little too big for him. Beneath this his clothes looked like they were once of high end quality, but now not so, with enough wear and dirt anything can look like rags. His skin was masked behind layers of grime and his longish hair hung in a tangled mop of grey from under a grubby baseball cap. His eyes caught mine and seemed to shine small, like raisins in the lights of the cafe. His large hands rested awkwardly on the polythene bag he held across his lap. His gaze was unwavering and unabashed, a cold shiver ran through me and caused goosebumps on my arms. I jumped, slightly unnerved as Tim stroked my arm, as if to warm me. "Are you ok Jaz, are you cold?" "Yes, sorry, I'm not cold, just thought I saw someone I knew." I replied. Goldie had seen the man too, "A dat Ed? Wah a wi gwine do?" I looked at her in total bewilderment, as she realised what she had just said and her face fell faster than a corpse in cement boots, her bronzed skin became slightly sallow and her mouth hung open. The thought had not occurred to me and I wasn't that sure that it was Ed Wrexham, although, now it had been said, I could see some similarities about the way he held himself.

Seeing both of us with mouths agape and in stunned silence, Tim took my hand and looking at us both said, "Do you want to tell me what is going on?" Just at that very moment, and without any signs of recognition, no raised hand or a brief nod, the man rose stiffly and with some trepidation from his chair and quickly disappeared outside. "Oh it's nothing, just thought it was someone we used to know, but I think we must have been mistaken." I smiled as I answered Tim. "Eh did Ed Wrexham fah sure Ave yuh hear seh ah him?" Goldie said loudly leaning over me and ignoring where she was.

As I moved her out of my line of sight, I noticed that Leroy was missing, "Where is Leroy?" I asked, Goldie looked around too, I hadn't noticed him leave the table. Tim was already standing up "For goodness sake you two, let's get after him."

How very strange, "Who, Leroy or the man?" I asked. Tim didn't answer as he was already outside the cafe, so we got up and hastened our pace outside to join him. It was all in vain, there was no sign of Leroy or the strange man, both had vanished into thin air. "Damn'" Tim uttered, before smiling at us both.

It was then I became aware of a gasping noise, breathing as if oxygen had been sucked from the air. I turned to see Leroy doubled over, hands on his knees, trying to catch his breath but only succeeding in making a wheezy, squeaky like noise, like some kind of weird instrument, quite worrying really, I thought he was fit! "Lost him, he gave me the slip," he eventually managed to sound out, "bugger," replied Tim. "Hang on a minute" I yelled out, "Do you two know that man, were you after him?" I had so many questions I wanted to blurt out, but I also needed the answers.

Tim looked at me and kissed my forehead, "Jaz, lies are a survival skill, but for you, there is always truth. He said, looking at his watch, four fifteen. "Well, looks like we have had a wasted journey, let's go for a rum and put the incident behind us, what do you say?" Tim stroked the side of my face as he spoke, I was melting, from his touch and the heat, so agreed reluctantly, but I wasn't going to let this go, something was happening, and I had plenty of questions, the incident wasn't going be swept away so easily.

Leroy seemed to have recovered very quickly and was now running to the car with Goldie on his back, smacking him playfully with her hand to make him go faster, I had to laugh. Tim took my hand as we walked to his car, why couldn't I act silly like Goldie? As that thought was running through my head and with no regard for where we were, Tim unexpectedly pulled me against his chest, his nose tickled my ear. I let out a tiny gasp and squirmed uncomfortably, I didn't like being so touched so intimately in public, especially as some of the cafes' occupants had come outside to watch the shenanigans.

It didn't seem to bother Tim as I felt his lips softly graze on my neck, I felt myself blush and begin to overheat. I managed to wriggle around so that we could make eye contact as we stood on the sandy, grassy ground, Tim cupped his hands around my face and let his lips reach towards mine, touching them lightly before the urge to kiss took over. In the minutes that followed, in that moment of the kiss we are our pure and vulnerable selves. As he pulled back he whispered, "I'm falling for you Jaz," the gathered crowd applauded and whistled, how common! I pulled away, my knees knocking together "Sorry, you are irresistible" he uttered. I smiled and licked my lips "it's fine, just not here." Was all I could reply. There is a shy side of me, a cautious spirit woven with an adventurous side and they must always accommodate one another's wishes, for today the cautious spirit had won.

We rejoined Goldie and Leroy, who were now under a coconut tree, scantily clad, their excuse being, they were trying to stay 'cool' whilst waiting for us. Tim and I looked at each other, 'yeah right!' After putting their clothes back on, Tim offered to show me around the newspaper office, he winked at Leroy, who then extended the invitation to Goldie, obviously the answer was no. She and Leroy had other ideas of how they would spend the next fews hours, we arranged to meet them at the Conch bar at seven.

As we drove to the BVI office, Tim was oddly apologetic, there was definitely more to this. "Really sorry about this afternoon Jaz, I'll try and sort something out for another day, trouble is, I have to wait for the source to contact me, they don't seem that reliable." "No worries, Tim is there something I am missing? There seems to be a bit more to this, what are you not telling me?" I asked. There was no reply.

By now, we had reached the BVI office and he was able to avoid continuing our conversation by helping me out of the car, ever the gentleman, and leading me through a short darkish narrow corridor to a square room divided into four other rooms, each with their own door and privacy shutters covering the windows. There was no sign outside saying BVI Beacon, no one about and there was no noise, just stillness in the air, all very odd. "This is me" pointing ahead as he ushered me into a tiny room no bigger than a broom cupboard.

It consisted of a completely empty desk, no files, no laptop, nothing. Two chairs sat to one side and a filing cabinet hugged the wall, it all looked brand new. Nobody came to greet us, not a single soul around, very odd for a newspaper office, normally it would be full of hustle and bustle, chatter, typing on computers, radios blaring. Really very odd!

Before I had chance to say anything more than "Tim," he stopped me in my tracks and said, "shh my darling" and closed the door behind me, I was so nervous but I tried so hard not to show it. He proceeded to wrap his arms around me, dropping his right hand to my thigh, pulling up my skirt that hung just above my knees. I couldn't move even if I tried, his fingers seemed to have short-circuited my mind in the best possible way. He turned me around and we tumbled onto the desk, his eyes searching mine. I smiled and kissed him, I felt his mouth stretching wider than it should, fighting between a grin and kiss.

Our lips fitted perfectly, as if it was meant to be, we continued to squirm against each other, feeling and caressing our bodies. Tim gently grabbed the back of my neck and I whimpered with pleasure. There's something about him that lights up my insides, touching him felt like I was being handed the holy grail, my heart mended even though I never knew it was broken. I found myself relaxing more and more as the moment just kept getting better.

I had every intention of not letting this go too far, that was until his hand massaged my breasts. The acceleration of my heart-rate had nothing to do with fear but everything to do with what my body really wanted. I glanced at the ceiling as if the ghost world held my attention, but he read me like a book, eyes on my chest, my breathing rate duly noted, he reoriented my face gently with his fingers. There was no smile on his lips, only the hot intensity of his gaze that we both knew was the start of the passionate inferno to come.

Tim's finger tips are electric, my skin tingles in a frenzy of static, as his hands move over my skin, my body has a transitory paralysis, my mind unable to process the pleasure so fast. His head moves around to my left ear and he whispers what's coming next. Suddenly my body is off pause-mode and I pull back for a kiss that's both soft and hard. Both of us begin to move in an intoxicated dance of limbs, never making the exact same moves twice. Inconveniently, we were interrupted by my phone. "Leave it" he whispered, but I couldn't it might be important. It was Goldie. "Yow fi mi fren, Wah a yuh up to? Ed Wrexham a alive an pan di Island Mi did si him cum outta an hul building. Yuh muss cum now." I felt myself hold my breath as Tim sighed, reached for the phone and silenced clicked off the call before I could reply.

But that was it, I couldn't settle, "Tim, I'm really sorry, that was Goldie, I have to go, Can we continue this again later?" What on earth was I saying? He smiled as he raised his eyebrows, but politely replied "Yes Jasmine, I would definitely like that, is Goldie in trouble?" As I had already ruined the passion by answering the phone, I decided to take my chance, after all what did I have to loose? "Tim, please don't deceive me, I am not stupid, there is something going on, this is not the BVI Office and you are not an editor." Did he respond to that? No, he did not, instead he caressed my neck with his lips and whispered, "Shh, I'll give you a lift back to the villa," then kissed me again. I was intoxicated by him, but I needed answers, I would just have to use my womanly powers to extract them from him and stop letting him over power my thoughts.

Chapter 17

As I strolled into the villa, Goldie was in the kitchen, wrapped in a towel, having just made lemongrass lemonade. "Well, what's going on?" She pushed a drink towards me, "Suh Mi did ah jus deh leff Leroy wen mi did si him he did di guy inna cafe wi did si Mia sure ah ih. Eh him a call wi yah mia sure ah ih." "Goldie, none of this makes any sense, what on earth is Tim and Leroy's involvement, I agree, I think they know Ed, but why are they pretending to be someone they are not?" I needed to think out loud and I didn't expect a reply, but I got one anyway, short and ridiculous, "Tim's ah spy." Goldie said looking at me with a straight face. I laughed, spraying the mouthful of lemonade across the room at the same time. "Goldie, you do spin some yarns, where on earth did you get that from, and what would be their motives?" She giggled, "Yuh a guh si. Anyway did tink wi cud gwaana di house an ave ah luk Si eff eh really a him" I stared at her completely taken aback from what she had just said.

As I stood there trying to process it, Tim is a spy, and she is sure it is Ed Wrexham, she wants to go the derelict house she saw him coming out of. It obviously took me too long, as she repeated it. "Ny way did tink wi cud gwaana di house an ave ah luk Si eff eh really a him," "I heard you the first time, I eventually replied, have you gone completely mad in this heat, why would we go looking for trouble Goldie?" She stared back at me with her serious face as I stood in front of her, I couldn't believe she had even suggested it, I really didn't want trouble, just a nice relaxing time researching and getting a newspaper story. Now she was suggesting that we get ourselves mixed up in some clandestine plan that would lead to a dangerous encounter, I could feel it in my waters.

Over the next twenty minutes as I showered Goldie chattered about the plan she wanted to hatch. It was to happen almost immediately, we would be safe as we were meeting the boys for the evening, so if we didn't turn up, they would come looking for us. Great fall back plan Goldie, if I am honest, I wasn't convinced this was a good idea but she was set on it, nothing was going to deter her and we needed to stay together to ensure our safety, so despite sharing my reservations with her, I ended up backed into a corner with very little choice.

After getting dressed and munching our way through some coconut dumplings we put her slightly reckless and not properly thought through plan into action, preparing ourselves mentally for any risks that lay ahead. It involved strolling to the other side of the Island, luckily, Anegada is small so it took us about three quarters of an hour in the heat, stopping for water on the way.

The neighbourhood on this side of the Island is quite different, it has been re-built for the most part, but there are still plenty of untouched derelict buildings remaining, clinging to the scenery, stubbornly refusing to die. As I looked at them, I thought to myself that derelict is such a harsh word, they are abandoned for sure, home only to the array of wildlife that shelters within them. Yet they have stood in all weathers, as if there is a pride in their lasting, a sense of a strength that could be renewed if asked.

There were a few local children running in and out of one of them with flashlights, eager to find anything worthwhile, or to use the place as a den. Goldie said that Leroy had told her there had been a few cases of children falling through rotten stairways or treading on needles. Most of the kids petty crimes were to get a thrill from making fires inside, but unfortunately it didn't go down too well with the teenagers who were believed to be using the buildings for drug taking, although that had never been proven.

We made our way inside a particular derelict house which Goldie had singled out. Its yellowed walls were peeling and blistering from the sun baked dryness, the floor was just a dusty concrete base. This house had discovered the company of the trees and wildflowers that brought brightness right up to its doors and windows. Goldie stared at me with a look of despair as she caught me standing in the opening for all to see, well only if anyone passed by. " Wah di hell a yuh a duh gyal Dis a nuh breaking an entering. Eh jus entering Bikaaz deh a nuh door." She rolled her eyes, as despite feeling very uneasy, I quickly did as I was told and stood by her side.

We sifted and sorted with our eyes, constantly on the lookout for any gleam of information that might help with the mystery of 'Tilly and Ed'. As we made our way further into the house I looked up at the open roof, letting the darkening blue sky bring us comfort. Stepping forward, I trod on one of the old fallen roof tiles, it cracked under my foot, "Shhh," Goldie said, this was ridiculous, we weren't going to find anything.

I was about to speak, when Goldie looked at me, "Hush yuh mouth Jaz." We were both silent, listening, suddenly a man's voice echoed through the walls. "I know you're here, I saw you come in, you are in my place, I know who you are." The outrage, the entitlement, the insistence in his voice really frightened us, as we stood, shaking and frozen to the spot, grabbing hold of each other for security. "I told you this was a bad idea." I whispered firming my grip on Goldie's arm. An odd shaped shadow appeared projected onto the wall to the side of us, it had to be a distortion of the light didn't it? My imagination took over, and I thought I saw someone staring at us with wide, horrific eyes. I gasped and stumbled backwards, jarring my shoe down the wall behind me. "Sh… Goldie covered her hand over my mouth to stop me from swearing and helped me up, we were still both trembling, "Wi need tuh git outta yah Faas." For once, I was in complete agreement, the faster the better for me.

We looked around, there was nothing here, just a stillness in the air remained. Have they now gone or are they laying in wait, ready to jump out on us, as prey? Where was the quickest and safest escape route out of here? To the left of us was another room, dust floating through the air caught in a swirl with the days final rays of sunlight streaming in from a wrecked window opening. If we lurched sideways now and headed through it we would be outside in no time, but we had to act fast. We couldn't go back the way we came, in case he was lying in wait for us, Goldie pushed me forward. "Guh, guh." We both moved clumsily to our left and as fast as we could, helping each other through the opening and onto a mass of vibrant weeds covering the ground below, then pulling each other along, we ran, ran for our lives.

The man appeared, he was right behind us, chasing, hoping for a capture. Our faces were flushed red, we were not fit and running in this heat was totally exhausting, I can't remember the last time I ran, but we kept going. We had a sort of primal fear, the kind that brings out every ounce of you, that empties your reserve tank and ignores your physical and mental pain in the pursuit of safety.

Being chased was nothing like it was in the movies, the actors made it look heroic and that they stay in full command of the situation. Reality was far removed from that fictional version of running to save your skin. I managed to trip over something and fell onto the hot tarmac road, I did feel a sudden but brief pain surge around my knee area, but before I had any time to think about it, Goldie scooped me up and pulled me along with her. The footsteps still sounded behind us as we turned a corner and ran down another road, with absolutely no idea of where we were going. Typical, not a soul around, we had to find somewhere to hide before we collapsed and he caught us.

Panting for breath I was ready to surrender, I didn't care, I couldn't run anymore. I stopped momentarily and leant forward hands on my hips to catch my breath, Goldie stopped too. "Wi haffi keep a go," she shrieked. From the corner of my eye, I noticed a backyard fence entwined with shrubbery with a broken gate, who cares if anyone lived there, safety is paramount. Without any further hesitation I pulled Goldie through, she fell sideways as I yanked her and we both fell into a crumpled dusty heap behind the fence.

We crouched as still as statues our hearts pounding in our mouths for what seemed like an eternity. We couldn't hear the footsteps anymore. Peering through the slats in the fence between the greenery we started to breathe a sigh of relief, it seemed we had shaken off our chaser, but we were still too scared to come out from behind the fence just in case.

Out of nowhere Goldie's mobile buzzed liked an annoyed rattlesnake, I had completely forgotten she had it with her. "Jus eena case." She had said. Goldie scooped it from her back trouser pocket, listened for a moment and then whispered some Caribbean chat, that ended in come and get us, it had to be Leroy. She replaced the phone back in her pocket. "Im a cum tuh git wi seemed tuh kno fi im fences

Cud'n geem real directions." She said, I nodded, "You mean Leroy?" She smiled and did a thumbs up as she peered through the fence once more. How on earth she thought he was going to find us by giving him directions in terms of fences and hedges, I can only wonder. "Mi tink wi hab laas him," she sighed.

After what seemed an eternity, a rattling motor announced the arrival of Leroy. He had parked by the fence and was now 'liming' casually beside it. "The coast is clear ladies, you came come out now," he said peering over the top of the fence. Cautiously we stood up and brushed ourselves free of dirt and grass, checking the vicinity to ensure he was correct. I have to say, he was right, there was absolutely no one else around, relieved we clambered quickly into the car. "Should I ask what you too have been up to on this side of the Island?" he smirked as he spoke, I think deep down, he knew. "Nothing, just got a bit sidetracked and sat behind the fence to cool off, we were lost and couldn't reorientate ourselves." I replied, hoping that would placate him but he was still smirking at me in the car mirror.

Goldie however, decided she was going to use the short journey back to reveal all and once on a roll, despite me prodding and trying to silence her, there was no stopping her. "Ed Wrexham a yah Wi gaan tuh dis hul house weh he a supposed tuh par Ih did empty suh wi smooched roun Den he cum bac. He did gwine kill wi suh wi ran an he chased wi Suh wi hid, den yuh rang." She uttered almost without

124

pausing for breath, I poked her a couple more times to try and stop her flow but she ignored me until eventually she finished. Silence fell in the car, Leroy looked in his mirror at us, "Honestly, you two, we need to let Tim know about your little adventure." "Why," I answered, Leroy just replied "because." Goldie seemed quite put out by his reply and uttered, "Eh all chuu Nuh yuh believe wi." Leroy just smirked.

It seemed odd that Leroy could actually understand Goldie as well and he had only know her for a very short time. It took me ages to learn the gist of what she says. Anyway on this particular occasion, she was correct in saying we were chased and that we went to this derelict house, but the only person who thought it was Ed Wrexham was her, she had convinced herself that she had seen him. I have to say, I don't know why we need to inform Tim though, why should he care?

As we arrived back at our villa, Tim was already there waiting for us. He was sat on the porch steps mopping his brow with a handkerchief. Leroy followed behind me with Goldie, "You might want to hear this," he said to Tim, raising his eyebrows. "What have you two been up to then? Leroy rang me to say he was going to fetch you, I was concerned for your well being." Tim hugged me tightly and then planted a smooth kiss on my cheek, at the same time, Lourdes appeared with a tray of 'Stamp and go,' dressed lobster and a jug of lemongrass lemonade and of course a jug of rum punch, just in case we fancied anything alcoholic.

"I took the liberty, hope you don't mind, thought this would be better than going out and I need to hear what happened, rather do that behind closed doors than in public," Tim said as we looked at him and all the food in bewilderment. "Dis feast a ah feast ah fi wi emotions Ah fi wi bonds Wid di bikkle as di perfect symbol ah an everlasting bond," Goldie said as she helped Lourdes arrange it on the table. "What exactly is Stamp and Go?" I asked Lourdes. She smiled at me, she had a lovely complexion with a few tiny lines etched around her eyes, the story of a happy life. Lines that spoke of laughter and told of a person who gave away smiles like they were wishes. "Stamp and Go, is a typical street food here in Anegada, it is a fritter made with salt cod and, or conch. I make this hot sweet chilli dipping sauce to go with it, my mothers secret recipe." She placed the sauce on the table next to the fritters, "Enjoy your meal," she said winking at Tim and then left us.

Chapter 18

As we all sat enjoying the food, Goldie and I explained to Tim what had happened, trying not to skip on any of the details. It seemed to take us forever, made worse by Leroy's constant interrupts and wanting clarification on certain aspects. I have to say it was really annoying, but I needed to have more patience, Leroy was just trying to gain a greater perspective of the situation. Tim, however just listened intently, his facial expressions not changing once, he just seemed to tune in and listen at a higher level than an ordinary person, occasionally asking a probing question in a certain way and at the right time.

Goldie was right, there was more to him, he watched our body language and followed our eye movements, he looked like he was taking mental notes of everything. Maybe he was a spy or some kind of secret agent, after all nothing seemed to be quite as it should be, least of all him. Should I ask him some questions? After all, since we had arrived he was hardly ever at the BVI office how could the paper run without him? Also the fact that newspaper office seemed to resemble a broom cupboard housing only him. If I give this a bit more thought, Leroy also seemed to have deserted his role at the bar whatever that was.

As an editor and 'boss' of a newspaper, you are ultimately responsible for what is published, assigning stories to reporters, liaising with the sub-editing and photography departments and deciding on the priority and the importance of all news articles. You also need to keep a constant check on the legal and ethical issues in a journalist's stories.

My old journalism professor at university used to say that a newspaper cannot run without the boss and when others present arguments based on only their emotions and prejudices, it was their role to acknowledge the emotions behind the comments but also be alert to any motives which may be hiding the truth, well he certainly was not there to do that.

For the rest of the evening, we continued to chat and I began to feel comfortable enough to trust Tim and Leroy. I found the strength to lower my emotional vulnerability shield and with the help of Goldie ended up explaining the events of what happened at Iberville with Lord Edward Wrexham, Lady Wrexham and Tilly. My tale concluded with Ed and Tilly escaping from prison and not being seen since, and I explained the odd feeling I had about the vagrant in the cafe who did bare a striking resemblance to Ed.

Goldie interrupted my train of thought by saying how brave I had been, going to court, giving evidence and writing an article in the newspaper about my ordeal. She finished by joking, saying I still looked over my shoulder if I had to go anywhere new, thank you Goldie, I did trust Tim but I wasn't ready to reveal my inner demons just yet.

By now, Leroy was handing around a spliff, we all took a drag and the conversation paused as our glasses were refilled with more rum punch, I was going to regret this in the morning that's for sure. From out of nowhere Leroy sat back on the chair and said, "According to certain sources, the government can now run all of your writings and audios through an artificial intelligence computer and from the choice of your words and language you use, they can determine your psychology, completely and literally read all your private thoughts.

If you have any online presence at all, especially, social media, you have no secrets, you are all bagged and tagged in cyber space." Tim sat still listening and only shook his head as Leroy realised what he had just said, Goldie and I were right, these two men had not told us the truth and we deserved to know. "Tim, Goldie and I deserve to know the truth, who are you both and what is going on?" I asked, Tim rubbed his head, obviously a bit woozy from Leroy's spliffs, but he was as chivalrous as ever, an exemplar of virtue. He replied. "It is getting very late and we should all retire for now, my brain feels like it has a low battery, we will talk more tomorrow."

I yawned, by now he was right, it was approaching midnight, "Would you like to stay?" I asked, God what was I thinking?

Tim nodded, "You know, we as individuals get to choose who we are, we can choose our better natures and build our own personhood, right now, there is nothing more human than feeling love." Tim said, as Goldie took Leroy by the hand and led him to her room, Tim took my hand too, how very forward of him! I could feel the chemical reaction in an instant as my sexual energy elevated and my stress levels reduced. Being with Tim definitely feels a lot easier than being apart.

Once in the sanctuary of my own room Tim and I climbed onto the bed. He smiled as he brushed my hair back from my shoulder and then moved in so close I could feel the warmth from his muscular body. I closed my eyes as he kissed me, as I reciprocated the gesture, he leant in further and began to caress my neck, slow and gentle with his tongue. I couldn't bare it, I wanted him right now.

He kissed my chest through my partly open top and whispered "I want you baby." Oh God, stop, I wanted him so much too, but my brain kept telling me that I needed to know the truth and this was all a bit too fast. I pushed him away slightly. "Tim, who are you really? Don't treat me like a fool, tell me the…" He smashed his lips against mine, stopping me, mid-sentence. "Shh, Jasmine, just stay cool," he whispered as he started to unbutton the rest of my top.

He was right, I should "shh," the power of love doesn't give me the right to meddle in his life, but I wanted to be his 'wonder woman' whoever he was. He was perfect in my eyes and to have the chance to be in his company for now was my little slice of heaven, his aura, an elixir. I became lost in the moment and started to relax, just as I had been ordered. As I let him continue disrobing and kissing me, working his way to my waist and then further, I shook with anticipation, every nerve in my body and brain electrified, its about being together in a way that's more than words, a way that's so completely tangible. Whilst my brain said, what the hell was I doing?

Before my brain could engage any further thoughts, we were both naked and the art of seduction took over. In one fluid motion I was astride Tim, our gaze lasting for only a full second, enough for each to take in each others faces. Nothing needed to be said, millions of years of evolution had already taken care of the message, he grabbed me gently and rolled me off of him and onto my back. The warmth of his flesh brushed my body, his electrifying energy soared through me, as a strong desire to play surfaced. His hands pinned me to the bed, I squirmed, curling my toes upwards, as his tongue caressed my body, leaving no part of me untouched, his hands stroking, always just a little higher than the kisses. My back arched, knowing where he would soon reach. My head rocked back against the pillow, a groan of shear ecstasy escaping from my lips. Our bodies fitted together as if we were made just for this, to fall into one another, to feel this natural rhythm as the showering sparks of positive chaos took us into the darkness.

Then we were lying next to each other panting, all dreamy eyed, until we caught our breaths. He rolled onto his side and pulled me close to him, his warm hand caressing my body, I shivered. "Jaz, that was fantastic," he smiled as he kissed me again. "You are right my darling, there is more to me." He wrapped his arms around me and I let my head rest upon his chest. He squeezed me tight, as if he needed to check I was really there with him, really there and really real and I was, in body and soul, completely open whilst he still remained mysterious!

Tim stood silhouetted against the open doorway of my bathroom, fresh from the shower but still wet in places, he has a perfect outline and he isn't wearing a stitch. He came back to bed and with one kiss my ambivalence shifted to enthusiasm. Then, there it is again, his finger tips electric as my skin tingles in a frenzy of static. His hands moved over me once more, my body has a transitory paralysis, my mind unable to process the pleasure this fast. His head moves around to my left ear and he whispers what's coming next, suddenly my body is off pause-mode and I pull back for a kiss that's both soft and hard. Both of us move in an intoxicated dance of limbs, never making the exact same moves twice, he was amazing!

We turned onto our backs once more staring at the ceiling, I was caught between the intoxication of the climax and extending a moment I never want to end, he was the man for me. Tim shifted awkwardly and took my hand, holding it tightly, "Jaz, I'm not an editor, nor do I work for a paper. I am a secret agent for the RSS." I swallowed hard, I never expected this, a spy! Goldie was right. It felt like a thousand knives had just pierced my heart. He had deceived me, he sensed that and squeezed my hand tighter, "I am truly sorry but it was a necessary disguise, I need to protect others, deception is a survival skill." He paused for another kiss and continued, "It wasn't just that, I knew that being a secret agent meant being a loner, not being able to commit, shutting the door on any romance because of the line of work, but then I met you.

Intelligence work always means having to look over your shoulder for the enemy, never able to stay in one place, a sacrifice none of the movies ever capture. There's a reason James Bond never settled down with anyone, except for a wife who was killed the same day he married her, the Bond character was always depicted as a lothario.

Tim rolled to face me, "Jaz, you have gone very quiet, are you ok?" I felt the tears welling up in my eyes, I couldn't make eye contact with him but I could tell he was regretting what had just been revealed, but we both knew I had to be told the truth. I sighed, the switch from reaction to reflection came on, I needed to process this and arrive at a good response. I felt kind of dejected, it's hard to want something or someone so much and then to discover that it might be beyond your reach. I wiped my eyes and nestled closer into his chest, suddenly the pieces of my heart that had been struggling to fit into this moment became quiet, it was as if they had found peace at last.

Tim held me closer than ever, "It doesn't change anything between us" he whispered. "How can you truly be sure of that" I said sounding melancholy. My brain was saying that I needed rest, but my heart wanted something different. "Tim, I know this is silly, but I am falling in love with you, I know we have only been together for a short time but I.." He held his finger to my lips then kissed me. In that very moment, I felt like we were in each others protective cocoon. "Let's sleep, you must know that I adore you too, don't you?" With that I felt so safe and secure that I closed my eyes and fell asleep in his arms.

Chapter 19

The following day, we were awoken by Goldie and Leroy's antics in the kitchen, allegedly they were making breakfast, but we decided to lay in for a while just to be sure. When we did decide to surface, what a sight to behold, the kitchen was a complete shambles, evidence of the great time Leroy and Goldie had had, disgusting, when food is involved! As the sensible couple, Tim and I began to clean up without saying much, so we could feel safe to eat our own breakfast without food debris everywhere. Thankfully by the time we sat down, their antics had moved to the shower, I wish I could be as brazen as Goldie!

Eventually both men left us, but made firm arrangements to meet up again later. We hadn't really been apart from them much since they met us, so it was good to get some girl time again. "Yuh ok Jaz Yuh seem laas," Goldie remarked as we strolled back to the kitchen. I sighed, "Tim started to open up to me last night and you were right he is a spy, now everything is ruined." She shook her head and raised her eyebrows before commenting. "Wah weh yuh a tink? Yuh shud hab bin a hav fun nuh ah third degree interview." "There was fun too, but now, there is no future for us and I really like him too." I replied looking forlorn. "Lovely, well kuff mi dung Mi kno in. Yuh lakka him nuh yuh Ih nut half change anyting Ih cud wuk eena fi wi favour." "Mmhm, how do you mean?" I answered slightly confused. "Cum pan Jaz Tink bout dis, Wah mek a he yah Wah mek a wi yah A Ed Wrexham here? He cud help wi fine di answers an yuh can still has ah criss time wid him inna process. Mi expec im areddi dug up di dirt pan wi Bill an fulljoy fi mi fren." I laughed, I hadn't considered he might look for information on us! If I stop to think about it, when we were revealing all about Iberville last night, he was listening to our words but probably at a deeper level than the ordinary person is able to comprehend. But to him it wasn't just words, it would have been the phonetics, the visual puns, the metaphors and our mannerisms. We were leaking a tonne of information without being aware of what we were giving away. I smiled and looked at Goldie, who was by now half way out the door yelling, "Cum pan Jaz, sea an sun a wah di docta ordered."

We strolled to the beach, spending the rest of morning working on our tans, larking about in the water and of course, drinking and eating. What a life, the only decisions are what order to do it all in! My skin, usually so pallid now had a warm, almost translucent glow. Even though I had lived in the Caribbean for a few years, I now had a rich caramel tone with a few dark freckles over the bridge of my nose. We placed our towels on the warm sand and I rolled onto my stomach, stupidly I had brought my phone with me, so was soon researching the RSS. I know I was on holiday, but I needed to know more so I wanted to ask Tim the appropriate questions, after all I didn't want to appear dim and uneducated.

The sand under my towel emitted a comforting warmth to rest on, matched by the sunshine filling the sky. Goldie was stretched out, both her arms and legs resembling a starfish again, her grin growing slowly into a broad smile. "Wah a yuh a duh? put unnu damn fone aweh an relax." She uttered as she pushed her sunglasses back onto her nose. "I am looking at what RSS is" came my reply. "Wah mek," "I am interested and I want to appear knowledgable." I said as she took the phone from me and put it in her towel bag. "Enuff empress jus relax an fulljoy di day Tap a tink." She was right, I always had to be thinking, one step ahead I suppose, I couldn't switch off. Luckily I had managed to find out a fair bit before she confiscated my phone, it was like being on holiday with your parents!

For the short time I had access to my phone and according to Google, 'The R.S.S' as it is commonly referred to, stands for Regional Security System, it is based in Barbados and headed predominantly by the army with government input. It consists of different units but serves mainly as a defence system for the Caribbean Sea, conducting specific secret operations, detecting and combating all cross-Atlantic and intra-Caribbean drug smuggling and protecting the sovereignties in the Caribbean. It also provides an assisted response to any security threats on any Caribbean Islands at the request of their respective Governments.

I rolled onto my back, relaxing and settling down to some serious sunbathing, trying to clear my mind. I pictured my mother calling me for lunch, my father sat in his deck chair, trousers rolled up to his knees, knotted handkerchief on his head and rustling a newspaper as he turned the pages. I was a little girl, playing with a red bucket and spade and making sandcastles, not a fear or worry to cross my mind, how lovely it would be to have the knowledge and wisdom of an adult but the innocence of a child.

Goldie suddenly sat upright as if some light bulb moment had occurred, I sat up, looking in the same direction as her. We both smiled at each other, as strolling towards us were Leroy and Tim carrying food and drink. Our own personal butlers, can't be bad, these two were joined at the hip, or so it seemed, where one was, the other was sure to be there too. I had to laugh to myself, maybe Leroy was Tim's side kick!

Todays picnic was courtesy of Leroy, when I say picnic, it was really a small feast, so much food. However, not that we weren't grateful, but as they laid the food before us, all I can say is it did not look appealing or in any way appetising. There was a light brown offensive smelling pile of scooped slush, apparently it was called Solomon Grundy and was a Caribbean delicacy made from pickled salt fish, minced and smothered in chilli peppers and spices, before being mashed into a pulp like pate, ready to be served on rye crackers. I have to say, when I did buck up the courage to try it, the taste wasn't as bad as I had expected. There was a bag of fried plantain, Johnny cakes and plenty of Caribbean salad to offset it, along with watermelon and pineapple.

They had also brought their snorkel gear, announcing that conditions are just right to see the reef. Leroy was really excited to show us the 'unseen wonders of the Caribbean' as he called it. I loved snorkelling, there was no greater wonderland on earth as far as I was concerned, than the community of corals and fish. So there was no complaints from me, Goldie also loved being under the ocean, "Mi can bi ah riva muma fah ah da," she would say if there were any reports I needed to do with the ocean.

We sat and stuffed ourselves full of food, chatting about the reef and Anegada. Tim explained how ocean conservation zones are becoming more pronounced, especially in Anegada, what was once over-fished has become abundant once more. Patience is indeed a virtue, and a part of ecological wisdom, if we fish less now, there will be far more later.

It was funny how we just all connected, as if we had been friends for many years. I savoured these moments in each others company and felt a sense of peace which comes from the feeling of being loved and protected. I was really desperate to ask Tim more questions but now was not the time, we needed to be alone and the moment needed to be right. What I didn't want was for it to appear as if I was nagging and make him run a mile, I wanted this man by my side forever.

We sank back down onto the sand, resting for a bit after eating, still chatting, venting and laughing, we could all be nearly honest with one another. It was so easy, so relaxed, a small happy family.

Tim stood up and stretched, I sat up and hugged my knees, staring at the distant reef which divided sea and sky, the bluest of brothers, together a covenant of everlasting beauty. "Come on, let's see what's out there," he remarked picking up a pair of green flippers. Excited we all put on our snorkel masks and flippers then staggered unceremoniously into the warm blue-green water. Of course, Leroy had this off to a fine art, as did Tim and after following some simple commands, so did we. "Concentrate on what you are doing, exaggerate your steps whilst you are on the sand, then when you are in the water turn and walk backwards, sliding your feet as you go." Leroy instructed, this was so much easier than looking like a demented penguin.

We swam out further and deeper until we reached the reef. I rolled onto my front, breathing steadily through the tube of the snorkel. The sea here bore no comparison to the murky grey-green of the English coast, it was crystal clear even this far out. In fact so clear that I could see some long strands of seaweed gently swaying in the current, a macro-algae responsible for providing oxygen and enriching ocean life. A large purple starfish tried to hang on to the bottom of it, they are intriguing creatures, every bit as beautiful close up in differing colours. I pointed and Goldie swam over, giving me a gentle tap on the back and nodding. I was mesmerised as black crabs scuttled quickly up the rocks and shoals of beautifully coloured fish darted in different directions, as if they couldn't decide which would be the best route to take, not a care in the world.

I drifted lazily for ages, in complete awe of the sea life below, it was so utterly fascinating. So many different species of fish, vivid and bright, with their own individual markings, they all thrived in these pristine waters, without any scars, their own heavenly paradise. It was definitely better than watching on any high-tech TV screen, there is a certain kind of beauty only found in the wild, where there is such freedom for organic shapes to grow and sway, building their own living art for us all to admire.

Tim swam over to me, waving under the water to get my attention and smiling at me though his mask, then he reached out and gently pulled me over to one side, pointing downwards. At first glance, I couldn't quite see what he was showing me, there was a large dusky pinky, creamy coral which did look stunning, but then I realised what he meant, a grin broke under my mask, the coral was home to many smallish yellow seahorses.

Their little tails curled tightly around the coral, eyes like lamps, on constant alert, their necks arching and their fins fluttering in the steady currents. I took a breath and dived down with Tim for a closer look. As we did, a beautiful orange seahorse glided right past us, so delicate, so refined, carrying the spirit of the entire ocean with such graceful ease. There really was no greater wonderland on earth than a community full of rich marine life. If I stop to think about it, the ocean has so many secrets, so many stories and wonders for us to admire and tell, it is so far from removed from the ordinary world, it is the wonderland of my dreams.

Goldie and Leroy were just as mesmerised as we all floated watching the ocean's life at its best. Leroy gesticulated that we should end our afternoon of snorkelling and swim ashore before the suns rays begin to fade. It's surprising how time flies when you are having so much fun, I loved the water flowing over me, I felt freedom, a release from the ordinary rules of gravity, a chance to experience weightlessness and be something or someone different for a couple of hours.

Once ashore we towel dried, packed up our stuff and wandered back to the villa to get changed ready for yet another meal. All we seemed to do was eat, drink, sunbathe and sleep. It's time to hold the fast food industry and advertising media to account, I wish, this was the result of our own over indulgence, oh well, the warrior queen will emerge from her cocoon and put a weight loss plan in place soon, well by soon I mean when I get home.

Goldie suggested that, rather than all go for a meal together, we might do our own thing with our respective partners, then meet in the morning. This was agreed by us all as a good idea and Tim announced he would like to maybe scuba dive in the morning, Leroy nodded as Goldie and I watched on.

Leroy was keen to show Goldie some dodgy street feast that was taking place called "Five nights at Freddies,"apparently, it was the most fun a person could have with pizza and Carib and all things magical. Goldie was very welcome to that, I'm no snob but that was not my cup of tea. Tim and I decided to cook some jerk chicken with coconut rice and mango salsa and then carry it back to the beach to enjoy with a couple of frozen strawberry daiquiris and some tamarind balls for dessert as a sort of romantic picnic.

As we sat on the beach, from the laughs, to the kisses, to the sweet silent exchanges, to eating our food, being with Tim nurtured every part of me. My eyes were open, but my brain was a perfectly empty horizon. I felt the soothing breeze and became absorbed in the chattering rhythm of the cicadas, letting the gentle energy of nature wash over me. Tim and I watched the sea, strawberry daiquiris in hand, we were lost in the musical percussion of waves on sand. I snuggled in close. "You're the only person I know that gives indefinite hugs." I commented, as our eyes remained steady on the horizon, staring at the last orange rays before twilight beckoned. He kissed the top of my head, "Well I can't think of anywhere else or anyone else I would rather be," he replied. I breathed more slowly, my body melting into him as every muscle began to loose its tension. This was life, my real life!

With the setting sun came a sky of fire, the orange ball reminding me of my auntie May's tangerine jellies. So big, so bold, looking over the earth, stretching out with sepia tones to everyone and everything below.

Instead of letting the romance and the atmosphere continue, once again I ruined the heat of the moment by bombarding Tim with yet more questions that didn't make sense to me, but I needed answers to them now. Surprisingly he was all right about it and answered as much as he could or dare. There was some official oath he had sworn on and I am sure I was not supposed to be told as much as I was. Tim scoffed, "If I tell you this, or you tell anyone, I will have to kill you!"

Chapter 20

Tim was formally known as a "Covert Human Intelligence Officer," in other words, someone who secretly provides information to an intelligence source or Government, a spy, with training in espionage and much more. He is able to speak many languages and interact alongside many cultures and faiths with a genuine soulfulness.

I tried to comprehend what he was telling me, but I have to admit it got a bit heavy in places. Especially when he was talking about diplomacy embracing global cultures, so that people's stress responses reduce to the point where real progress between people with conflicting ideals can be made.

Anyway, there are different types of spies or 'Intelligence Officers' as they like to be called. Firstly there are those who are highly trained in espionage techniques and the use of agents. They can either operate openly, declaring themselves as representatives for foreign intelligence services, or they can operate covertly under the cover of other official positions such as diplomatic staff or as trade delegates.

These officers rely on agents such as Tim, they are the most significant information gathering assets and report to specially trained officers known as agent handlers. Some information gathering can take them a long time, sometimes years.

Some intelligence agents operate under non-official covers in order to conceal the fact that they work for an intelligence service, they can pose as a business person, student or journalist for example. In some cases they have to operate under "deep cover," assuming false names and nationalities. These people are dubbed as "illegals" because they operate without any of the protections offered by diplomatic immunity.

Tim explained how the methods used by intelligence agents vary, limited only by their ingenuity. Often they are able to take advantage of the latest technology, using it to eavesdrop, tap telephone calls and communicate secretly. However, they still need to interact with other intelligence agents, a key element of espionage, Tim couldn't divulge how. Agents also often operate by developing trusted relationships and positions to obtain sensitive information often exploiting vulnerabilities among those handling secrets. I was quite shocked, I had seen Bond movies but never knew any of this, but then why would I? I suppose I was quite naive.

So this was why Tim was posing as an editor for a newspaper, but for what purpose? Still waiting to get to that bit. As Tim continued to offer up as much information as he dare, it transpired that he was part of a covert operation to stamp out drug trafficking on the Caribbean coasts of Venezuela,

Colombia and Honduras. Recently there had been a major increase in marijuana and cocaine trafficking, largely directed by mafia type gangs in the area. With the support of the Drug Enforcement Agencies, they had already arrested a few hundred of cocaine smugglers, cutting the total supply chain of cocaine entering the Caribbean by ten percent over the last two years, but they still needed to source and stop a new increase in activity in certain areas.

This was all very interesting, but it still didn't explain why Tim pretended to be an editor and contacted the Alise, ensuring that Goldie and I travelled here, why were we singled out? There was a pause in the conversation as we shifted our bodies closer, Tim kissed me and pulled me even closer, he knows that once he kisses me again, my resistance will crumble. After just a few delicate touches of his warm lips, my hands will start to do his bidding, they will fall down his back as my head swims, all previous thoughts stopped in their tracks. There will become only one desire, one wish, and we both know it's just a matter of time before it happens.

In the dwindling light, our fingers caressed each other's skin as if afraid a heavier touch would break the heady magic, we were becoming one, one mind with one goal and purpose, utterly drunk with love for the other. I took control and pulled away, "Lets not do this here, talk to me more," I whispered. Tim smiled, " You are terrific, sexy, intelligent, passionate…" I stopped him, "No you silly man, about your job and why we are here." "Oh, that," he smirked before reluctantly continuing.

Information revealed to him, was that a member of the drug trafficking trade had been possibly sighted here, on Anegada. He was given the lead by a source he could not reveal, saying that a large shipment of cocaine was expected to land on the Island and would then be broken into smaller more manageable shipments ready for distribution around the US and British Virgin Islands. After further investigation, the details of which he could not divulge, but suffice to say, it turned out that Ed Wrexham, known locally as Rex, was the contact who would receive and process this particular shipment as he needed to make money fast. I shifted uncomfortably when Tim revealed that my nemesis from Iberville was alive and involved.

Let out of prison in April two years ago after a mysterious $325,000 'donation' in lieu of bail, and after serving only a year in jail, Ed Wrexham and his partner Tilly Colspur then failed to show for a court hearing and they both just vanished. It is believed that they managed to board a flight to Honduras, with the help of the cartel, the mob, the most emotionally indifferent monsters of the money-nexus, they are evil. Ed, somehow, had past dealings with them and during the last two years became more involved, making many trips involving money laundering, drugs, human trafficking and extortion all for a fee thought to be a minimum of forty-five percent of the total sum.

But then Ed got greedy and branched out and now exports industrial volumes of cocaine, marijuana, heroin, and methamphetamine. His operation is thought to be responsible for as much as half the illegal narcotics that cross into the Caribbean. He has become one of the most powerful drug traffickers and the most wanted fugitive. Governments promised to bring him to justice, even offering a five-million-dollar reward for information leading to his capture. But part of his fame stems from the legend that he is uncatchable, so he has continued to thrive and has now consolidated control of all key smuggling routes.

Recently the Federal Drug Enforcement Authorities nearly caught up with both of them, as by now Ed has extended his operations into new markets across more than fifty states. However, as usual, once close to catching them, they had already had advance warning and fled. Using Ed's routes and contacts, Tilly has become specialised in gun running. She helps organise the purchase and shipment of all guns, she knows she requires licences for dealing and exporting, but she has decided not to comply with the law, instead she makes sure that her illegal activity remains hidden, with proceeds from the illegal trade finding their way to a bank in the Cayman Islands.

A tip-off led us to a room near here and following a search of the premises, we discovered emails from a computer that confirmed she was an integral part of the illegal trades. We also used mobile phone records to trace her movements, proving that she was somewhere here in Anegada when making the shipment arrangements, however she must have cottoned on to the that fact that she had been found out and the authorities were closing in on her, because she changed tactics and both appeared to have gone into hiding yet again.

Once the criminal overclass, often the elite rulers of society, use their powers to influence the law but that has all now changed, the world has become upside down. Nowadays, the mob rule the overclass, it's a complete mess. I couldn't believe what I was hearing, why on earth would Tilly do such a thing? Tim had said he couldn't reveal much but 'blimey' I think he had told me more than I ever thought he would. There is still the big question of why us and why were we here?

Tim hugged me tighter, in his embrace the world stopped still on its axis, there was no time, my mind was at peace. I felt my body press in, soft and warm. He is my drug, one touch and his intoxication is instant, just his scent is enough to send me into a heady trance, one that doesn't end until our bodies are warm and snuggled in as close as two souls can be. I moved in even more to Tim's personal space, I wasn't very good at seduction, I hadn't had enough practice for a start, but I was willing to get better. I kissed him, sensually and much deeper, pushing my body with a blend of relaxation and tension into him and he was so responsive to my touch.

As Tim started to respond more to my art of seduction, I pulled away, "This time I'm in control, so you be good and tell me more, then I will drive you crazy." I know this wasn't the right time, but I wanted to hear the rest of the story. I know Tim was slightly taken aback at my response, but just replied, "You are such a tease!"

Tim was sent here to Anegada on undercover drug trafficking surveillance to try and apprehend the perpetrators. Whilst sitting in a cafe drinking a Cuban espresso, he caught sight of a person matching the description of Ed Wrexham, alias Rex. All of this came to an abrupt and fruitless end as Rex disappeared once more without a trace, so he needed to try a different tactic if he was to catch him. I laughed, it was just like playing a part in a spy film. They all seemed to meet in public places, so as not to draw attention to themselves, sensitive conversations getting lost in the general hubbub of what other customers were saying to each other. To quote from a film I once watched, which I can't remember the name of, 'Restaurants and cafés are in many ways the lifeblood of espionage.'

Anyway, as part of the new plan, Tim decided to dig even deeper into Ed Wrexham and found information about his and Tilly's involvement in the murders of his wife, Candice and Winston and of my abduction and their brief spell of imprisonment. He knew how I had escaped and had read my newspaper account of my adventure, I use that term loosely! I became quite curious as to how he managed to collect this information, but he was not willing or able to divulge these details. I thought this might be the case, but at least I tried, I wanted to know more about the ways he gathered data and information about targeted organisations, as a journalist, it was close to what I did and so interesting. But all Tim would tell me was that the practice was clandestine and by definition generally unwelcome. In some circumstances it is a legal tool of law enforcement, but sometimes the way it is carried out may be illegal in certain countries and could be punishable by law, that's if they catch him in the act!

Chapter 21

To cut a long story short, otherwise it may go on for ever. I really wanted to know more about the espionage industry and being a spy, you see, but Tim was beginning to keep repeating himself, telling me he could not reveal his sources or saying he was unable to answer this or that as I probed further with my journalists head on.

Tim did reveal that he had posed as an Editor from the BVI Beacon as cover so that he could invite Goldie and myself to enjoy an all expenses paid holiday courtesy of her majesty's secret service and to do a story promoting Anegada as a tourist destination. He knew I would not come alone, so needed to lure us both to the Island. News spreads fast in the Caribbean Islands, so hopefully Tilly and Ed would get wind through the cartel grapevine and they would want to finish what they started three years ago, and that might just bring them out into the open. I see now, Goldie and I were the bait to flush them out so that they would be caught unawares, captured and put behind bars for good this time. Nice to know!

In order to get us here, Tim went to a lot of trouble of intercepting our emails and diverting them to a fake but secure site and responding with an untraceable email address just in case anything went wrong, nothing could be traced. He also managed to place listening devices in our office. Wait a minute, I pulled away from him and stood up cross. "That was an invasion of our privacy and you want to use us as bait!" After thinking for a further moment, Why would he bug the offices of the Alis, we had done nothing wrong?

My brain stuttered for a moment and my eyes began to take in more light than I expected, every part of me went on pause whilst my thoughts caught up. I stared down at him, he had deceived us! "Jaz, you wanted to know everything and now you do, if you don't like it, please don't judge me," he uttered as he took hold of my hand and held it tightly.

I was shocked, it was as if I was stuck underwater, everything felt slow and warbled. All I managed to ask was "How and why did you bug the office?" "Do you remember when you signed the contract with cable TV and someone came to install an updated version of your frequencies for easier communications?" "Yes," I answered beginning to mellow, he smiled at me and kissed me on the cheek, "Well, that was when we bugged you, with RF, Radio Frequency devices. We placed them into your internal telephone systems, they are your run of the mill spying device and with our specialist equipment, we can keep an eye on whatever we need to know."

His eyes desperately searched mine, waiting for a reply, for anything. I had to say something! I searched my mind for something sensible and unprejudiced to reciprocate, but I couldn't, I was completely stunned, why should I help, I never wanted to see Ed or Tilly ever again, why couldn't I speak? He had deceived me, but I just know I'm going to forgive him as I loved him.

Tim wrapped his arms around me and I let my head rest on his chest, he kissed my head and then spoke softly, "Jaz, it is war that deals in such things, deception, hate and fear, love deals in trust, honour, bravery and empathy. I seek one that deals in love, one who lives in the same reality as I do. I love you, this doesn't have to change anything between us. I am sorry I deceived you, but I couldn't tell you everything before, do you trust me?" I nodded, feeling stupid but remaining nestled into his chest. "We need to keep this between ourselves for now, ok?" he said as he placed his finger under my chin and lifted my head and kissed me, a kiss that was the sweetness of passion, a million loving thoughts condensed into one moment, "Lets go back to the villa, it's getting a bit cooler." He said taking my hand as if to lead me.

As we stood up, I managed to speak, angrily I asked, "Why did you bug the Alise if you were after Ed and Tilly and how do you plan for us to flush them out?" Tim looked at me and stroked my face, "Shh." Was all he said, well this was like a red rag to a bull, "Don't shh me, answer me." I uttered, "Later Jasmine, not here, not in the open air." That was kind of weird, he had no difficulty in revealing all in public so far, maybe this was one of his tactics to try and throw me off course, still simmering, I did as he said and let it drop for now anyway.

We packed up our stuff and took the short stroll back to the villa in silence, there was a slightly uneasy tension in the air, well on my part anyway, lots of thoughts were going through my mind as I tried to comprehend what he had told me. Once inside, my insecurity returned, I faced Tim, "Will everything be okay, really?" I asked him, he had a serious look about him, but still his eyes were warm, "So long as you're by my side, sweet angel, the rest of the world will take second place" he replied smiling and that was just what I needed to hear, that he's mine for now and probably into the future.

That's when Tim pulled me close, his emotions telling him he needs more of a connection, or that I do, though I guess in reality it's both of us. His eyes are so different in moments like these, more soft than I knew eyes could be. The professional man is gone and instead it is the eyes of one who wants to love deeply. If it were anyone else I would drop my gaze, but with him I'm drawn in closer, always wanting more. Then he says the words I need to hear, "Jaz, I promise I will always protect you, I am so sorry I had to deceive you. I will always make sure you are safe, you can trust me." I smiled and nodded, as he kissed me.

I felt his lips widen against mine as he swept my hair aside and continued to kiss me just over the collarbone, I sank myself further into his arms. I was in his protective cocoon, I took in every moment for my memory, knowing that this is the medication I need to survive the next few days. He buried his face in my shoulder curve, his hands flexing around my back, as he gave a reduced groan. "I love you so much." And then I knew that in all the world there isn't another like him, he is my soul mate, my eternal flame. I melted as, with a laugh, he lifted me right off my feet, carrying me towards the bed, letting me fall with a soft bounce on the mattress.

We locked eyes for just a moment, then he was all business, undoing my clothes and taking them off, then kissing from my toes upwards. I felt the electricity in my skin, the rising of my animal self. From there on in it was raw passion, intensity, intoxicating. I was completely smitten, I couldn't worry about the petty deception or of being cross, all I wanted to do was enjoy the ride and be taken to levels I never knew existed before.

Chapter 22

The following day, we all reconvened at the villa for a day of scuba diving as Leroy and Tim had previously proposed. I was so excited as I had read about some of the wrecks here. Our first dive was to be on the MS Rocus, a steel Greek freighter that sank in 1929. It is said that she was on route from Trinidad to Baltimore with a cargo of cattle bones which were to be turned into fertiliser. A storm came in and washed her onto the reef, tipping her over, she took on water and then subsequently sank. She now lies beneath the waves, a gallant grand dame of the seabed. For some time her bow used to project out of the water and many ships used it as a navigation aid, however, many hurricanes have put an end to that. Apparently she has become home to an abundance of marine life, a support structure for new life and an iconic structure of beauty.

Leroy headed over to the fridge sneaking out a cinnamon bun, forty-five seconds in the microwave and it's as good as new. "I wouldn't go too mad before your dive" Tim uttered as he watched Leroy demolish the bun, Goldie laughed tossing her head back as I just stood there staring. Oh gosh, he really was so handsome, from the depth of his eyes to the gentle expressions of his voice, I was intoxicated and incapacitated with a burning desire for him, I do have it bad! "Are we about ready then?" he winked in my direction as he spoke, we all just laughed and grabbed our bags.

Goldie and Leroy skipped out the door to the waiting truck, laden with diving gear. As I followed, Tim grabbed my arm. "Jaz I mean't what I said last night, I really do love you, I would defend you with my life even if the odds were insurmountable, I promise I will never betray you, never give up on you and I will never put you in danger no matter how noble the cause may be. There will never be a higher calling than protecting and caring for you." The kiss that followed was steeped in so much passion that it ignited the promise of years of real love to come, this was definitely not a holiday romance.

Following the confessions of last night, I really wanted to be indifferent and not make it so easy for him, but after our night of passion, I couldn't stay that detached. Coupled with the fact, that on this occasion Tim pushed all the right buttons and my resistance crumbled immediately. I had the chance to learn deeper love, to nurture and listen to my heart and for once I didn't want to loose that.

We strolled hand in hand into the morning sun, Goldie and Leroy had got fed up of waiting and were now otherwise engaged in romantic antics of their own, using the truck as a prop. His hands plunging inside her dress, dragging her closer, as she groaned with pleasure. Tim looked at me and raised his eyebrows, I giggled, embarrassed by their very public show of affection. Goldie also slightly embarrassed removed Leroy's hands away, "Latah Cyaan yuh tink ah anyting else?" She told him as we piled into the truck.

It wasn't far to Horseshoe reef, this would be the best shore to swim out from. In an effort to protect the reef, the BVI government has made anchoring on Horseshoe Reef illegal but you are allowed to still dive on it providing you have a permit. According to Tim and Leroy, it is one of the largest barrier coral reefs in the Caribbean and due to its shape and depth it has caused hundreds of shipwrecks, including the two Leroy had picked for us to dive on, MS Rocus and apparently tomorrows dive, HMS Rhone which sunk in 1808 and lies deeper on the reef.

Once we were parked up and unloaded, we donned on our short wet suits and tested our gear. I had really been looking forward to this although I was slightly apprehensive as I hadn't dived for a few years, but hopefully it would all come flooding back, a bit like riding a bike! Leroy reminded us of the acronym BWRAF, as we checked our own gear and that of our partners. It stands for buoyancy, weights, releases, air, and final ok.

I needn't have worried as it did come back to me, as we tested the gear, I had however forgotten how heavy the air cylinders were. For the purpose of this dive, we had ten litre cylinders, which should give us about forty-five minutes to do a dive, down, look and get back, as Leroy put it.

Both Tim and Leroy went through some more dive checks with us, making sure we knew how to equalise frequently as we dived, keep checking our air gauges, stay with our buddy, don't exert ourselves and plenty more. Tim also told us not to touch anything, as the corals may be sharp, some of the marine plants are poisonous and creatures at that depth may bite if they feel threatened, ok duly noted.

Leroy held on to his spear gun as we made our way into the tranquil turquoise water. It was just in case we became entangled on sharp rocks or came up against any sharks. Goldie and I tried to remember how to walk in our fins, just as we had been shown when we snorkelled. We walked into the shallow water, until we were just about knee deep, lifting our knees a bit higher than normal, then slid the fins across the sand bed until it was deep enough to swim. Tim and Leroy seemed to have it off pat, but we looked quite awkward, wobbling and splashing.

Tim looked around checking our location and the sea current to ensure everyones safety. It didn't take long before the water to cover our heads, air bubbles made their way to the surface with every exhalation, they were the only things down here that were ready to leave in a hurry. We all did the ok sign and began slowly continue to descend, staying together as we made our way down to the wreck.

As we kicked deeper, I felt the pressure of the water against my wet suit, the current was changing. I looked up, the sunlight now a soft diffuse glow, those once golden rays from above are now only blue in this water, and the deeper I swim the less light penetrates, the glow becoming even more distant, it was a strange feeling, apart from my air bubbles, it was eerily quiet. No distractions, no noise, my mind was completely free to simply dream and admire the beauty that can only found here. The water flowed through my outstretched fingers and I could feel my connections to this magical underwater world growing deeper.

Even this far down the water was very clear, schools of bright-hued fish inquisitively swam up to me, there was a temptation to extend my hand to them, but I resisted. Under the water the rocks are ever more beautiful, bejewelled by barnacle crowns and sea anemones in an array of colours, gracefully waving stinging tentacles, stretching out waiting for their prey. They are known as the flowers of the sea, meat-eating animals that typically attach themselves to the rocks waiting to feed on any small and unsuspecting creatures that swim by including me.

As I swooped down towards the sandy bed below, the rocks were beginning to resemble silhouettes, but were still adorned with corals, jewels to the human eye. They are all individual, their beautiful colours swaying in the current, some have rods as skeletons like the delicate sea fans whilst others have a more jelly like structure, It is an exuberant carnival, this is the earth's most diverse ecosystem, providing shelter and food for all marine life, it is truly a three dimensional world.

We switched on our headlights, the beam powered into the sea ahead, cutting right through the eeriness and glinting off the strange creatures as we invaded their domain. It was beginning to get colder, more than I imagined it would be. I naively thought that the heat of the Caribbean sun would warm the water all the way down to the bottom. I let the filtered light from my headlight caress my arms and wish I didn't need this air tank to stay, but I do, the fluidity of life far below the waves has brought a sense of freedom and levity, as much as I love this watery world, I can only be a visitor for a short time.

After what seemed an age of precision descent, we found the wreck, it was well worth the dive, truly awesome. The Rocus wreck is now mostly broken up, but you can still make out the boilers, anchors, winches and chains. The most unexpected part is the cargo of cow bones still scattered around the wreck, which makes for a spooky seascape. There was a clear path around the outside from which we had a good view of the stern, deck and railings. There was some brilliant marine life there too, barracuda, triggerfish, durgeon and nurse sharks, all swimming amongst blue elk horn coral.

The most iconic element of the wreck was its enormous rudder. I felt so ecstatic as we swam between the rudder and the keel, all covered with orange cup and fire coral. As I looked around I could be see more cow bones, hundreds in fact, I was amazed at how well preserved they were, quite macabre really. According to the book on famous Anegada shipwrecks I found in the villa, the Rocus had been renamed by the locals in Anegada as 'The Bone Wreck' and bones were still washed ashore in hurricane season as the ocean floor was churned up.

For some reason, I glanced upwards, I could only see the rays from my headlight, I was surrounded by water, I had never been this deep before and my desire to explore was now starting to evaporate, I wanted fresh air and land. I could feel my heart pounding, resonating in my ears, I didn't like it, I felt a sense of panic, but this was the worst thing I should do down here. I took some deeper breaths and kept telling myself I was ok. Tim must have seen my exaggerated body movements as despite trying, I began to flounder. He took my arm and pointed upwards and then levelled with his hands, meaning not too fast. As he held me around my waist, I started to kick with my flippers, gentle but powerful strokes, heading for the world above, Goldie and Leroy following closely beneath us.

As we continued to ascend from the deep resonating blue below to the lighter blues above, I felt the panic ease and become replaced with a feeling of safety. In Tims arms, I could brave any storm and push fear aside, I trusted him.

Our heads all bobbed above the waves once more and we made our way awkwardly and unceremoniously onto the beach. We stripped off the diving gear, checking the air cylinders were off and everything was intact. Leroy suggested another dive tomorrow, slightly deeper and with much more to see, I knew Tim would keep me safe, so, despite some reservations, we all agreed, it would be fun. Tim and Leroy said they would set it up, what did they mean by that? Surely we had permits, so we could just do what we did today couldn't we? I meant to question it, but sort of got lost in the moment.

As we looked back out to sea, not too far out, Tim pointed out something black and long which seemed to be swimming in a circle, followed by a million flashing lights caught in the bluest of waves as the sun hit the water. Suddenly two dolphins leapt high into the air, from their shiny grey topside and whiter under bellies water droplets flew about, cascading down, bejewelled in the light. Their bodies arched and tails flipped as down they fell with an almighty splash, white spray erupting around as the warm blooded mammals rejoined the waters' surface. We all clapped, what an end to our dive, it had been the perfect day.

Leroy and Goldie dried off and made their excuses to leave, they could not keep their hands off each other. Leroy's sex drive seemed to have the kind of power that roared with the lightest of touches. Power and control with a touch of silk, whatever was a woman to do! Goldie said, "Lover Yuh a fi mi medication." Leroy looked at her and took her hand as they made their way towards a local bar, Tim and I decided to stay on the beach for a bit longer.

Tim and I were now alone, when I say alone, I mean completely alone, not another sole anywhere to be seen. We both lay naked in the sunlight, waves hushing the shoreline. Tim draped his arm over my waist, I lent in for a kiss, the kind I wanted to last forever, but I withdrew and instead was mesmerised by the face I loved so much smiling back at me. Tim glided his hand over my skin working his way to my face, brushing away a little sand. "I love you." Tim said, a wide sincere smile sitting on his face. I grinned, "Really, tell me again," I shook my head as I tried to fight away my cheshire-cat grin.

Tim's hand was now pushing my hair back from my face. "Well, I do, and do you know what?" I could hear the words he was about to utter before he said them. "I always will, I want to be with you for ever." I smiled and then in one fluid motion I moved, I was now astride Tim, my hands on my thighs.

Our gaze lasted a full second, nothing more needed to be said, as we both rolled over the luxuriant warm sand, playfully bumping into each other, giggling like children. I leaned forward, whispering into his ear, "This time Mr Meyers, I'm going to drive you crazy, I'm just going to do naughty things to you until your mind and body explodes."

He laughed, "That's fantastic Jaz, I would truly love that to happen, but maybe we should wait until we are somewhere a little less public." I didn't care, there was no one around so I drew him closer moving his head up to my moist lips and in that split second every nerve in my body and brain became electrified.

Chapter 23

Thankfully Tim spied Goldie and Leroy heading back with the picnic food. Quickly, we began to dress, not fast enough though, I was embarrassed by amount of nakedness still on display but it didn't seem to bother Leroy and Goldie, they did not batter an eyelid.

We laid out the food on our towels, there was enough to feed us six times over and the vivid colours spoke of its freshness and the bold flavours to come. Leroy had managed to con Lourdes into cooking up this exotic feast and drive it over to us. There was a variety of seafood, some jerk-chicken, the usual fried-plantains, ackee saltfish, spring rolls and a small pepper pot stew which included aubergine, okra, squash and potatoes. To accompany everything was rice and beans and of course a rich rum cake and plenty of chilled Carib beer. One thing was for sure we weren't going to starve or be sober for long.

Leroy had bought a large radio with him from the car. He turned up the volume and music soon filled the air without effort, from giddy reggae beats to stoic tones, it brought both mirth and wisdom to our beach picnic. We continued with our chatter as the lively tempo of the music began to lift us, moving us to wanting to dance. After far too much alcohol for some of us, the silly dance moves turned into an even worse "dance-off," with the promise of anything you wanted going to the winner. We decided that the winner was to be the one who made everyone laugh and had the worst moves.

Leroy chose to go first, he listened to the music and then it was like liquid adrenaline being injected into his blood stream, turning him into some barking mad freak. He was a cross between a deaf Micheal Jackson and a demented octopus, arms and legs flailing in all directions, how we laughed, he liked the attention. Goldie, point blankly refused to dance, which was unlike her, the excuse being that she had eaten too much, which to be honest was true of us all. After a lot of cajoling, she did a quick take on a very bad rendition of the river dance, leaping into the air and kicking her heels, difficult on the sand and completely out of sync with the music.

I was dreading my turn, I really couldn't dance, I had two left feet, my father used to tell me that I should have been a bloke with my lack of rhythm, nice to give your child confidence, but he was probably right! Tim must have had some sixth sense as he decided we would perform as a pair, I was relieved that it would be both of us acting the fool together. The song, "I'm Every Woman" by "Chaka Khan," came on, very apt, he grabbed hold of me and twirled me through the air without any effort. I felt like I was floating, but in truth, I looked like some wild dingbat, limbs so uncoordinated, being spun around by a man who could barely find his feet in the sand, it ended badly with us falling in a crumpled heap laughing.

Leroy announced, "And the winner is...da da da... Goldie, for her inadequate rendition of the river dance." Well, that was a forgone conclusion, she was always on a promise. I have never laughed, clapped and whistled so much in my life, it was like being at a football match, as the ripples of our laughter turned into great waves of hilarity, about absolutely nothing. This was the best, such good memories to keep forever.

It was beginning to feel a bit cool as the sunset had arrived without us noticing, its boldest blaze with a graffitied rainbow-flame as the fire filled sky lost its glow. We all nestled in together and sat in silence, our eyes steady on the horizon, faces shining with the last of the reflected orange rays before twilight beckons the stars. Lost in the rhythmic percussion of waves once more, just enjoying each others company. Goldie spoke first, "Lets guh bac an ramp cards," an exhausting groan sounded from the rest of us, it had been a long tiring but great day and I for one wanted to sleep. We packed up our bits and pieces and drove back to the villa.

Once arriving we climbed out of the car and crossed the marram grass that brought life to the sandy ground, moving in the gentle breeze like tiny green flags. "Duh dis grass remind yuh ah anyting?" Goldie asked, we all looked at each other in complete bewilderment. "No, what should they remind us of?" Tim asked, "Dem troll-dolls Di green tufts a fi dem ier." She replied, well, the hysterical laughter reappeared, how we managed to put one foot in front the other to get to the door after that was anyones guess. But she was right, they did look like the troll toys with tufts of green hair.

Once inside, Leroy headed straight to the fridge and extracted a bottle of rum, which he placed on the kitchen table. "Is that a good idea my friend?" Tim announced "Just one," Leroy replied smirking as he high fives Tim. "Nothing for me thanks and only a quick game of cards, I know what you are like, Mr Hamilton." I looked at Tim, who did not meet my gaze in return, this was the first time he had used Leroy's surname, I am sure these two have known each other for some time.

The card game was called 'All Fours' it is a traditional Caribbean card game once very popular amongst the gentry. What started out as an innocent gambling game until the end of the nineteenth century, had now become a well known trick-taking card game. The aim is to be the first player to reach the number seven four times in a row by tricking your opponents. I was totally rubbish at it, I kept being dealt kings and queens.

After about and hour and half of Goldie cheating and winning every game, I decided to call it a night. Tim asked again if we were definitely sure about going diving again tomorrow. The wreck he suggested was the RMS Rhone which had sunk in 1808. The wreck was deeper and right on the edge of Horseshoe reef, where the currents were slightly different from our position today. They could change at a moments notice, so it would be a bit of an adrenaline-thrilled adventure dive.

Goldie and I both agreed enthusiastically that we were up for this dive, but for me, the thrill of flying over a reef, pushed onward by a strong current and being one of the most exhilarating experiences in diving didn't excite me, more like scared me. Goldie looked at me, "Eh will bi fine probably nah as bad as dem a a mek out Jaz." She was probably right. But diving in strong currents can lead to problematic situations if you're not vigilant and I already had a little panic attack today, I decided I could always change my mind, after all no one was forcing me.

I had read that there are a number of factors that can cause strong currents, including tides, wind, and unstable water columns. Usually all currents run horizontally and these are perfect for drift dives. But on this particular dive, sometimes the current can run up or down and if we got caught in one of these currents it could lead us to be in a dangerous situation. I would stay close to Tim so he could keep me safe as he had promised.

We said goodbye to Leroy and Tim and followed them out to the jeep, we were going to have a night to ourselves. They would come for us in the morning around ten and we would assess the weather and sea conditions then. Goldie and I cleared up after they had gone, amid our usual banter and Goldie's insistence on knowing my exploits with Tim. She stood there, listening and laughing as I revealed what I wanted her to know, it was like she couldn't have been more proud of me. She, on the other hand, was very open about her and Leroy, I had never heard about some of the stuff she mentioned, I think she noticed my awkwardness. "Oh Jaz Yuh need tuh experiment gyal." She said grinning from ear to ear.

We eventually retired to our rooms feeling very tired, I laid down on the bed, hoping to sleep, but no such luck, I tossed and turned, with all manner of thoughts going through my head. I picked up my phone and began to research the wreck Tim had talked about for the next dive, I found myself quite engrossed in it. Anegada prided itself on it being one of the best dive locations if the sea conditions were right. With everything crossed for tomorrow and a feeling of trepidation I read on.

Chapter 24

The RMS Rhone was built in 1865 in England and then sank in 1867, on the reef off Anegada. It was a UK Royal Mail ship, owned by the Royal Mail Steam Packet Company and it carried mail, passengers, horses, and cargo on regular scheduled routes. The Rhone was an innovative ship for her time, she had an iron hull and bronze propeller. Having said that, the history I was reading said that the Rhone proved her worth by weathering several severe storms, including one in 1866, which destroyed its cutter and two of its lifeboats.

In October 1867 there was a hurricane so the Rhone dropped anchor in a harbour for "bunkering". At first, the hurricane caused very little damage, but its ferocity had led to the Rhone dragging its anchors and the captain was worried that they would be driven onto the shore. They decided to set sail for the open seas which was usual practice at that time, however, just as they were passing Black Rock Point, which was less than two hundred yards from safety, the winds shifted to the opposite direction and Rhone was thrown directly into Black Rock Point. Wow, I can't image what those poor passengers and crew went through! As I scrolled further, it went on to say that the crash onto the rocks sent its Captain, who was making a drink at the time, flying overboard. Local legend says that his teaspoon can still be seen lodged in the wreck, how bizarre, but I must have a look for that when we dive. Fascinating!

The impact had broken the ship in two and seawater invaded her hot boilers which then exploded, killing everyone aboard. As I continued to read on, absorbed by its history, Goldie appeared at my door and clambered into bed beside me. "You can't sleep either?" I commented as she snuggled up close and peered over my phone. "Nuh Wah a yuh a luk at?' She replied. "Its about the wreck we are going to dive, it is really interesting." With that she clambered off the bed, retrieved her phone from her room and reappeared within seconds, clambering back into my bed. "Wah site a yuh pan?' she asked as I showed her my phone and she typed in the same site, scrolling through the pages and photos.

I went on to read that it sank swiftly, but only into relatively shallow water, her mast remained sticking out of the water until it was deemed a hazard to other vessels and so eventually, in the 1950s, the stern section was blown up. Despite all of this, the wreck is still relatively intact and well preserved, apparently still with some historical artefacts on board. "Eh one addi tap wreck dives Fi eh historical interest an eh teeming wid lots ah marine life." Goldie piped up, I was now more excited about exploring this wreck.

I went on a different dive site which then dampened my excitement, as it started by saying that conditions on the reef remained treacherous at times and it is not recommended for beginners or tourists to dive the wreck unless accompanied by trained divers. Goldie must have seen what I was reading as she said, "Dem a," she paused as I glanced at her, "what?" "trained divers," she finished, we both laughed.

Anyway, Goldie then found a site which does organised night dives on the wreck. It proposed that it was a fantastic way to see what goes on at night, lobsters, eels, and barracudas all turn up making for some great dive buddies, as you encounter a guided dive around the middle and stern sections of the wreck. It also boasted that you would see giant sleeping turtles, nudibranchs and basket starfish amongst the wreck. "Ah nite tuh memba." Goldie said, I yawned "so will this one be, if we don't get some sleep." I looked at the time on my phone, it was now 4am, "Goldie I need to sleep," I uttered placing my phone on the table next to the bed, "Suh duh mi," she replied, then with a stretch and a yawn she rolled onto her side and fell asleep. Lovely, looks like she here for the night then, I smiled to myself, oh well and with that blackness fell and, sleep arrived as my magical rest and let my brain take control of my fantasy world once again, dreaming of being carried along by a shoal of fish.

I was woken at some point by thunder and a roaring promise of rain which arrived shortly after, quenching the earth, water for the parched soil. I climbed out of bed and looked out the window, as the thunder bequeathed a percussion of rain on the roof, lightning illuminated a brilliant pathway across the

sky. However long this storm decided to last for, the day would always be that much brighter and refreshed.
I noticed Goldie was gone, I tiptoed to her room and there she was, snoring loudly, oblivious to the storm. I went back to bed and listened to the roar of heaven's drum for a while until it must have rocked me back to sleep.

Chapter 25

The following morning, Goldie arrived in my room swinging two rackets she had found underneath the villa, "Cum pan Jaz Git up Mek wi ramp ah quick game ah tennis before breakfast eh nuh dat bashy yet." I rubbed my eyes and slowly swung my feet onto the floor. Having not slept particularly well, I was still quite tired. My body wanted more rest, yet my mind wanted to get moving. I laughed, "Are you mad?" I replied, "Nuh Cum pan Eh will bi fun. Im gwine fine sinting tuh kunk." she shouted, halfway out the door. I attended to the necessities and got myself ready.

As I joined her she was practising her swings, it was already getting warm but without the intense heat as the early morning storm had freshened everything up. "Fine one ah unnu socks fashioned eh inna ah ball." She said as she handed me my rickety racket, it had been strung and restrung and still brandished holes in places. I surmised that having found it under the villa, it was probably destined for the rubbish, but good on Goldie for being innovative at this hour.

We put the two plastic chairs from the porch on the sand, then she drew a line in the sand with her finger. "Dis a fi wi net ok?" She shouted, then with all the poise, grace and acrobatic aggression of an elephant ballet dancer, she leapt into the warm spun air launching the scrunched up sock. It propelled hastily into the sky, I was ready, my feet began to dance, I angled my racket ready to return the volley with great finesse, dancing backwards but, yep I missed it. With a thud, it plopped down to earth, landing behind me just as I had fallen over, making a fool of myself. I picked it up and, taking the most professional tennis stance I could, I held my arms high into the air, ready to launch the sock as hard as I could. Goldie was yelling and cajoling me, but it had become stuck in one of the rackets' holes. I extracted it and fiddled with the strings before propelling it into the sky once more with my best ever tennis groan helping it on its way.

Brilliant! Goldie, took a swipe but missed it as she leaped unceremoniously into the air before ending up prostrate in the weedy sand. She then announced that she had to rest for a second after hitting all the aces! If truth be known, she probably winded herself a bit. We were the worst in the world at playing tennis, but the best at laughing so freely, We had no poise, grace or aerobic aggression as the tennis players at Wimbledon do but we had fun despite our lack of sleep and that's all that counts.

We were startled by a man's voice announcing, "And the winner today is the number two seed Ms Jasmine Tormolis, please take a bow." I turned to see Tim holding up some fried plantain and dumplings, Goldie took great delight in this and clapped as he yelled, "Yo Jasmine." "Breakfast," swinging the breakfast bag forward as if to usher us inside.

Clowning around is so underrated, such innocent antics. Tim was still laughing as we sat down to eat. His laughter was so free and pure, so childish despite his adult years, we couldn't help but join in such generous mirth. "Where's Leroy?" Goldie asked. "He's busy, he will join us later, there is a change of plan today." Tim replied. Goldie and I looked at each other before I cautiously uttered, "Ok…. What?"

Tim took my hand, "Please don't get annoyed, I need your help, you will be safe I promise." Before he said anything more, I felt a wave of apprehension wash over me, I need to be brave instead of being a puppet of fear. "Ed?" I managed to say. Goldie gripped my hand tight, "Wi can duh dis empress." She said smiling at me. "No, not Ed," Tim answered. Instantly, Goldie and I looked at each other, bewilderment doesn't quite cover it, I felt like someone had just taken my spark of wonder and poured oil on it. The smile that was on my lips on the outside didn't adequately reflect what I was feeling on the inside, every thought in my head is trying to fire off in different directions at once. I stood up and went to the kitchen, "Anyone for coffee?" I asked as I removed cups from the cupboard, I needed this before Tim went any further. If I drank a warm coffee and hugged the cup so close, all would be right with my world, how naive was I! They both nodded as Goldie put her elbows on the table, "Tell wi all den."

Tim smirked as I sat down with the coffees, it was an announcement of sorts that he was about to release his magic. He sighed and took a sip of his drink. I watched, wishing I was his morning coffee, touching so lightly upon his lips. He began, Goldie and I listening intently desperately trying not to interrupt, if I am honest quite stunned by what we were hearing.

Unbeknown to us, Tim had put a plan in place to flush out Ed today, the day of our dive, so that was what he needed to sort out. He was unable to say anything to us and then launched into a sentence about espionage, confidentiality, protection etc, in order to cover his back. Anyway the previous evening after leaving us Tim was given some information by a reliable source that Tilly Colspur alias 'Tabitha' had been sighted at the harbour asking questions. As expected, word had got around the Island that Goldie and I were here from the Alise and Tim was confident that she wanted to find us. The person she had asked was held at knife point, and was able to give Tilly directions as to where we were staying. Once she had gone, he made contact with Tim in order for an immediate plan to be formalised.

Meanwhile, Tilly, now armed with this information, would have gone straight to Ed, alias 'Rex'. If I am right, she will come here to find you, I shifted nervously in my chair, "Its ok, she will just want to talk and possibly use some scare tactics to warn you off," Tim said, sensing our uneasiness. "Wah mek scare tactics?' Goldie asked, staring at Tim, "She thinks you

181

are looking for her to gain revenge." I stood up "What" I shouted, "Sit down Jaz, stop being over melodramatic, neither of you will come to any harm, I will be here, albeit out of sight, I really need to do this to get to Ed." "How dare you, what if she does want to kill us?" I questioned Tim. "She won't try anything in daylight, she needs to be in and out before her cover is blown, she will be aware she may be being watched."

I could not be more at a loss for words if I had learned the art of metamorphosis, quite unbelievable, shocking really. My mind was sent reeling, unable to comprehend or process the information it had been given. The realisation that this time we didn't really have a choice, if we said no, Tim couldn't put his plan into place and she was coming for us anyway. Goldie must have felt the uneasiness too, I had never known her to be silent for this long.

The silence was broken suddenly as Goldie asked "Wah hap'n eff deh a unexpected problem dem?" There will be no problems, I promise, this has been meticulously planned." Goldie nodded and looked at me, smiling a fake smile that simply said, 'I am actually scared and slightly uncomfortable'. "Tell wi more missa Meyers," she uttered. Tim touched both our hands and kept eye contact, "I swear to you both, there will be no danger, if you can be brave and do this for me, you will remain safe no matter what." I wanted to trust him, I did trust him, I think. Goldie was one step ahead, before Tim could tell us more. "Suh Wah duh yuh waah wi tuh duh?"

He put his hand in one of the breakfast bags and pulled out a small bullet and some small buttons with wires on them. He is so clever, I never even noticed until now that one of the paper bags contained spy bits or that there were three bags not two. Tim continued to explain that the small bullet had a GPS tracker device inside it and if we could plant it in her bag, he could track her movements, catch her and ultimately Ed too. "Aren't you going to apprehend her, when she is here?" I asked Tim, "No, I need her to lead me to Ed first, once I have him, she will be easy to catch, she will slip up when looking for him." "Oh," was all I could say, it made sense to catch the big cheese first and the mouse would scurry along after so to speak.

Tim stood up and began to search the rooms with his eyes, "Wah a yuh a luk fah?" Goldie asked, I was stood next to him by this time, he handed me one of the small button things, "These are the listening devices, I need to find somewhere to put them." He replied smiling. They were tiny, the size of a ladybird, "I will be in the villa next door listening to your conversation, they only have a certain frequency range, so I can't go too far, can either of you wear contact lenses?" Tim asked. "Why?" Came my reply but once again a now excited Goldie was first in line, " Mi Can," she was really into this espionage stuff. "Ok, here we are then," Tim handed her a small box, she opened it, he was right, they were contact lenses. "Put these in your eyes just like contacts, they won't cause you any harm, there are optical bugs, basically I can see what you see as well as hear you." Amazing!

There is something intoxicating about watching an excited Goldie, bouncing, pouncing, squealing and whooping into the air, so funny. Tim was transfixed, watching her as her arms jangled around like a demented puppet. He turned to me, "Do you want some too? I would like to see you like that!" He smiled pointing to Goldie, "I think I will give it a miss," I replied laughing. "Ok, I want you to lead the conversation," His serious spy head was back on now. "What do I say? I don't know what to do." I stared into his eyes, I needed to see the real Tim, there are times he gets lost, when he becomes the man the world demands of him, oh god, I really don't want to mess this up.

Tim gazed back into my eyes with the promise of protection, "I will do anything to keep you safe, I will be next door, all I need you to do is glean as much information as possible from her, let her know you are just on holiday and the information is wrong, that should throw her off. Trust your instincts and you will be fine, I just need her to lead me to Ed, remember that."

I tried to mask my fear, but it was my survival essential. I always get nervous when I'm about to do something big, but I need to find my bravery spark. Tim took hold of me in his arms and hugged me close. It felt so warm, so right, it even smelt right, if that makes any sense. I let my body sag and my muscles start to relax.

In his embrace all my worries loose their sting and my optimism raises its head from the ground. He brushed my hair back with his fingers and kissed me gently. "I would be more concerned if you weren't worried, because there is a difference in the world between brave and foolhardy, you are brave, it's a good feeling to have, it makes you more reliable and solid.

Chapter 26

Goldie came between the two of us, "How will wi kno wen shi a a cum?" Seems like a very good question, if you ask me, but all Tim replied was, "You will know." Just as he finished those three words there was a knock on the door, oh no my nightmare gate was about to open! We all stood rooted to the spot for a second before Tim handed Goldie the coffee cups and ushered her to the sink, then he kissed me quickly and disappeared out of the bedroom window at the back and hopefully into the villa next door without being seen.

There was another knock, the silence was so absolute that my breathing sounded loud in my ears, I noticed Goldie putting in the spy lenses as I walked to answer the door. I turned to look at Goldie, who nodded, I took a deep breath in and opened it. "Hello, is it ok if I have my containers back from the picnic I made you, I need them for someone else." It was Lourdes, I just stood there and at that moment I realised I hadn't understood her words, it was as if she had been speaking a different language, I guess I found myself dumb with astonishment and sheer relief.

Goldie arrived beside me and handed Lourdes the containers, "Hush bout Jaz Wi a expecting ah fren tuh cum an si wi an wi nuh si dem fah ah lang time." Lourdes grinned and wished us much happiness with our old acquaintance. I closed the door and stood up against it staring at Goldie, "Yuh nearly mek ah mess ah dat." She uttered. There was a delicious moment where my face washed blank with confusion, my brain cogs couldn't turn fast enough to take in the information. Every muscle of my body had just frozen before a grin crept onto my face, it soon stretched from one side to the other. Just then I jumped out of my skin as the door vibrated from another knock, my grin disappeared, this time it would be for real. I opened the door cautiously and there she was, Tilly.

She had the look of someone who had woken up to find that her youth had passed by before she had, had any fun. She gazed at me as I moved out of the way, letting her in. I was just a moving mass of nothing she could focus on and not care about. The smart suits she had so elegantly worn as an editor had given way to elastic waist-banded pants and long flowing tops. Her face knew how to perform all the right gestures, but the passion behind them had long since abandoned her.

She still had brown hair, now swept up with a plastic clasp, I suspected this was not to look professional, but was to hide the fact that she was overdue a shower. Her sunglasses were so much wider than her face, comical and not at all stylish, behind those tinted lenses her eyes could have been anywhere at all, maybe even closed, except everything else about her said she was deeply immersed in getting this over with, which was fine by us, although the gun in her hand pointing our way was a little disconcerting!

She lowered her sunglasses and looked around the room, eyes searching all the time, her smile was taut and there was a slight tremor in her cheek, she was tense. "Hello Tilly, would you like to sit down? This is Goldie, do you remember her?" I gestured in Goldie's direction, Goldie gestured a nod, "Yes," was all Tilly replied as she sat down at the table, still on alert. She would be very clever, as once she was a puppet taking direction from others, but now she had taken control of her own strings and we were just a commodity, an interruption amongst her bigger schemes.

She lowered the revolver to the table, keeping it close as she placed her small shopping bag on the floor, then put her sunglasses on top of her head to get a better look at us. There was a dead quality to her eyes, as if her soul had long departed and left this zombie-woman instead, a monster to do the bidding for the dark force. "So, you are still at the Alise then," she said replacing the glasses back onto the bridge of her nose. "Yes, I am editor there now and Goldie is one of my finest reporters, she always gets the best stories." Oh no I shouldn't have said that, I panicked as quickly, Tilly stood up and moved behind Goldie, grabbed her hair and yanked her head backwards, holding the gun to her head. Goldie flinched her eyes moving from side to side erratically, "Either of you report this or say anything to anyone and you are both seriously dead, got that?" Tilly replied. "Sure ting Wi nuh even si yuh." Goldie answered as Tilly let go, "Mmhhm, you make sure of that," came her reply.

Goldie put her thumb and forefinger to her eyelids, opening them wider and leaning in as she did so, to try and give Tim a better view of the scene. I gently pushed her back into her chair, not wanting her spy craft to be too obvious. Knowingly, Goldie smiled and tried to relax. Tilly was clearly on edge and unnerved as she stood up once more, twirling the revolver around her thumb, like she was attending some cowboy rodeo. "I heard you were looking for me," she said wandering around the room, looking, searching, moving things and putting them back. "Nah chuu Wi a pan holiday wid fi wi mon." Goldie replied following behind Tilly. "For Christ's sake, sit down girl or I swear I will kill you both right now," Tilly uttered. Goldie immediately did as she was told and scurried back to the table, saying, "Wah a yuh a duh pan Anegada?' "Work" was all Tilly replied, I interjected, "What kind of work?" "This and that, its none of your business, why do you need to know, why did you want to find me?" No matter what you said and how politely you spoke, Tilly was right back at you, all our nerves were straining now.

I needed to try and get her on side, "We didn't, would you like a drink of anything?" I asked. Without taking her eyes off of us for a second, she reached into her bag and pulled out a bottle of water, "Can't be too careful, she said as she placed it on the table in front of her." Goldie was beginning to get quicker and got in there with, "Ah wah?" "Anything, they bug and fingerprint everything these days, I bet you, I am being watched and you have been bugged as we speak." Goldie lent in as Tilly's facial expression became straighter than a poker player. I sat her back and glared, she giggled.

Every muscle on Tilly's face tightened, her eyes narrowed, her chin jutted outward, as she held up the gun at a jaunty angle. "What's the matter with you, why are you laughing? If you know what's good for you, you just don't try anything girlfriend" I changed the subject quickly, this was not going well. " How is Ed?" "Who? Don't know who you mean" came her snappy reply, I went again, "I thought you two had got married," and there she was, "don't be daft." It was like playing table tennis. "Is he here with you on Anegada?" I questioned, "Sometimes," came her reply. "So you do live here all the time then?" I asked, no reply followed.

This really was the most awkward and shallow conversation I had ever had, we were on the edge of our seats the whole time, with a sense of danger, non-acceptance and prejudice. "So you have seen him then." I said catching her gaze, "Did I say that" came her reply. "Well, have you?" I needed to try and get some information, so I tried to chat about old times, not that that helped in any way. "Did you know Petra has left the Alise and is now married and living in England, do you ever go to England?" Tilly just got up and wandered around the room, peering out the side of the closed windows. This really was hard work, "Do I need to?" She asked, looking at both of us. "Duh yuh liv yah pan Anegada wid Ed?" Goldie interrupted, "Why do you keep harping on about this? Its none of your business, if you know what's good for you," came the stark reply, oh god, if we are not careful, there will be a reason for the secret service to cordon off this area before long and it won't be to catch Tilly. "Can we meet up with you and Ed before we go home?" I asked her, not sure why I would even say that. The reply was still as quick, "I don't think so, we are not friends, you hate him don't you? Anyway I don't know where he is."

Goldie folded her arms and in doing so, accidentally knocked Tilly's bottle of water across the table, as I went to get some kitchen roll she shouted, "You stupid girl, leave it, Jaz sit down. As I sat down a waft a petrol hit me, "That's an unusual scent," I said to her, "what is," "the petrol smell," she sniffed her top, "from a petrol station" came the reply. I looked at her quizzically, "I didn't see your car outside," that's because its not there." Goldie uttered, "Duh yuh liv eena ah petrol station?" "What, no a house" came her reply, ok then, were we about to glean some useful information after all?

During the confuffle I noticed Goldie managing to place the bullet tracker into Tilly's bag, "What are you doing Goldie?" Tilly said reaching for her bag, as Goldie sat back up at the table, "Nutten Jus picking di tap aff unnu bakkle up addi floor," Goldie held out her hand and Tilly took the bottle top, staring at her in a disbelieving manner, God that was close, quick thinking on Goldie's part. "So can you arrange for Ed to meet us before we go home then?" I asked, Tilly stood up and turned to face me, I decided to try and throw her off guard a little. "Tilly, what happened, happened, there are no hard feelings, I don't blame either of you, I would like to stay in touch, we got on well once, didn't we." Tilly took a step backwards, then pointed the gun right at me, "Did we," she replied, clicking off the safety trigger. "I wouldn't do that if I were you." I replied staring at her. "Why would that be, are you about to try and take me down?" She uttered, putting her arm around my neck and holding the gun barrel against my head.

I closed my eyes, waiting for her to fire and hear the bullet resound in my skull, seconds that will be all it took, I wouldn't feel anything, death will be instantaneous. "Remember you have seen nothing, go home or be killed, don't mess this up again." Suddenly, we were all distracted by a knock at the door, I opened one eye and squinted at Goldie, unsure as to whether we should attempt to answer it. Goldie was already there, opening the door to a man, who sort of looked like Tim. "Hello, I thought you were supposed to be having a kite surfing lesson today, but you didn't turn up, can I come in and go through some paperwork" he said peering in.

I felt her grip release my neck so I opened my eyes fully, Tilly had gone, disappeared into thin air. Tim walked in, "You do a very good instructor impersonation," I uttered, slightly unnerved from it all. Tim held his finger to his lips to silence us as he searched the villa, just in case she was hiding somewhere. But alas she was gone, probably through the back window that was still open. He checked outside before coming back into the villa and removed the bugs or RF's as he calls then and Goldie took the lenses from her eyes. "Hush wi didn't git very fur fi yuh," she said, "yes ditto," came my reply. Tim looked at us both in turn, "On the contrary ladies, you did very well, he was cut off mid sentence as Leroy swung in the door, "Got her." He said looking at Tim.

What did that mean, was Leroy a spy as well, surely Tim would have revealed that when we had our heart to heart wouldn't he? Leroy was now inside next to Tim, I'm not sure why a simple baseball cap rendered him so very handsome, perhaps it brought the focus to his eyes, deep brown eyes, anyway Tim must have anticipated my next question as he said, "Before you ask, does this man look like he belongs to any intelligence source?" We all started to laugh, "Hey, mate, thats uncalled for," Leroy uttered, but Tim was right, he didn't look like spy material if there is such a thing. Goldie stood up ready to defend her man, "Yuh a ah cruel mon missa Meyer's Ave yuh luk inna mirror Leroy a fi mi spy." Well, that just made everything worse. Despite what had just happened, we seemed to have recovered quickly and all fell about laughing.

Chapter 27

Helping himself to a cup of coffee Leroy spilled the beans, I am not sure it was an entirely truthful version in my opinion, these two were still holding stuff back from us. Despite everything that had been said and for all the larking around, I am now convinced more than ever that Leroy is a spy working with Tim.

Anyway, Leroy's version of the truth, is that he was driving here when he saw someone who looked like Tilly disappearing through a bush, he managed to follow her and found out where she went, some derelict house behind an unused petrol station, he thinks he saw Ed too but couldn't swear to that.

Both men sat at the table, discussing and making plans to revisit where Leroy last saw Tilly at dusk. If this was correct information, they may be lucky and manage to catch Ed and Tilly unexpectedly. "Can we come too? We won't get in the way," I asked "Certainly not, this is work" came Tim's instant reply "So how come Leroy is coming with you, if he is not a spy?" I questioned Tim. Leroy answered, "He said I didn't look like a spy," Mmhm, anyone smirking with such electric glee in my book has stories to tell, but I let it go for now.

Tim put his serious head on, "I need you and Goldie here, just in case," "in case of what," I answered him. His brows creased and his face tensed, his tone became casual, I sensed I had pushed it too far, so I retreated, "Ok," came my reply, still not a hundred percent sure what we would be waiting for here at the villa. I looked at Goldie who winked at me, oh no, this meant she had another harebrained plan in place, did I really want to hear that, probably, we had to get rid of the men folk first though. If they could be secretive, so could we.

That actually didn't take long, as they made excuses about reviewing their plans for a dusk raid and had to leave. We said our 'see you laters' and once they were out of sight, poured some lemongrass lemonade as Goldie excitedly revealed our own mission.

We were to invite Tim and Leroy back for a light bite before they went off at dusk, we would leave the villa before them on the premise that we were going for a walk, but in reality, we would climb into the back of Leroy's truck and hide under the tarpaulin, which was covering the diving gear. We would then be taken to where Tilly and Ed were and could make our own investigations from there, if anything happened the 'spies' would save us. Ok then, just like they did in the films! I listened intently to Goldie's plan, before explaining the flaws in it. Supposing they went in Tim's car or Leroy removed the diving gear from his truck so as not to get it stolen. How would we get in to wherever we were going, what would we do? Tilly or Ed were not about to welcome us for a chat or a sit down meal and furthermore, how do we get back or explain our antics to our men?

I could have walked away from this ridiculous idea, had it not been for her smirk, the little rise in the corner of her mouth, it tickled me. "Duh yuh akcep di mission?" she asked, jumping around the room like some excited child, I sighed, I guess I was a born curious and I always wanted to be a detective. Goldie was right, we did both want to figure out this puzzle and the only way to complete it was to close it bit by bit until we had a full solution. "Mission is go," I replied, which sent Goldie into a flurry of activity, chattering, organising and texting Leroy to get them both back for supper first.

I know this sounds bad, but there was something about our mission that warmed my core and brought a surge of energy that was more pure than anything I'd felt before. It gave me a fire, a passion that went from a spark to a fire within. We would be in danger that was for sure and just by going could seal our fate, it was weird, I wasn't afraid this time. Leroy texted back, Goldie showed me the message, "Agreed good idea, Are we on the promise of insane naughtiness after? Heart faced emoji, smiley face emoji. We can make sure you are safe before and on return, possible objective complications," what was he on about, Goldie seemed to understand. The rest of our afternoon was spent indoors finalising things instead of being out in the lovely weather, still it would give our skin a day to recover.

Dusk came sooner than expected and just before the last of the sun's rays faded behind a soft grey cloud, Tim and Leroy arrived. As I opened the door to them, the outside had taken on a look of an old photograph, every familiar thing a shade of greyish orange. Goldie was at my side, "Dem ave cum eena Leroy's chuck an di tarpaulin a still deh." She squeaked. "Are you two ladies ok?' Tim asked, maybe noticing that we were behaving differently, we needed to keep this as normal as possible.It was hard, we both felt quite excited about our betrayal to the men and night ahead.

I had made some vegetable sushi bowls with a pasta salad under Goldie's watchful eye and the food was devoured in no time. Tim gave instructions that we were to go to the beach bar and stay there until their return, we would be untouchable there, should anything go wrong. We were given a get out password of "Indie." Well, that worked in our favour, if we went to the bar, we didn't have to make our excuse of going for a walk. We did as we were told, heading out of the door, luckily for us Tim and Leroy were clearing up. Call themselves spies! We climbed onto the truck and hid under the tarpaulin where we laid on our fronts, our hearts in our mouths, ants crawling around our feet.

Tim and Leroy climbed in. As the truck started and rolled off the dirt track onto a black tarmac road, we pulled back the tarpaulin slightly to see the bright headlamps illuminating the road. We jolted and jostled around in the back and as Leroy picked up a little speed I could feel the gentle rise and fall of the road beneath us. I couldn't imagine what lay in store, but somewhere at the end of this journey we might find some answers as to what that could be.

The car came to a sudden halt so we covered our heads once more. Goldie put her finger to her lips as we listened to the sound of Leroy and Tim whispering, we couldn't make out what they were saying, then there was silence, I peered out from under the cover, there was no one around, so as quietly as we could we slid out from under the tarpaulin and got down from the back of the truck.

We stood for a moment, taking in where we were, my ears became sharper, my mind full of paranoia, any slight noise was a predator, my brain jumping to the most fearsome thing it could be and my body was preparing for flight, fright or freeze. Goldie took my arm, "Wi need tuh bi eena an out before di bwoy dem si wi an bac unda di cova otherwise wi a laas. Wi stick togedda ok?" "Yes , let's get a move on then." I answered. She handed me a touch which she retrieved from her trouser pocket, why hands't I thought of this? Great idea! "Nuh put di torches pan until wi agree." She whispered. "Ok" I whispered back.

Creeping behind the petrol station, we tried to be as quiet and invisible as we could, safety is paramount to the success of our mission. In front of us was the house, abandoned but standing in a composed way, as if it had chosen solitude for itself, its door was half off its hinges the knocker dangling with gravity but the walls still had perfect brickwork, the mortar holding back the weeds that had overtaken the neighbouring paths. We crept up the path as quickly as we could so as not to be seen. Luckily we could still see without our torches for now, but it was getting darker every second.

As we entered, the spirit of the house seemed to have rescued itself by sleeping in the walls, retreating into the welcoming wood away from the dust. The floors were bare and the paint was in need of loving care, there were still odd bits of furniture lying around without the warmth of its family, standing all the same, strong beneath the flakes and dirt of years.

Suddenly a movement in the shadows had us frozen, it was no more than a rustle but in this eerie darkness it was enough to put the fear of God into us. We stood still, feeling the aches in our legs, stillness and cold are never a good combination, more noises came. I took a step back, my lungs rapidly inflating and deflating, adrenaline surged through me, Goldie held me tight. I felt my feet touch something soft, I stared at Goldie, our fear taking control, thus provoking a reaction in place of a response, a lack of self control. We wanted to scream, but we didn't, instead we both turned round and bent down feeling our way as we did.

I took a deep breath in, as we turned on the torch, we gave it a moment before our eyes became accustomed. As we looked down we realised the soft thing that I felt on my leg was actually that of a human form bulging beneath cloth, it smelt of exhaust-fumes, as we shone the torch nearer, the cloth was actually a coat. "Oh fi mi big massa Ahuu a ih Mi tink mia gwine bi sick," Goldie whispered. I wanted to answer her, but I couldn't, the child in me wanted to scream sheer terror, telling of a mind that was lost in absolute fear. Goldie put her hand over my mouth, "Christ Jaz Hush yuh mouth Yuh waan tuh git wi killed?" She was right, the body groaned, whoever it was, was still alive, just. It took both of us more courage than you can image to move closer to this body, shining the light onto them just incase it was Ed, lying in wait ready to to kill us. Neither of us were sure of our next move.

Goldie took the torch from me and shone it, trying to hover over the face, but we couldn't really get a good enough view, they were quite well camouflaged under the coat and the torch beam had never been that great in the first place. I put my hand onto the fabric and felt a stickiness, "Shine the torch here," I whispered to Goldie. As she did, I could just about make out a dark patch on the fabric, it was the stickiness of blood I was sure. Their breathing was a noisy rattle, we didn't know what to do, then there were silence. "What are you doing?" I whispered once more as Goldie was fleecing the coat, "You don't know what's under there, take your hands away." She put the small fading torch beam to our hands which felt quite sticky, patches of red adorned them, definitely blood. "Whats fi wi plan now? Wi cud bi dun fah murda Dem ave fi wi fingerprints pan dem." Oh no, she was right, I didn't even think of that.

Just then we heard voices and saw torch beams, thankfully it was voices we knew. We were in deep trouble already, so being in even deeper didn't matter anymore, we needed help. "He…..lp, over here, help us," we screeched at the top of our voices, I hadn't heard Goldie dream in the English language before, but there is a first time for everything. The torch light seemed to find us quickly, and as it shone on us, there was Tim and Leroy. Leroy shone his torch in front of us to reveal a body with a knife in its chest and then Goldie and I standing in a pool of blood.

Both men stood there completely aghast until Tim uttered, "What the hell are you both doing here, how the hell, you could have jeopardised the whole operation, you stupid…" he stopped in his tracks, I could tell from his voice that he was really angry, but then within seconds it changed, "are you both ok, lets get you out of here before you get yourselves mixed up in things you can't get out of." What did he mean by that? Tim helped us both outside and told us to remove our blood covered shoes, which he then placed in a bag he just happened to have in his pocket before giving it to Leroy uttering, "Leroy dispose of the evidence." "Jaz wait here, do not move," he said as he picked up Goldie and carried her back to the truck, before returning for me.

Once in the truck, Tim removed some tissues and a bag from the glove compartment, use these to clean yourselves up a bit, he looked at us concerned, "I am going back to help Leroy, stay here and don't go anywhere, lock the doors and keep the windows up." We both nodded, "Wi a hush," Goldie whispered, "we will discuss this at length later, not now." He closed the door and disappeared, we did as we were told. "We have probably ruined everything," I said to Goldie's as we wiped the blood from our hands, she nodded in agreement, "Duh yuh tink dat did Ed?" She asked, "I am not sure, I don't think it was. We are in serious trouble, we have broken Tims and Leroy's trust. I think our first priority is to get them back on our side, Goldie smiled, "Dat a chuu Buh ih will bi aright Dem a nuh tuff nuts tuh crack despite wah dem tink." I wanted to laugh, but instead, I just sat there feeling quite sombre, we had consciously betrayed Tim and Leroy for personal gain and I may have shattered Tims love for me into a million shards, I have broken all the rules, he won't want a relationship with me now I had destroyed the trust.

Chapter 28

Both men returned to the truck and climbed in next to us, removing their black gloves. "Are you both all right?" Leroy asked. Very subdued and embarrassed, we just nodded. Leroy started the engine and we drove back to the villa in complete silence, both men staring ahead at the empty road.

When we reached the villa, Tim ushered us inside," Get yourselves showered whilst Leroy dispose of all incriminating evidence and traces of us." Tim said curtly and we obeyed his command as if we were children, although Goldie did click her heels together and salute him. As I nudged her to stop and pulled her to our respective bathrooms, I could have sworn there was a small grin trying to appear on Tim's face.

It was quite late once we were all sat at the kitchen table, but we needed to get this out in the open, so we were in for another late night. Leroy made us all hot chocolate as Tim broke the silence. "So then, who would like to explain what the hell you thought you were doing?" His eyes were wide and angry, he had switched gears again, from a warm empathy to a cold emotional and professional determination, his softer self had taken a backseat for now. I felt so guilty, ice-cold inside, what had we done, everything was now completely ruined, our romances over forever. I was sure I had lost the man of my dreams, I need him to show his warmth so that I know we are still ok and he still loves me regardless of tonights events. I looked at Goldie, who looked at me, we both felt the same, sick to the stomach.

The few moments of silence that followed was unbearable until Leroy said, "Don't fret ladies, forgiveness and judgement used to be redundant attitudes that consistently failed to develop creative problem solving skills, which in turn eventually led to a real comprehension of issues and preventative solutions." What? As I was processing exactly what he had just said, Goldie nestled into him "Yuh big twit." She smiled. Maybe I should do the same to Tim, it might soften him, although I have to say a bit of righteous anger in the right moment, in the right situation, can be a good thing.

I smiled awkwardly, "Well, anyone got anything to say?" Tim said again, this time his tone slightly softer. I cleared my throat and began, "Tim, Leroy, we are really sorry we put ourselves and you in a position of danger, we should have known better and stayed at the bar. We really wanted to see for ourselves what was going on and where Tilly and Ed were, we wanted to help you and also for me I wanted to lay my demons to rest before they found me. The trouble is your world is in an exciting frontier, possibly a battleground at times, you can be the good force or the evil force, but also your world is a confusing mess of love and emotional indifference, of profound beauty and profound suffering. For a short time we wanted to see what it was like to be in your world, focusing on the protection of the planet and…." "Ok enough, we are not angry, just can't quite believe what you did, it was a daft thing to do, supposing they were there and tried to kill us all." He replied, we nodded and Goldie added "Wi a hush Buh duh yuh tink wi wud mek gud spies?"

There was no reply from either of them, just a guffaw of laughter, their faces changed into a vision of relaxed joy and unrestrained mirth, humour bubbling around them, until just the sound of their gales, snickers, giggles, was enough to transport us all far away from our worries and the tensions. Tim looked at his watch, "Goldie, Jaz, I will say this for the last time, you could have jeopardised the whole operation or got yourselves killed or harmed, however on this occasion you were lucky, but it won't happen again, when we ask you to do something, you need to do as we ask for your own protection, tonights antics stop now and this is an end to it." "Is Leroy a spy then too?" I asked, "His bitch more like," Leroy replied quickly, they both smirked at each other.

I needed to put this to bed too, so I asked, "What exactly was tonight all about then, can you tell us that?" looking at each of them in turn. Tim nodded and Leroy spoke carefully trying not to incriminate himself. "I drove Tim to where I had followed Tilly the other night, Tim's intelligence source had confirmed that was where they might be hiding out. Anyway when we arrived there was no one there, no traces of them or trails that might lead to their whereabouts, for all intents and purposes they had vanished. The only evidence that they might have been there was the furniture, but to be honest that could belong to any of the local hobos."

Tim took over, explaining that even under their hi-tech laser devices that emit a particular wavelength, or spectrum, there were no fingerprints, absolutely no sign of them ever being there. Goldie interrupted and made us laugh, they couldn't stay mad at us for long, "Fingerprints can bi fine pan practically any solid surface including di human bady especially wen deh a blood dirt ink paint etc. Mi read ih sumweh." Tim continued, "They did a good job of clearing out, must have been pre-warned by someone and must have had help as they only had a few hours before we went in. We searched the place and came across a vagrant who had been stabbed in the chest with a Schrade SCHF9 Extreme Survival knife, its grip had been wiped clean, we were outside looking for traces of further evidence when you screamed. The stabbed man was clean, we checked, I think he was a victim of unfortunate circumstance, probably came across the place to rest and disturbed Tilly or Ed or both and ended up being stabbed." "What will happen to him now?" I asked Tim, "He will bi blown up an cut out nuh traces," Goldie sniggered, "Goldie, take that back" "what! Yah hush dat did ah bit below di mark." "His body has been moved to a safe place and handed over to the authorities," Tim replied, "oh, will they have to investigate further?' I asked, "No, it is our baby and once they know we are dealing with it they back off, they will try and identify him and if they can, they will proceed to contacting any next of kin, but if that draws a blank, he will have a silent cremation and be laid to rest." "An Tilly an Ed Wah ah them, will dem git addi Island?" Goldie asked looking at Leroy for an answer. "I doubt that very much, they might be clever, but not that clever," he replied, cuddling Goldie. "We have surveillance on all exit routes from the Island, so unless they know of a secret shipping lane from here, they can't leave. I suspect they will lay low for a while and probably move their trafficking handling to someone and somewhere else for a while. Have no fears, we will get them, but our main priority now is protecting you two." Tim interrupted, he moved closer to me and cupped my face in his hands kissing my forehead. "Wah mek" Goldie asked looking confused. Before Tim could say anything, I answered for him, "Tilly and Ed will think we told someone and they will want to kill us, remember what Tilly said," "oh, Yah Buh wi didn't tell nobady," came her reply, "but they don't know that." I answered, yawning.

Leroy put the cups in the sink, "We should all get some rest." He was right, it was half past midnight. "We will stay with you both tonight," he uttered leading Goldie by the hand into her room as if she was some naughty school girl. Tim did the same with me.

As we cuddled in bed, I was transported into a serene space, a place of loving restoration, I still felt slightly ashamed of myself, I had let Tim down, but I think I was forgiven and thank goodness he still loved me. "Tim," I said, "Mmhm," came the reply, "I truly am so sorry, does it change anything between us?" There was a brief moment of silence, as if he didn't know the answer, but in truth, he was trying to fall asleep. "Love transforms our emotions Jaz, into healthy perspectives and good thoughts that build us into better selves, I love you dearly, it's late, please can we go to sleep." I smiled to myself, before one last stretch and yawn. By now he had snuggled right into me, he was the big spoon, I was the little spoon, in his arms was my safe place, my cocoon, I fell asleep, content and without saying another word.

Chapter 29

The following morning, it was as if the previous nights events hadn't happened, we all ate breakfast together, laughed and chatted. Tim and Leroy decided that to take our mind off things we should complete our dive on the RSS Rhone. They looked at the weather forecast, sea conditions and wind direction. "If we dive at eleven thirty and limit ourselves to no more than three hours, we should be ok. It will take us twenty minutes to swim down to the site, how do we all feel about it?" Leroy uttered putting all the maps and compass to one side. Despite the nerves, everyone seemed to be in agreement so I wasn't going to let the side down.

By the time we had eaten our fruit, cleared away and finished getting organised, it was time to go. We climbed into the truck and Leroy drove us back to Horseshoe reef. We hauled our diving gear onto the beach and I mean hauled, we had bigger tanks this time, so we could do a longer dive. We did our pre-dive checks and then buddy checks once more after putting on our gear. "We really must stay together and be extremely vigilant, if it is too dangerous and the currents change we come up, ok everyone?" Tim said with his serious head on, we all nodded and did the 'ok' sign with our fingers, then made our way out to the reef. This time we were better practised so we didn't look like demented seals going out to play.

As we made our way slowly, there is no amount of poetry or words to describe the images and memories of the marine life we saw. It is a world apart from anything, yet so dependant on us to be able to thrive, the marine life needs our empathy, not to just think of them as food or a good day-trip to an aquarium.

It is so beautiful, brightly coloured fish darted and snuggled amongst the flowing coral, it was their shelter, their home. A crab with raised pincers ready for battle scuttled with some difficulty over the rocks, clinging on for dear life as the water currents fought against his small body. He had darker coloured legs and yellow eye-stalks, his shell mirroring the two shades. Leroy pointed out more seahorses curling their tails around pieces of coral, fluttering their fins so gracefully.

We kicked deeper, the glow of the surface becoming dimmer and more distant. An octopus with its rounded body and bulging eyes swam past me, stretching and retracting its eight long arms to get home. Even through my wetsuit I could feel the temperature of the water beginning to drop, it isn't like a winter chill, bringing a shiver to my skin, but more like the welcome coolness of an autumn breeze.

The further down we descended the rocks became like silhouettes, shadows that give the impression they are moving eerily, we switched on our head torches to improve the visibility. From time to time I was surprised by a lone fish, completely invisible to me until it entered the beam of my headlight. I am so free to turn and move as I wish, the ties of gravity fading into nothing. I felt more pressure on my suit than I did on the previous dive, but as I sucked on my mouth piece, taking in more oxygen and stealing a glance at the gauge, I looked over at Tim and I knew everything would be all right. Tim saw me look and touched my arm, then nodded, I nodded back, I am ok. He pointed below as we neared the wreck.

I looked down, the shipwreck was shrouded in a fine mist, it was a beautiful skeleton, it would have been an imposing craft in its day, now it rests in this truly three dimensional world. I nudged Tim and pointed below, he nodded, we all swooped down for a better look, a truly majestic sight, in another century there may not be such a distinctive outline, perhaps simply a bed of sand studded with bits of ironwork.

As we dived in and out the wreck, a giant green moray and several octopus swam past us, oblivious to our inspection of their home. The ship had split in half as it sunk, so the bow and the stern are about fifty feet apart. The bow lies on its starboard side, its foremast complete with the crow's nest is still attached, the cannon is pretty spectacular too, all encrusted with beautiful coral and overrun by schools of yellowtail snapper fish. I grabbed Tim as a barracuda swam right up and around me, I later learned that he is a local 'pet' barracuda who lives on the wreck and has earned the name Frag from the regular divers visiting his home.

We continued to swim through the mid section, I checked my gauge again, despite my reservations I was really enjoying this dive, I was glad I read up on the history beforehand as I had more sense of what we were seeing. There were several artefacts laying on the floor of the wreck, a few bowls and coins and others which were difficult to make out, however one thing that did catch my eye was a set of giant marine spanners. Goldie seemed very excited to see them and indicated for us to follow her. She and Leroy showed us some large and roomy openings at either end of the wreck allowing us to swim through, joined by a graceful turtle, gliding next to us and keeping a watchful eye. We spotted a few brass portholes that were still visible, including the 'lucky porthole' a brass circle which had survived the storm and remains intact with its glass today, it is quite shiny, as most divers rub it, apparently it is said to bring good luck, well we just had to do it didn't we!

We swam inside the wreck, its exposed ribs covered in orange sponges and yellow cup coral, the wooden decks had rotted away, but still provide excellent habitats for lobsters, eels, and many more. There is a huge propeller which features its own short swim-through drive shaft and a group of black-and-white tiles that looked like a chess set, known as 'the dance floor,' allegedly part of the ships bathroom.

It is amazing to think that all this time the wreck has rested here on the sand and despite the site being used for dives, it was still in relatively good condition. We even found the silver teaspoon embedded in the side of the wreck. Legend has it that the teaspoon belonged to Captain Wooley and that he had been using it to stir his tea when he was thrown into the sea. I do remember reading about this, but never expected to see it so clearly. There are also numerous coral gardens, cleaning stations and nurseries throughout the debris field. Sergeant major fish dot the area with their purple eggs, along with small pufferfish, damsel fish, green moray and octopus which are all common visitors.

Leroy looked at his watch and indicated the time we had left on the dive, thankfully it was long enough for us to explore a bit more. We swam in a different direction this time, taking in the wrecked guns, misshapen by colourful sponges and crinoid, a swarm of brightly adorned fish swam past me in an effort to reach home before it was invaded. We also found one of the huge water boilers which had once made steam for the engine, it was laying on its side, spilt open from the explosion. There was a surge of temptation to keep a few of the smaller artefacts as souvenirs, but these dives were monitored closely and anyway they wouldn't hold the same meaning as they do down here.

Even though the sinking of this ship was a tragedy and many people lost their lives, today it serves a new purpose, it has become part of the living reef, no longer a tomb for the dead, but a home for all marine life to use and help in marine conservation.

Chapter 30

The feeling this dive gave me was surreal, a feeling of awe came over me, never before had I felt more like a mermaid, I wouldn't trade this incredible experience for anything else in the world. I tapped Tim and pointed inside the wreck, he nodded, then without waiting for the others and without giving it a second thought, I just swam through the cracked hull of the wreck.

The interior was considerably darker than I imagined, I think I might have taken a wrong turn, but if I focus on finding the swim-through I will be all right. My heart began to beat rapidly as I clung to a thin line I had found, hopefully it will guide me through. With every exhalation, bubbles floated upwards to a large cloud trapped in the hull, time seemed to slow further with every breath I took. I was so frightened that I barely noticed the light trickling through every crevice in the wreck. I continued to swim a little further forward until I realised that the beam from my head torch in these shady conditions was disorientating me, it was a like a maze and I felt lost.

Suddenly I was grabbed from behind, thank goodness, Tim had found me, but it didn't feel like Tim! This grip was rough and the more I tried to squirm, the tighter the hold, I saw the silvery skin of a shark cruise past me, the wolf of the ocean. What was I going to do, I was on my own? Was this just Tim or Leroy messing about? No, they wouldn't do that. I tried to get my hand loose to punch my attacker, I had never been in this situation so never attempted this underwater before and the resistance of the water, coupled with the lack of space slowed my motions, my attacker was getting the better of me.

The light from my headlight decided to die faster than the heat from a winter campfire, destroying what little visibility I did have, all I could hear was my own bubbling. I squirmed again and managed to break free for a second before my regulator was punched out of my mouth. I moved backwards and then managed to land a punch in the divers stomach, he sort of bent in half which gave me enough time to fumble and find my mouthpiece again. I took some quick sharp breaths as a dark hand came forward trying to aim for my mask and rip it away from my face, I managed to bend my knees and aim with my flippers, jarring myself on the side of the wreck. As I went to go forwards once more I found that I was now stuck, the section between my tank and me had become snagged firmly in one of the crevices, I couldn't free it, I couldn't move. My assailant realised this and came at me once more, this time with a knife in his hand. I managed to deflect his knife hand, hoping the knife would fall but it didn't.

My regulator fell down and dangled somewhere at my side, I wanted to scream inside my mask, but I needed to conserve energy and no-one would hear me anyway. I was running out of air and running out of time. I felt an overwhelming mix of intense loneliness, stupidity, frustration and an adrenaline rush. I had to collect my thoughts in a last bid to stay alive, I had to do something. But what? There was only the weird squeaks and squeezes coming from the rubber of my suit, I had no means of defence.

As I fumbled for my regulator again, I felt my head beginning to pound, I was becoming dizzy and more disorientated, every cell in my body was screaming for oxygen. I have to keep fighting, I have to take a breath. I managed to find it and put it back into my mouth, albeit momentarily. They came again, this time ready to finish me, I felt defenceless, I really didn't know what to do, pure terror surged through me, I was underwater, gasping for air, I was going to die, a knife in me would only make it quicker.

They came closer to me, ready to plunge the knife in, I looked straight at them, peering through their mask. A wave of shock pulsed through me as I recognised the dark sinister features of Ed Wrexham, I wasn't going to let him be my killer no way! My head was about to explode and everything was getting darker, the ocean wanting to swallow me whole, but with every once of energy I had left I took one last swipe, hitting his mask, his regulator fell from his mouth and his head rocked backwards a little as he hit the side of the wreck.

Just as I was about to try again, I felt something above me, then in front of me, phew, it was Leroy. As he moved to try and free me Ed slashed him across the shoulder with the knife, the cut oozed blood into the water. Two more sharks appeared, their streamline bodies gracing our space, smoothly swimming back and forth. Contrary to popular belief, sharks do not go for human blood, unless they are great whites, on this occasion we were thankful they were not.

Leroy turned and smashed Ed into the side of the wreck, a creaking noise followed, it felt like it was all going to cave in. It gave Leroy enough time to cut the snagged cord to release my harness as Ed came again. Someone hauled on me from above, in my sheer terror, I hadn't even noticed an opening above me, not that I could have got out with my tank cord snagged. I looked down and saw Leroy surge forward, his harpoon gun pointing and then firing at my assailant, sealing Ed's fate pinning him to the side of the wreck. Leroy's blade met no resistance and a fountain of brilliant emerald green came from the wound, the ebb and flow of the wound killing Ed all the faster.

From my diving course we had been taught that any blood from a cut underwater would be green due to the different frequencies of light travelling at different speeds. Water slows light down so as you dive down into the water, the first colour to be filtered out by the water is the slowest, which happens to be red.

As I continued to be hauled up, I felt myself start to panic, I kept telling myself, this was the worst thing I could do. I took a deep breath to try and calm myself, but no luck, I couldn't get control. My brain became so bombarded by fear and disorientation that my actions became erratic. I was grabbed tightly and as I looked up I realised I was now in the safety of Tims arms, he put his mouthpiece in my mouth and I sucked as much as I could before squirming again, I had to stop this panic escalating, if I didn't, I will put the others in danger.

Goldie grabbed hold of my arms and smiled through her mask as much as she could, trying to calm me. She gave the ascent command, Tim held his mouthpiece in place and still holding me tight, we slowly made our way up, we needed to do this properly but we were all nearly out of air.

Ascending slowly, my breathing was still very fast and I could feel myself hyperventilating, all I wanted to do was get back to the surface before I passed out, if I passed out now, there was a chance that I might not make it out of the water alive. I looked at Goldie and Tim who were helping me, I had Tim's air so Goldie and Tim were sharing air, but there was no sign of Leroy. I felt my head tilt, I needed to sleep, then as if by some divine intervention Leroy was there, he moved his hands to support me despite his bleeding wound, coaxing me to move my legs and I kicked my flippers with my last reserves. It felt like ages, as we had to complete our decompression stops. Tim held onto to me all the way, he was my safety net.

Eventually our heads broke through the waves and we all relaxed a little now we were nearly safe. I could feel Tim dragging me through the water until we were near enough to the shoreline, then he picked me up and carried me as my legs felt like jelly. Tim gently laid me on the sand and removed the mask from my face, I coughed and spluttered with exhausted relief.

The others fell on the sand beside me like crumpled puppets suddenly released from their strings. It was hard to make anything out, it was all a blur, but after a while I could just make out Goldie attending to Leroy. Tim held me in his arms as I closed my eyes. He shook me, "Jaz don't go to sleep, you have to stay awake." Goldie held my hand, "Jaz, Taak tuh mi Seh sinting." I heard Leroy's dulcet tones saying, "Ambulance on its way, I am going back to remove Ed," that was all I remember hearing before I passed out.

Chapter 31

When I woke up, I felt quite strange in more ways than one, my clothes didn't feel right and I certainly did not recognise the room I was in. I was lying in a bleach tinctured room on crisp but thinning white sheets. A green patterned curtain hung in front of me on a shiny chrome rail, it smelt of disinfectant, like a hospital, but why would I be in one? I couldn't remember.

I sat forward and immediately came over quite dizzy, I felt a crick in my neck, all my muscles ached and a pain in my head surged from back to front with waves of nausea that added to my misery. I felt my lungs crackle as I coughed so loud that it could have woken the whole ward, gosh it really made my head throb when I coughed. I laid back, resting my head on the pillow, I felt something tug, I put my hand up and felt something me my nose, which I duly pulled out. I stared at the pristine white polystyrene tiles on the ceiling, hoping if I lay still the nausea and swimming feeling in my head would soon pass.

Suddenly the door opened and a nurse entered the room without slowing her stride at all, one moment she was in the corridor, the next she was grabbing my hand to take a pulse. She replaced the nasal oxygen back into my nose and stared into thin air. In this exchange she neither made eye contact or spoke, she didn't even introduce herself, I felt sub-human, as if I no longer qualified as a person at all, but right now, I didn't care or feel up to doing anything about it.

The nurse's face was like an overstored apple, round and full, yet crinkled worse than a brown paper bag after all the candy is gone. Her eyes were small, mean looking and bereft of any make-up, she smelt of garlic and detergent. As I wiggled my nose to avoid her odour, she adjusted the nasal oxygen prongs in my nose which had become loose once more and then fiddled with the intravenous drip that I had just noticed in my hand, "Whats that for?" I asked her. She made a weird clicking noise with her tongue before pursing her withered lips and uttering, "It is to keep you hydrated, you have visitors outside, do you feel up to seeing them for a short while?" "Um, ok" I replied, I didn't really want to see anyone but it would be rude. As she disappeared out of the room, taking her soapy, herby smells with her, I heard her say, "Not for long, mind, she needs to rest." With that, my handsome visitor appeared at the door, he walked over to me and sat down on the bed.

Tim entered the room looking concerned, as he sat down on my bed he kissed me on the forehead and took my hand, his expression changed to one of relief. "Please don't kiss me," I said, he expression changed again, "why, have I done something wrong?" "No, because it hurts my head" came my reply, he smiled, "So, I guess you are feeling as pretty rotten as you look then? You had us really worried, we have all been waiting outside." "Thanks." I started fidget in the bed to try and get comfortable, I felt like I was going to be sick, Tim held on to my shoulders and gently laid me back on the pillow. "Try and lay still, try to rest. Can I do anything, do you want me to get a nurse?" "No, I will be ok, just feel a bit sick, how long have I been here?" I asked, he stroked my face and brushed my straggly hair to one side, then glanced at his watch, "About four hours" he replied, "Are you sure? It feels like I have been here for days," Tim laughed, "I'm afraid not, just a matter of hours." I have to admit, I managed a smile at this point too, I suppose its my brain fog causing my slight disorientation, but that will soon disappear. Tim moved closer to me and took my hand, "Do you remember what happened on the dive?" "Yes, I do now, its all beginning to come back to me," came my reply. "Well, once we got you onto the beach, you collapsed from decompression sickness, we had to get you to hospital to administer some oxygen."

I felt completely embarrassed and ashamed. "Its ok, don't worry, you just need to stay in tonight for observation, I will come back for you in the morning, unless you want me to stay with you?" I ignored Tim's question for the time being and instead asked, "What about everyone else, are you all ok? Leroy? He was stabbed." Just as I finished my sentence, wave of sickness came over me, Tim looked at me, "Jaz?" "I think I'm going to be sick," came my reply. I had never seen him move so fast to collect a plastic bowl from the side and hand it to me, just in time.

He then passed me some water and removed the filled bowl from me, "Rinse you mouth round and spit into this bowl he said." I obeyed, "Anymore? He uttered taking both bowls outside the room. "I don't think so," I replied. He smiled and despite asking him not to, he kissed my forehead once more. "We are all fine, including Leroy, get some rest my darling, I will come back tomorrow." With that he got up and left with a brief wave. I needed him to stay but I wanted to be alone, I felt so ill, if I sleep it will help my recovery and might take my mind off how bad I feel.

Just as I nestled under the sheet and closed my eyes I was disturbed by a nurse. "Remember me? Nurse Nicola?" She wasn't the least bit familiar, probably came in when I was sleeping. She took my arm. "You must need the washroom by now? Come." I shook my arm free, the last task I needed to do at the present moment in time was to move. "Get off, I don't know you, don't touch me," I said sternly, she didn't seem the least bit surprised. Quite the contrary, her expression said she'd heard it all before.

I really didn't want to get up, I wanted to sleep, but insistently she helped me sit up and swung my legs off the bed, my head swooned and I thought I was going to pass out, but instead I vomited again everywhere, on her and the floor, it was amazing how far it actually travelled. Well, I did warn her to leave me alone! The next few moments were a flurry of activity as she laid me back down on the bed and called for help. Her colleagues responded and helped blitz the room with Dettol or something that smelt very similar.

Now another nurse stood at my bedside, taking my pulse and observing my respiration rate, one glance at her ebony skin against her starched white uniform and I felt myself relax. "Is this a hospital?" I asked her. Her speech started with a liberal dose of terms of endearment, "Honey, sweetie, sweetheart and love." "Honey, It's a health clinic, you can only stay as a day case or one night, anything more and you have to be transferred to the main hospital in Tortola, sweetie." At least she spoke to me like I was a real person, a person who mattered. Her gaze fell on me, it had the warmth of a mother's eyes and her voice was deep yet honeyed, in her presence my pain seemed to subside and I could feel myself beginning to fall asleep. She made sure I was tucked in tightly before washing her hands and leaving the room, I felt cocooned and snug and must have fallen asleep straight away.

I awoke to loud shouts from across the corridor, presumably from another patient. I listened and caught the pain behind each shout, they became so loud and frequent that the peaceful air became polluted. I knew it wasn't their fault, they needed help. I glanced at the clock on the wall in my room, six twenty am, this patient was going to test my patience, if you pardon the pun. If it carried on for much longer, I swear I would find an illegal use for a pillow.

Just then another nurse entered my room, this time in blue scrubs, washing her hands at the sink and looking like she was lost entirely to worrying thoughts. When she came over to me, her face softened into a smile and she introduced herself, "I'll be your nurse this morning before you leave us, my name is Maya. Do you feel better, how was your sleep?" She smiled again, "Much better thank you, I have a bit of a headache but I don't feel sick or dizzy anymore, I think I slept really well." Nurse Maya listened to my answers whilst taking my pulse, blood pressure, looking in my eyes and pinching the nail beds of my fingers and toes to make sure there was enough oxygen going around me. She had a permanent fixed smile whilst doing a head-to-toe assessment and making her notes.

Occasionally she would ask a pointed question but other than that the chatter was no different to when she got her hair done. She removed oxygen prongs from my nose and the drip from my hand, delicately applied a plaster and helped me to the wash room. She fussed with the sheets then tidied around the bed whilst I made myself presentable, I did actually feel much better, tired, but almost human again. Her final job was to raise the head of my bed and plump the pillows behind me, saying that some food was coming soon. She left, sterilised her hands, made her final notes on a folder outside the door and then disappeared. The yelling patient was silent, probably by some tranquilliser. I sighed, I will be glad to leave here today, Tim had promised he would come for me later but it was still early morning.

The door opened again and Goldie ambled into my room with a tray and a beach bag. The tray was loaded with soft pancakes, maple syrup threaded on the top and a mountain of berries. They smelt delicious and were as warm as they had been in the sun, they were accompanied by two cups of coffee. "Hi, where on earth did you get all this?" I asked, "Nuh one did roun Suh helped miself Mi get extra eena case yuh did raw," she replied, as she sat down on the bed and started to share out the pancakes onto two plates, munching one as she did so. "How a yuh feeling? yuh fraid mi Mi did tink yuh did gwine drop out." She asked, mid pancake chew, she took a sip of coffee as I answered. "I feel much better, I have to admit I felt like I was going to die, Tim said he is coming to get me out of here later, he is isn't he?" I asked her, piling the berries on a pancake, I was hungry, I hadn't eaten since before the dive."Yep, Wi a all a tek yuh yaad." came the reply.

We carried on munching amid the banter, until the loaded tray was completely empty. Our banter was bonding, it was our friendship and I needed our daily fix now more than ever. Goldie bent down and picked up the beach bag, "Cum pan lets mek yuh luk gorgeous Ruff yuh sum fresh clothes unless yuh waan tuh cut out yah eena ah diving suit?" We both giggled as she helped me to the washroom to get dressed and laid out all the creams and make up in the world.

Once doused in an array of creams, dressed in my own clothes and with my make up applied by Goldie, I felt and looked more human, possibly more on the clown like side of things, (Goldie was always heavy on the make up!) At least I was out of those red oversized hospital gowns, they were functional but not at all modern or desirable attire.

We sat back on the bed waiting for Tim to arrive both chattering at the same time. "Yuh fos." Goldie said giggling. "I was just going to ask about Leroy and Ed Wrexham that was all. Was Tim annoyed that I went off on my own?" "How cud Tim bi mad at yuh he did very concerned bout yuh paced di floor all day Mi shud'n wonda. Leroy, hav feem arm eena ah sling deep cut, mi ave bin nursing him." She really was my best medicine, poor Leroy, I bet Goldie as a nurse has a whole new meaning. "Ed a well an truly dead harpooned tuh di side addi wreck he will bi ah out a road artefacts," she said in her mischievous manner, it is somewhat childish, I grant you, but she just made me feel alive.

I was taken aback for a second, the thought of Ed Wrexham being dead and pinned to a famous wreck, just his luck, he dies and will still go down in history, but they wouldn't leave him there, would they and why did Leroy spear him?" Her answer to that question was, "Bikaaz he cud he nuh regret ih." She giggled, now I know that bit was not true.

Chapter 32

For the next hour, Goldie had laughter in her eyes and a smile twitching at her lips as she revealed everything. Tim had been honest with me, but I guess the mystery started from what he didn't say, from what I had lacked the courage to ask. Thankfully there was no holding her back.

In order that I understand Goldie precisely, I will relay her yarn in English rather than her own dialect, otherwise it will get to confusing for me and I didn't need that.What she said was, "Leroy is also a spy, but he belongs to National Security Agency, NSA for short and is part of a program nick named Somalget. He locates International narcotic traffickers and special-interest alien smugglers. His agency has been closing in on Tilly but Ed heard that we had been commandeered to help flush her out, he wanted in on the action. Ed wanted to kill you as he thought we had leaked information to their where's and want them dead. Anyway Leroy leaked some information about us all going to dive on the wreck. Well, Ed heard and came after us, they knew this would happen. What Tim didn't bank on was you swimming off in the wreck and becoming stuck Ed had you just where he wanted you, all alone and vulnerable, we found you from you regulator bubbles when it was out of you mouth. Leroy swam in to where you were and saved your life, Tim and I hauled you out and gave you air to get you back to the surface. Leroy injured himself harpooned Ed.

I think I just about got the gist of it, despite her own take on things. "So, Ed is definitely dead, we can be sure, can we?" I asked her. She nodded, "Yep, he a as dead as ah dodo, A bi eaten by tiger sharks as wi taak hopefully." Goldie pressed the call bell and nurse Maya appeared almost immediately, still smiling. "More coffee please, wi a celebrities." She uttered, "Goldie, this is a private clinic, not a hotel." I said, but I had to smile as Nurse Maya, washed her hands and disappeared without uttering a sound just nodding. She returned very quickly with two more cups of coffee and some biscuits.

She had the bearing of a soldier, her every action was precise and purposeful, she smiled at us but this time in a distant way professionals do. I can never seem to relax around such false expressions, I need a genuine face, preferably with a smile, but if not I'd rather they didn't fake it.

There was screaming from another room again, only stopping momentarily to draw in rasping breaths. Her face broke, this time she was not amused, she spoke with an American accent and with each word her fine fingers would flourish into the stagnant hospital air like birds, then settle, "Do you know it is already a quarter past nine and I haven't started organising the medications yet, let alone actually administering them, hear this, I am not a waitress." With that she washed her hands, spun on her heels and left the room, we had been reprimanded!

As I looked towards the door, both Leroy and Tim were stood there, smiling. "How long have you been there?" I asked. "Long enough." Tim replied as they entered the room, "Jus bin a tell Jaz everyting, nearly finished." Goldie remarked, "The short version I hope." Leroy answered.

Leroy had his arm in a sling, "Does it hurt much?" I asked him as he strolled over to the bed, Goldie stood up and kissed him, "No, my nurse helps make it better" he said smiling at Goldie. Yuk, "No seriously, it's just a flesh wound to the shoulder, should heal in a few days, need the stitches to heal first though." "I am so sorry I let you all down, I feel really ashamed that I put you all in danger, I really owe you big time." I said, making eye contact with them all. Goldie stood up of the bed, "Nuh worry Nuh feel bad, Wi a all alive an dem get di result dem waah shall mi finish di story?" She uttered, "Well, not quite, Ed is dead, granted but it would have been nice to have him alive and see him squirm." Tim joked. "Serve him rite" Goldie exclaimed as she finished her coffee. "What about Tilly?" I questioned, "Nuh kno Dem a still a luk fi har."

Goldie took my hand, her face fell into an expression I would never have associated with her features before, as if she was going to break more sombre news to me. Under that exuberant personality was someone more vulnerable than I could have guessed. "Tilly mite cum fah wi wid guns Wi need tuh tan wid fi wi mon. Eh suh kool knowing spies a nuh it? mi an Leroy a gwine git hitched wi ave decided, a yuh gwine marry Tim?

Translated for us English speakers what she just said is, Tilly might came for we with guns, we need to stay close to our men. It's so cool knowing spies isn't it? By the way Leroy and I are going to get hitched we have decided. Are you going to marry Tim?

Marry Tim! I was lost for words, confused even, I needed to gain greater perspective and take a step back to see the wide angle version. I knew there was something between Tim and Leroy, but I never connected Leroy with NSA and the Somalget Program. He doesn't look like the kind of guy to locate International narcotics traffickers and special-interest alien smugglers, intercepting and derailing plots, but then, I suppose that's what they want, someone completely unassuming. The two of them were complete opposites, a 'Morecambe and Wise,' serious and funny.

Tim broke the silence, "We are not without a heart," "that's right" Leroy replied, "I did try to save Ed, as I took out my spear, he winced and I held my hand to the slash, but no matter how much pressure I applied, the blood still gushed between my fingers and oozed under my hand. I watched his skin turn pale in the mask, until his eyes became still. I went back to get him but a tiger shark swam through the wreck and latched on to Ed's leg, shaking it, so I made a hasty retreat, the shark will dispose of Ed for us." "Shall we get out of here, or do you want to spend the rest of the day in this clinic?" Tim asked, "My preferred answer would be let's get out of here please." I replied without any hesitation.

Chapter 33

I pressed the call button and waited to see which nurse would arrive in order that I could get the all clear to leave. Despite his injury Leroy seemed to be doing a good job of pinning Goldie to the wall, kissing and clearly igniting their primal desires. You see these are not the actions of a spy, Tim wouldn't do that, although a girl always fantasises about being taken by surprise. "Leroy, for goodness sake this is not the time or the place, behave, put Goldie down and put your tongue away!" Goldie smiled as she reluctantly let go, "A yuh jealous, Wi a passionately eena luv."

For such a shy person my sexual urges and fantasies are anything but restrained, but I try to keep what I am thinking in my inner secret diary. However Tim, being a man of some intelligence sensed this, there is something ultimately very bonding about secrecy and privacy, perhaps it is the tethering between the two that keeps tantric emotions alive. Tim smiled, "I could rise to the occasion in more ways than one, if you are feeling better Jaz." He remarked, I was just about to speak when Goldie interrupted, draping her arms around me she said, "Tap ih Shi a ah sick person Dem ave germs Enuh." Despite the laughter that filled the room I felt myself blush, my embarrassment was immense, I really wish I didn't blush so fast, in an instant my cheeks are always rosy and everyone can see my feelings, I might as well write them in little notes and hand them out.

A different nurse yet again, entered wearing green scrubs this time, I wonder what all the different uniforms meant, or was it just that there were not enough of the same colour to go around, this was quite possible in the Caribbean. Her black hair was tied low in a pony tail, she had an Asian look about her large brown eyes, neatly lined in black and an easy smile of one visiting a dear friend, her movements were unhurried, choreographed and deliberate. "Can I help," she said softly, "Wi waah tuh tek Jaz yaad now please," Goldie uttered before anyone else could say anything. "Do you now, let's see," the nurse said, as she stood next to me taking my pulse once more and checking the paperwork on the board outside my room.

She returned, standing beside me she asked,"Do you feel fit enough to leave? I nodded, "Ok, all your observations are normal and you have eaten and drank so I will get your release papers and leave them outside, take care of yourself. I would suggest you take it easy for the rest of today and keep off any alcoholic drinks, you will be back to your normal self by tomorrow." Leroy followed her out of the room as Tim picked up the bag and helped me off the bed. As he offered up his arm to escort me out of the room and down the corridor, Goldie uttered, "Duh yuh waan ah wheelchair? Mi kno weh one a Wi can push yuh." "No need, I am not an invalid, my legs do work, I feel fine really" came my instant reply, the thought of Goldie launching me down the corridor in a wheelchair doesn't even bare thinking about. "Yuh did tell tuh rest Jasmine." She said, her eyes searching to make sure we hadn't forgotten anything, I did like having her around, she was funny. "We will all rest when we get to the villa." Leroy said catching up with us and grabbing Goldie's arm.

The health clinic hallway was like something out of a Star Trek movie, everything that could shine, did shine. The floors were a shiny grey colour almost like stainless-steel and the artworks on the walls were all natural images in colours as bright as a glacier melting to water in the heat of sun. The air had a pure fragrance, not at all sterile. As we made our way to the exit, music played in the background at just the right level to give the patients and staff an emotional lift, a sort of classical meets Tubular Bells, quite calming actually.

I looked up at the ceiling which was completely clear with high arches, the glow of sunlight glinting through the fanlights. It was like standing out in the open but without the risk of any rain showers. Tim must have seen me look up. "This is what a private clinic looks like in the Caribbean, nothing but the best for you my beautiful Jasmine." He definitely saw the shock register on my face before I could hide it, this must have cost an arm and a leg, nothing came cheap out here, how was I going to repay this? A small smile played on his lips, "Just teasing" he said smiling again. "Teasing what? That my stay here didn't cost the earth or that you called me Jasmine?" There was no reply, I sighed and let the happiness soak right into my bones, I was happy I was with Tim, I loved him so much, It didn't matter that he called me Jasmine, I just wanted to savour the moment, I felt serene and quietly laughed to myself.

We came to the door of the clinic, Tim disappeared to bring the car around, whilst Leroy stuck right by our sides, waiting for our chauffeur to reappear. "Are you sure you are alright?" He whispered in my ear. I nodded as Tim arrived back with the car, "I am now," I replied. Goldie cupped my face in her hands, "Yuh a gorgeous Jaz." She said smiling, "You too, my friend," I replied.

We all climbed into Tim's car and drove off leaving the health clinic behind us. He dropped Goldie off at Leroy's place before taking me back to the villa. Goldie kissed me on the cheek, "Si yuh first light empress, jus rest," with that they were outside the car waving as Tim drove off.

Leroy's 'house' was nothing like I imagined. Tim saw me eye up the imposing facade, "I will take you in there one day" "It's not really Leroy's place, it's what we call an offensive safe house for Leroy and I to stay in, courtesy of the Government here. Leroy and Goldie will stay there tonight, I will stay at the villa with you, we can swap tomorrow if you would like to?"

When they say house, it was more like a mansion. It looked quite posh and was in an area of Anegada with minimal inhabitants, including wildlife, so Goldie had said. Anegada is beautiful but so odd, it is only a small Island but the neighbourhoods vary hugely, from small brightly painted wooden houses to old large buildings in grey stone and some derelict and long deserted areas. The only dwellings that were consistent were the churches and they were still well attended and held in high esteem.

Anyway, this mansion was huge, it stood all alone as if the surrounding nature had embraced it, from what I could see, the flora flowed within it as much as around it. Tim said that the architect had loved the trees so much that there was a mighty tree in the centre forming the pinnacle of the place and the house had been built around it. The outside was a pale green painted concrete with tall glass windows, blackened by closed blinds for essential privacy and for complete solitude. "Yes, please I would like that." I said.

I touched Tims knee, I wanted to be more mischievous, but he was driving, so I asked a question instead. The smile that came upon his face, showed me he knew what I wanted to do. "Tim, why did you call it an offensive safe house, it looked very nice and safe to me?" Tim glanced at me and laughed, "It's not what the building looks like, keep your hand on my knee, I like it. In our line of work there are two types of safe houses, a defensive safe house, which is one where we can hide people to keep them safe or secure during any investigation and an offensive safe house which serves as a place for us spies to conduct covert surveillance operations. "Oh, I see." I laughed leaving my hand on his leg.

Chapter 34

We arrived at the villa and once inside Tim made sire I was comfortable on the sofa and poured me a glass of cold lemongrass lemonade, "Is that it?" I asked "I'm afraid so, for today anyway, do you want to rest here or lay on the bed?" "Rest on the bed for a little bit, will you lie with me?" I replied heading to the bedroom and climbing fully clothed onto the bed, "Sure," Tim replied and followed me with a book to read. "You try and sleep for a bit, not too much strenuous activity for now, doctors orders." I nodded and snuggled into him.

He felt so warm, in his embrace the world stopped still on its axis, I could feel his love flow around me and in this moment of togetherness, we are at the centre of our own divine vortex. Tim cradled me like a cherished child but always gives me the respect of an equal. His hug was stronger than anything I'd ever known, as if holding me wasn't quite enough, he has to feel every ounce of me pressed into him. I yawned as he opened his book, closed my eyes and must have fallen asleep.

I came to suddenly, awakened by a clattering sound. I got up, sorted myself out before strolling into the kitchen. Tim had made an evening meal, what a mess! The kitchen had become a place of great art with absolutely no orderly system, everything was everywhere, I smiled, he wasn't perfect after all. He looked up, "Sorry I didn't see you there, how are you feeling? "Much better," came my reply as I ventured into the unknown. "Its a bit of a mess I'm afraid, not very organised in the kitchen area, my excuse is, its not my forte as you can see!" We both laughed, it was part of our loving bond, we were safe in each other's heart. "Make yourself comfortable on the porch and I will join you in a moment," he said, taking my arm and leading me there.

He had set a beautiful table, he removed a tea towel from his chair and placed it over his arm asking, "Would madam like some lemongrass lemonade?" as he went to pour a glass, I answered, "No thank you kind sir, I would prefer a small rum punch please." Tim looked concerned," Jaz, I really think you should take it easy, remember the nurses orders." Ah yes, I remember, no alcohol for today.

Forceful in my approach, I replied, "Nonsense I am fine, stop fussing, and bring the rum." "Just one then," he sighed, disappearing inside, returning with a small jug of rum punch. "Much better, thank you" I replied taking a sip and savouring the moment. A growing happiness fell on his face, he liked to please me, his gaze held the promise of protection and more. He really was so handsome, from the depth of his eyes to his generous opinions to the touch of his hand upon mine. I loved the way his voice quickened when he sparkled with a new idea, or was so enjoying one of mine that he lost himself

241

for a moment and lowered the professional mask he wore for his work. I have relented, giving him my heart and keeping his safe, my mother will be so pleased if I can keep hold of him.

The food smelt delicious as he brought it outside, it was a Picadillo, a friends recipe, made from chicken with a tomato sauce base and then raisins, green olives and lots of spices. Tim had prepared some coconut rice to go with it and there was a traditional rum cake with a coconut cream for dessert, bought obviously. As we tucked in, our conversation was alive with the adventure of our dive and its outcome, his work, my work, Goldie and Leroy's engagement and of course the fact that our holiday on the Island was nearly over.

As we were just finishing our last mouthfuls of dessert when Goldie and Leroy arrived "Yuh luk suh much betta empress Duh yuh feel criss?" She shouted as they made their way towards us carrying a brown paper bag. "I do, so much better." "Mi hab brought doubles," she said as she plopped the bag in front of me. "Oh lovely, more food, thanks, we will be huge soon, maybe save them for tomorrow if that's ok?" She giggled with an innocent kind of mischief.

Doubles were invented originally for the poor as a staple diet, I had had them before and loved them. Basically they are a sandwich made from homemade dough, which then you pat down into two flatbreads, fry them and fill with curried chickpeas, they are then dipped into a pepper sauce and green mango pickle before taking a bite, they clear your head that's for sure.

Tim took the bag to put in the fridge, "Lets go inside," he said as he glanced at Leroy. I took the plates through to the kitchen and Goldie turned herself into a whirling dervish and before you knew it, had cleared away the mess to reveal the kitchen work surfaces once more.

Leroy walked into the kitchen, there was something different about him tonight, a little hippy-ish, he moved for all the world like he was walking to his own beat, literally, like there was music playing in his head. There was a softness to his appearance, a kind of warmth married to a shyness, the look of an honest soul who had fallen in love. For some reason he had on jeans and a duffle coat, as he removed the coat, wincing slightly, he revealed a tight t-shirt with his muscles popping right out, I had never noticed him like that before.

He returned a smile as he caught my admiring glance, "Is it feeling better now?" I nodded towards his shoulder, "What" he replied, "your shoulder," I said nodding in his shoulder direction again, "oh, yes, sorry, it's a bit sore but I can't bear the sling, it prevents you doing lots of things." "Isn't that the point of it?" Tim laughed, I looked at Goldie, "Wah? He calls di shots Nah mi, Mia feem duggu-duggu slave." She uttered quickly, revealing far too much information, not that any of us were going to accuse her of anything.

Our little chirps of laughter came in bursts, bringing smiles to our faces, until laughter filled the room. I collected an aspirin and a glass of water to remove a slight headache that was coming my way and sat down next to Leroy, "I told you it wasn't a good idea to drink rum," Tim said, watching me swallow the aspirin, "yes, yes, alright," I replied, I hate it when he has the upper hand.

Goldie poured fresh juice into clean glasses and emptied a bag of crisps into a heap on the table, "I think I owe a proper explanation to both of you," Leroy said. "Wi kno yuh a spies Dat a hul news," Goldie interrupted. Leroy kissed her hand, "We have told you both independently about our work and you have done well to keep it secret from each other." "Wi hab passed di tess." Goldie interrupted again. "Shh, be quiet Goldie," I nudged her as I said it. Tim smirked as Leroy seemed oblivious and continued, "I have been here for about four years investigating computer hacking attempts that take place on national telecommunication devices as well as the banking infrastructure." Tim interrupted, "We met each other by chance, chasing after the same people, Ed and Tilly were top of Leroy's wanted list too. Leroy nodded, "Yes, so after a brief consultation with our bosses and the authorities it was decided to cohort our investigation, two heads are better than one and all that, but we became good friends as well as colleagues."

Goldie stuffed her mouth with some crisps, they were the most nosiest crunchy munch of the night, she sipped the juice and said, "Enuh yuh a di knights eena fi wi day an nite Di ones dat mek ih safe fah wi Wi tink yuh a courageous an ih a bikaaz ah ahuu yuh a dat wi hab fallen eena luv Yuh an di duggu-duggu, well." Leroy laughed awkwardly slightly embarrassed, Tim looked confused, "I actually have absolutely no idea what you have just said, he uttered.

I laughed and told her, "Goldie speak English for once." She raised her eyebrows, giggled and finished another mouthful of crisps before speaking. "What I said was, You are the knights in our day and night, the ones that made it safe for us, you are courageous and it is because of who you are, we have fallen in love you and the sex well." Tim blushed for the first time. "That is why you are better off not knowing what she says half the time," Leroy uttered before continuing. "Neither of us meant to put you in any danger and we are truly sorry for what happened, no-one could have foreseen those circumstances, but nothing about this whole charade with Ed and Tilly has been truly predictable."

Tim nodded in agreement. "Ed, is well and truly out of the picture, although it would have been good to take him alive, however, it is what it is and he will be fish food by now, there wasn't much meat on him in the first place." "Won't you have to be tried at a Court of Justice? You know prosecuted for murder?" I asked. "No, not at all, quite the contrary," Tim replied. Leroy looked at me and smiled before saying, "Just like James Bond, we really do have a licence to kill with immunity granted by the government or government agency in order for us to initiate the use of lethal force in the delivery of our objectives, we can justify it as self-defence or the protection of life." You can tell they had read the book of spy rules after that sentence!

Tim smirked, "We are an odd bunch, we learn to live rootless, able to transplant ourselves into the strangest of situations and still appear as normal as anyone else, well I do anyway." He nudged Leroy, who said, "Hey dude, we've been at this game so long we can only approximate what being normal is, we protect the 'normals,' it's what we do."

Goldie singled handedly finished the packet of crisps and piped up changing the subject, "What about marriage?" she asked "What about it?" Tim said with a slight upward curve of his mouth. I needed to ask this, to gain Tims response, so glared at Goldie not to say anything, she got the message."As a spy are you get married or maintain a serious stable relationship?" Leroy and Tim both looked at each other and then at us in turn. "Sure you can, Goldie and I plan on getting married soon, but she wants a ring first." Leroy replied. "What about us?" I asked gazing at Tim, he made eye contact but cleverly avoided the question and changed tactics. "We still need to find Tilly? Hopefully that's the easy bit, she will wonder where Ed is, she can't be without him for long, she is too heavily reliant on him. Word will soon get around that he is dead, she will want to make sure and then focus her efforts on revenge for his killer." "Isn't that dangerous?" I questioned, "No way, Tilly is a pussycat to take down, its catching her that is the problem." Tim replied. Seeing my frustration at Tim's apparent lack of commitment, Goldie said in English for Tim's benefit," "Don't you think she will suit a wedding ring of white gold the best? It will go with her cool complexion and her neutral clothes." She winked at me, but again it fell on deaf ears.

I started to fidget and my eyes kept flicking to my phone on the kitchen top, my attention span was wavering, I could feel my face sag into boredom, Goldie tried to steer the conversation back around to affairs of the heart, "Tim, when you and Jaz get married can you tell her about your missions? Leroy said he will tell me about his." Tim leant over and kissed me on the cheek uttering, "We are usually allowed to tell our wives where we work but can't discuss every detail of what we do, we can talk about general areas we are working on and what we do on a day to day basis, you never know, Jaz, you might be able to help me find the solutions." Well, it was not a complete 'yes we will get married' but in a roundabout way, I knew we would get there eventually.

Chapter 35

By now it was getting late, my headache had all but disappeared but I was quite tired, we left the crispy crumb mess on the kitchen table and retired to our respective rooms for a good nights sleep.

I snuggled into Tim once more, stroking his chest, "How come I haven't been to your offensive safe house yet and Leroy has taken Goldie on lots of occasions? Don't you love me enough?" I asked. I felt him sigh, "Jaz, I thought you were tired?" "I am, but I just want to know why." He sighed again, "Its got nothing to do with how much I love you, I am a higher ranking than Leroy and can recruit other agents, sometimes I have to set up a refuge for defecting spies in that house, so I just have to be more careful, I can't be seen taking people in there just in case. How about I break some rules and take you there tomorrow evening? We can stay the night if it makes you happy." "Promise?" I answered, "Promise, now please go to sleep and I do love you a lot." He whispered.

I looked up at him and bit my lip, his eyes looked deeply into my mine, my breathing became softer, my pensive look melting into a smile as my body squirmed just a little to get closer to him. "Tim what about us?" I asked as he continued to gaze at me. He stroked my face, "Oh, Jasmine." I smiled, "I know I am sorry, but do you think we will we get married?" He smiled a sweet smile with all the love I'll ever need, but said, "Not if we don't get some sleep, stop talking, close your eyes and go to sleep, it's late." "Will we?" I said propping myself up on him, I know I was being annoying and we were both tired, but I needed to know that he wanted to stay with me, that I was worth something to him. It was important, I wanted to see if he'd risk his single spy life for me. He leaned his head forward and kissed me, our lips locked together in a burst of passion, the world itself ceased to exist, blurred and indistinct as an impressionist masterpiece. He still hadn't answered the question, I hoped it was just that he needed to sleep and maybe the courage to ask so I needed the patience to wait.

Despite our tiredness, a spark of passion had been kindled and before I had chance to think or say anything further, we were naked, our skin moving softly together silk on finest silk. I felt his hand enter from below moving fast, our tongues entwined in a kiss, and then he was in control making my breathing change with every thrust, my moans timed to his body. The cool room now felt considerably warmer! Tim stopped momentarily before kissing me again from my breasts to my stomach, his hands light, he began to lick me and use his fingers all at once, watching my reaction, feeling how my legs moved, watching my body writhe. He told me he is going to make me beg for it, I just let out a moan, unable to articulate a proper response. I couldn't move even if I tried, his fingers have short circuited my mind in the best possible way and it is so hard to hold back and make the moment last. Isn't it always the way, so caught between the intoxication of the climax and extending a moment we never want to end, but this just keeps on getting better, a pure night of passion is just what the doctor ordered.

Afterwards, we fell back on the pillows, perspiring, panting, we were so relaxed, we both yawned and snuggled into each other, two spoons in one bed. Falling asleep in his arms was my safe place, my cocoon, two souls mingling in the quiet moment of stillness.

In my dreamland ideas of love were transformed from pure imagination into real magic. I dreamt that I was stuck in a maze with seventeen ways to go, I became confused as to which path to take, so I just sat there all day, completely lost, resigning myself to the fact that I would never get out. Just then gardener Tim appears, his shears slung over his left shoulder as he makes his way heroically through the maize stems and onto the still sunlit path. I was in awe of such a magnificent species, nothing was going to stop him until he reached me. I sat staring at this adonis as he gazed lovingly, towering over me. Smiling, he beckoned me to follow, I stood up and wrapped my arms around his loose cotton shirt. He picked me up with one swoop and carried me to safety, a gentle giant, walking right through the stems below him.

These days, since meeting Tim, sleep was almost as active as being awake, for in my gentle slumber I dreamed a new and better world and my future with him. He was the best thing that had ever happened to me, always speaking about the situation with logic, confirming his emotional reality before seeking to expand his perspective to the needs and views of others. He was a reliable and safe place for me to anchor my heart, to feel that my soul was nurtured and valued. He was the strongest and softest person I had ever met, one who realised that true power is lifting others up. That's the power of what love is, rather than suppressing and controlling its elevating and educating.

Chapter 36

I woke early the following morning and watched Tim sleeping, he looked quite cute, I am so attracted to him, it is an intoxication, he is my soul mate and fierce protector too and even before we speak, the attraction between us is a tangible thread in the air. I kissed him on his cheek, feeling his warmth at my lips, as I did he opened his eyes and held my gaze. "Good morning" he said, lifting his hand to stroke my face. He kissed me, it was the sweet way we began, a little tickle that opened our hearts, that's all we ever needed to connect, Tim and me, often no words, if we were mute our love would be just the same.

We were rudely interrupted by a knock on the door, our moment of calm shattered. Goldie's dulcet tones echoed "Jaz, Tim, A yuh both up? Leroy an mi a cum eena." Oh no, that's all we need first thing in the morning, "Just give us two minutes," I replied as we quickly made ourselves respectable, just in the nick of time, as they literally counted two minutes and then strolled in. Goldie was prancing around the bed practicing a royal wave before she eventually walked towards us. "Luk at dis ring Leroy an mi a engaged." She was so excited, she thrust her hand forward as she plonked herself down on the bed beside me, I took her hand. Tim smiled as he climbed out of bed to make room and shook Leroy by the hand. "Congratulations old fella," he uttered sincerely.

I looked at the ring, "Goldie it is beautiful, congratulations," she giggled, "Mi will bi Mrs Hamilton soon," she said taking off the ring and handing it to me for closer inspection. I twirled it around, "Gwaan try eh pan," she said squealing, "no Goldie, it's yours, I'm not trying it on, it looks very expensive." "Nah knock aff." She, gazing lovingly at Leroy, "Thank you Goldie, it cost me at least a months wages." Leroy replied raising his eyebrows towards Tim as he smiled.

It was an elegant platinum engagement ring, three strands woven together to make one, almost as if they had grown into unity over time, housing two emeralds, neatly entwined into the ring itself, I can see why he chose it for her, it fitted who she was. I kissed her on the cheek and we hugged as I handed the ring back to her. "I am so pleased for you, Mr and Mrs Hamilton to be, you are both made for each other." I said as our embrace loosened. "Yuh an Tim nex. How bout ih Tim A yuh gwine put ah ring pan har fingga?" I nudged her and mouthed shut her up, blushing a pink champagne colour. I didn't want Tim to think I was keeping on at him. However, our holiday would end in a week, I would return to St Kitts and Nevis and who knows what will happen to him and I then? Long distance relationship, I should wonder, oh well. Tim moved awkwardly to the bathroom, uttering "what will be, will be!" I just had to try and be patient, but it was growing increasingly more difficult.

By now we had all mustered in the kitchen and were eating breakfast, "You know what we didn't do yesterday?" Tim said as he took a slice of watermelon. "What!" We all replied at once, he smirked as if there was something cheeky about to explode in my general direction, instead he said. "I promised Jaz I would take her to see the flamingos fly, let's go there this morning and then go for a bar meal, do you feel up to it Jaz?" Goldie and I nodded in agreement,"Yes I feel fine today, thanks." "Is it really worth it? The look out I mean?" Leroy commented, "They are elusive creatures, you and I haven't seen one since we have been here Tim!" "I know, but the ladies can see the salt water pond if not, it will do us good to get out." "A fun packed mawning den!" Goldie replied sarcastically nudging me, I grinned, we cleared up and the general consensus was to give it a go anyway.

The Flamingo Lookout is basically a wooden structure built on the edge of a large salt water pond on the West side of the island and is alleged to host a large flock of flamingos. The locals here believe that they are making a comeback and eleven chicks have hatched this year so far. There used to be flamingo hunters who patrolled the pond, killing them for their tender meat and feathers until the dumb (or not so dumb) birds got wise to this and fled so until recent years they were a scarce sight on the Island.

As we arrived at the lookout and climbed the wooden steps with our binoculars in our hands, it was quite clear that in fact Leroy could be correct. We stood poised on the top platform, peering across the lake but there was not a single flamingo to be seen. Suddenly Goldie shrieked, "Deh Ova deh suh Luk towards di trees at di bac addi pond." She pointed as her excitement took hold, everyone strained their eyes, looking through the binoculars and eventually four pink blobs appeared in the distance. I was slightly disappointed, but we knew the probability of not seeing them was high.

Tim leaned in and put his arm around my waist. "I want you right now" he whispered, even with the lightest of his touches, he made my body want to roar. I giggled, trying to maintain some decorum and dropped the binoculars, luckily Goldie was quick and in one swift move, managed to catch them before they hit the deck. "Everyone seen enough? Its eleven forty-five, everyone want to head to the beach bar" Tim asked, removing his hands from my person, his ability to stop on a dime is without rival, mmhm, power and control with a touch of silk, whatever is a woman to do?

We piled back in to his Audi and headed the short distance to the bar, stopping for a brief moment at the grocery store for some provisions. It was the kind of shop that housed tins that would be considered antiques in England, the gems of times past, like spam fritters for example, the delivery from Tortola had not yet arrived, so our selection was very limited. We wandered about, looking for anything that we needed, then, Leroy had a sudden brainwave, "Lets get what we need from the beach bar, they will help us out for a couple of days until the next delivery arrives, it will be better than here," Whole heartedly none of us disputed that.

Luckily Leroy used his persuasive charm on the beach bar cook, Marta, she donated a food parcel for us, he was quite cunning, but then I suppose spies have to be, as a way of survival, these con artists make up their own laws. Between him and Tim they also managed to persuade Marta to do a picnic lunch for us and Marta did not let us down.

Marta saw a brilliance in food with its potential to make people feel better, she wanted everyone to know how sublime taste was, it was simply a mixture of the ordinary. It was her genius at play, I guess that's why we called it her 'culinary magic,' joking that her spoon was a wand carved from a spirit tree. Her food fed body and soul, brought smiles and made bonds that made everything and everyone feel better. She appeared from the kitchen with our salt fish and egg spring rolls, fried plantain, jerk chicken and plenty of lemonade lemongrass. Two large brown bags laden with food and a picnic with style.

Marta was a wonderful woman, I had not seen her until now, she was pink in the face with blonde bangs pasted to her forehead from either steam or sweat. She was child-like in proportion but clearly an adult, from the crows feet around her eyes, I would say she was probably forty-something. She asked Leroy sarcastically, if he intended doing any more bar work sometime soon. "Yeh yeh, Marta soon, I have been injured in the line of duty," came his dismissive comment. After the exchange, Marta made a small bow and retreated, the smile vanishing from her diminutive features and her pace stretching out wider than it looked comfortable for her.

Tim put the bags in the car as the rest of us walked about a hundred yards to the beach for lunch, with our picnic, the new plan, apparently, instead of eating at the bar.

We sat on the beach and tucked into our wonderful tasty lunch, laughing and joked with and at each other. In this easy going camaraderie we had ignited the kind of friendship that will be part of our onward lives forever. I looked at the white sand stretching for miles, my mind wandering off, this holiday will come to an end in a weeks time, Goldie was settled and had firm plans, but what would happen to Tim and I? "Do you fancy a stroll?" Tim asked.

We decided that it was a good idea, I didn't feel like doing much today and Leroy still had stitches to care for, so we strolled, talking, holding hands, linking arms and beach combing. I loved doing this, it was a wild and random treasure hunt without a map or compass, just the rhythm of the waves. I found a soft unusual shape of driftwood, bleached by the salt and the sun, my mind turned to a use for this piece, a simple candle holder, possibly.

Before we took stock of things, we had walked for miles, collecting bits of the beach and now had to walk back, it was nice to just relax in each others company

Chapter 37

We met Goldie and Leroy back at Tim's car, they had packed up and we waiting, well other wise engaged with their usual antics. We drove the short way back to the villa, chattering and laughing. Leroy's truck was still parked outside covered in sand, it was as if there had been a sand storm whilst we had been away, very strange! We took the food parcel and went inside, I was beginning to feel quite excited, it was my night to be at the offensive safe house or 'Ouch' as they both referred to it.

As I opened the door, I trampled on a piece of paper, I picked it up, thinking it was from Lourdes, asking if we needed anything, she was a great host. But it wasn't. I stood there dumfounded and motionless, Tim nudged me in further, "What is it? Can we all come in and close the door?" I didn't know what to say so just handed him the piece of paper. In extremely bad handwriting it said and I quote; "You bastards, you killed Rex, your sins have found you out, we are your worst nightmare, we are coming for you, you will all meet a sinister demise." Tim looked at Leroy, "What" he said as Tim handed him the note, Goldie stood over his shoulder reading it." "Jaz, Goldie, pack everything in your suitcase as quick as you can, we are all going to Ouch, it is no longer safe for you both to stay here." Tim said with an insistence in his voice.

Leroy nodded in agreement and repacked the food in the bags. "Fast as you can." He uttered.

Goldie and I did as we were told, as we threw everything into our cases quickly, I saw the look of concern on Goldie's face, I'm scared too, I could feel those bad memories wanting to invade my confidence and erode the person I have built since Iberville. "Goldie, we will be safe, our spy radars will make sure that." I uttered trying to convince myself. She smiled and replied, 'Heroes nuh dread Dem buckle up an brace themselves fah impact." She was right of course, but despite her bravado, I knew deep down she was a frightened as I was.

We returned with our suitcases, everything squashed inside within an inch of its life, I'm surprised we managed to get the lids closed. Leroy took our backpacks from us and said, "We will go in Tim's car and leave mine here, that way Tilly might think we are nearby and still staying here." Yuh think dis a Tilly's wuk?" Goldie asked. "Yes, let's get out of here now." Tim replied taking our cases out to his car, checking before stepping outside. "I thought you needed to catch her and it will be easy." I muttered as we got in the car, "We do and we will, but our way, not hers. We will splat her like a fly, you'll see." Leroy replied.

Tim drove us to the 'Ouch,' discussing options with Leroy in the front, whilst Goldie and I kept our heads down chatting quietly about trivia. "You two ok back there? Remember to stay out of sight as best you can." Tim said peering in his drivers mirror at us. Leroy turned his head to check, "Yes they are both fine."

Arriving at the safe house we turned onto a driveway of imprinted concrete, a shade of grey with a hint of blue, its edges lined with trees and drove up to a garage. The mansion looked different somehow, rejected, although that is not the best word to describe it. As I peered through the car window, close up it looked like it had been abandoned for sure, but as if there was a pride in its lasting, a sense of a strength that could be renewed at any time. Tim opened the garage door remotely and drove the car straight in, the garage closed behind us. With another flick a light came on and Leroy opened an inner door, showing us into a large room whilst Tim retrieved our cases from the boot of his car.

Goldie stood in the middle of the room, "Yah wi a den Jus wah yuh hab bin deh wait fah," she smiled, looking at me, Leroy raised his eyebrows, "stop teasing princess." The room was quite odd, large with polished wooden floors, two red leather sofas, a table, bookcase and a huge fireplace which dominated the room, there were no other doors or stairs. As I walked around the room, which took all of two-seconds, I said, not wishing to sound rude, is this it?" Tim smiled, "Possibly," he replied taking my hand," Goldie snorted, "Yuh will si empress Dis a di Bond moment," what on earth was she on about?

With that Tim led me past the huge fireplace towards the bookcase. I couldn't help but notice that on the richly carved mantel stood an exquisite porcelain box, heart-shaped, covered with china forget-me-nots, a silver drinking-cup, a small oval portrait of a beautiful young woman, framed in a richly chased gold, the inner rim set round with pearls and next to it was a blue pitcher. Tim has very poor tase if he thinks these things look nice, but then I don't suppose he had much to do with the interior.

We stood in front of the bookcase and, like the rest of the room, it was just something else that looked like it had been picked at random to decorate the room. It was old and basic but somehow, it still had integrity, the wood was straight and it hugged the wall, on closer inspection I could see it had quite a few scratches. Tim began to playful search for a book, running his fingers along their spines. "What are you looking for, are we just going to sit and read?" I asked him, getting slightly impatient, he had promised me a good time in a nice house and this was very far from the truth. "A book called Frenchman's Creek by Daphne Du Maurier's" he answered, ignoring the second part to the question I had asked.

Exasperated, I extracted the book from the shelf, it was plainly obvious that it was right in front of him. "Here it is," I replied as I removed the book from the shelf and handed it to him. Stunned and shocked I stepped back, as with ease the bookshelf parted into two halves revealing a portal to something new. "Si James Bond Nyam yuh heart out!" Goldie exclaimed, I smiled, looking at Tim, wow, totally amazing, all my exasperations disappeared instantly, "Well go on, the only way to find out what's in there is to step forward." Tim aid gaining from ear to ear.

Metal stairs twirled upwards towards a skylight and a balcony grew from the top looking down over the room below. The metal had a patina of ocean greens and blues, or perhaps it was more the early evening light that softened it, either way it was beautiful. If I stood on the balcony I could be Juliet and Tim my Romeo, gosh this was stunning, from what I could see, wooden doors led off in different directions, probably the bedrooms and bathroom, but I had plenty of time to investigate later.

Downstairs was one huge room, completely open plan. Pastel sofas adorned with scatter cushions, just enough order, just enough chaos, true perfection, a large wooden table and chairs and a modern functional kitchen. All were equally pieces of great art, alive with colours that spoke of the ocean, wave-kissed lands and rocks, they sang of the movement of the water and echoed its sound and aroma. The room was lit in lamp-light glow, electric rays spreading like petals on the walls, illuminating the sweet-toffee browns of the wooden floor, then bouncing onto a giant redwood tree which stood tall in the centre of the room, a resident of that natural place.

Tim had been correct in his description when he said that the house was born from an architect's dream plan. The giant arched windows at the back showed the sea below and you could just about make out that this house lived and breathed in the rock formations, its foundations perfectly sound and set to stand for generations to come. "Well, go on Goldie, show Jaz around whilst Tim and I get your things upstairs," Leroy instructed, wincing slightly as he picked up one of the cases. He never complained of his injury, but I am sure it was still quite sore, noticing that I had seen him wince he went on to say, "Its ok, I will take the stitches out tomorrow, it won't feel so tight then." "He seh mi can dweet wid fi im pen knife." Goldie joked as she took my hand and continued to steer me darting in different directions, ensuring I didn't miss anything.

The clean lines brought a calmness and peacefulness to the house, it was so modern, an ode to science and art, woven together in such beauty. It could have been beamed there from the Starship Enterprise, yet it felt like a home, albeit from the outside it was a complete contrast.

As the daylight continued to dwindle I could feel a tension growing in me. Tim filled the kettle to make coffee, "Are you ok?" He asked, putting on some music as the kettle boiled and clicked off. I smiled, "Yes, sorry, it's just that," Tim hugged me, "it's just what?" he said, "Something doesn't feel right," he looked at me in complete bewilderment, "what doesn't feel right? You are completely safe here, no one can get to us." "I know, sorry, I will be ok." I said trying to force a relaxed smile.

Tim poured the coffee, "Jaz, you know, we create our own roadmaps of survival and each is unique because we are unique as are our experiences and circumstances. In being okay with not being okay, we get to open up instead of closing down. Our worries fade from red to silver, we share everything with each other and inside we begin to roar." I think I understood what he was saying, slightly embarrassed I nodded and smiled. "Another sermon? Tim, my man." Leroy uttered as he and Goldie sat down for coffee.

Chapter 38

We were all quite happily enjoying one another's company, sitting together on the sofas and drinking coffee. Goldie was acting the fool again attempting to lighten the mood from the dark images I had managed to create. When my mobile rang, I looked at it as a silence fell on the room and all eyes focused on me, "Its Lourdes," I said, "answer it and put it on speaker phone," Tim replied, I did as I was told.

I could sense of tension in Lourdes voice as she spoke and there was quite a bit of background noise to contend with. "Jasmine," "Yes," I replied looking at Tim in case in needed to prompt me. "Thank goodness. Is Goldie, Leroy and Tim with you?" "They are." The concern in her voice seemed to ease a little, she had got to know us all quite well. "Thank goodness," she repeated before continuing, "Jaz, I need to speak to Tim." "I'm here mum, are you alright?" Came his reply. I looked at Goldie and mouthed the word "Mum," I couldn't believe it. "Um Tim, there was this terrible crashing sound and when I went to investigate, Leroy's car had exploded into a fireball. I called the fire service and they are here now, but the flames have continued to flare up in the evening sky as if they challenged the heavens to stop their consumption, they have spread to the villa, its burning Tim. They can't get it under control yet, everything is nearly ashes, the fire service are trying to stop the fire spreading further, the destruction is terrible, my business." Lourdes fell silent.

There complete silence, as Lourdes then burst into tears, we could feel the enormity of her sobbing through the phone, it was as if she could bleed an ocean through her eyes, she sniffed. "Sorry, they think it was the result of an arsonist," she blew her nose. "Mum, we are on our way, we will be with you in minutes. Who is with you?" "Just Marta and the fire service thankyou darling, I will see you soon." She answered before the phone clicked into silence.

We all looked at one another, "This is Tilly's work," we all remarked at the same time, "bitch," Goldie commented and I was inclined to agree with her. Piling into Tim's car as fast as we could, I know we all felt the same, shocked and disgusted that she could stoop so low and destroy us through Lourdes. "Good job, we moved you out of there, otherwise we would have more than building ashes on our hands." Tim said, driving at warp speed to the villa. " Wah duh yuh mean?" Goldie questioned, "Our bodies," I replied squeezing her hand, she looked thoroughly shocked at the thought, "Wi cud bi dead," she said, "exactly," I answered her, wiping away a rogue tear.

Nearing the villa the black night and more stars than the imagination can ever conjure was broken by the flashing brilliant blue lights of the emergency vehicles, a contrast to that of the roaring red and orange of the flames still trying to take hold. We spotted Marta first then Lourdes, she was standing like a broken child behind a taped barrier that had been erected to keep the growing crowd of onlookers a safe distance from the fire. Locals had come from nearby to be with Lourdes and Marta.

We walked up and hugged her, even now as we looked at the burning villa, the heat of the flames still spitting at us, it felt surreal, "They are trying to stop it spreading next door," she said releasing us but retaining a firm grip on Tim, Looking at him for the support and to know it will be alright in the end, he could fix this."Lourdes, I don't know what to say, except we are truly sorry, nothing we say is going to make up for this." I said. She tried to smile but her eyes were red from smoke and tears, this was her life, her bread and butter, a place of many memories and to watch it burn was really hard. Tim hugged her tightly then kissed her, "Mum, I promise I will sort this, I know that this is the worst night of your life, but the person who did this has no power over me. They are a tyrant to others and a prisoner to their own warped beliefs. Their dominance and cowardly need to do this at any cost is short lived, I am truly sorry, it wasn't meant to happen like this, it will be fixed and rebuilt in no time."

Lourdes nestled into Tim and kissed him on the cheek, she sniffed again and Leroy handed her a clean pressed handkerchief from his shorts pocket. "My business, that awful girl Tilly, you kill her so it hurts, Tim." Lourdes uttered starting to cry again. Tim embraced her tighter,"Shh, mum, it will be ok, she came for us, she thought we were in there, I will make sure all this is rectified quickly, we will get the insurance and builders sorted within a couple of days," he really was a true gentleman. But wait a minute, does Lourdes know Tilly, how does she know it was her? Why didn't Tim say Lourdes was his mother, was it to protect her? So many questions, but right now with all these emotion let loose was not the time to look or ask for answers.

By the time the fire service had done their job and dampened down the smouldering ashes to stop the fire spreading to the neighbouring villas, a new light of day was dawning. Our once beautiful villa now looked skeletal, as if an artist had sketched it in charcoal, the fire had taken all it could, yet the walls of stone remained firm but black. As I stared at the charred remains of the car and villa, I believed every word Tim had promised Lourdes, I could see it in my mind a beautiful new villa on the site, the picture simply needed completing. The rebuild would be a phoenix dwelling, what is charred will be soothed with plaster and made pretty once more with a little patience and a lot of love.

We made sure Lourdes had everything she needed and then all returned to our respective properties for some well earned rest as we were all tired from the nights events and dirty from the smoke and dust. She dint want Tim to stay with her or come with us, she said her and Marta would be fine. "Poor Lourdes," I said as we got into Tim's car for the short journey back to their house, Goldie and I in the back, Leroy in the front. "She will be fine, good job we moved you both, it could have been a very different story otherwise." Tim said softly. Goldie and I sighed, the realisation of a different outcome was now very real in our minds. "Cheer up ladies, we are all fine, you are both fine, we promised we will always keep you safe and we will." Leroy said turning to face us, we both looked at each other, believing this to be true.

Arriving at the 'Ouch' house we went through the same rigmarole as we had previously to get inside, then we all hit the showers completely exhausted and although it was almost morning, we fell asleep together in each others arms, despite Leroy saying we could not sleep for long as it would disrupt the whole day.

Leroy had set his watch alarm to ring with the sounds of nature, well birdsong for the most part, there was a soothing quality to waking up that way or so he thought. As Goldie and I opened our eyes, Leroy and Tim were already up, warming up as they called it, stretching and flexing their muscles, it also helped their thought processes apparently. I just yawned and stretched as the vibrant glow of a new day glistened though the window. It was already eleven thirty am, so not entirely the best nights rest as we didn't go to bed until four o'clock.

We got up and attended to our ablutions, ate a late breakfast and generally made a nuisance of ourselves with Leroy, as

Tim was on a silver mobile phone, which I hadn't seen before, sorting out things for Lourdes. "Its a special spy phone," Leroy joked, seeing me glance at Tim, Goldie laughed too, "yuh tink dat's bad, aal tia appliances a spy tools, de vacuum cleanah has been collecting dut fah years!" She said in absolute hysterics, "Goldie, that has to be one of the worst jokes I have heard in a while." I replied, "Sorry, I didn't get that, what did she say?" Tim asked, replacing the mobile in a drawer. "It was a bad joke, If you think your microwave is spying on you, then you won't be surprised to know your vacuum cleaner has been gathering dirt for years!" Tim grinned, "Yes that is quite bad, do you mind if we nip to see Lourdes and then would you like to do a bit of kite surfing, we can grab a sandwich or some fruit to take with us?" Before I answered Leroy piped up, "Ouch Goldie, that actually hurt quite a bit."

Goldie had him stripped to his shorts and was digging away with his penknife to remove the last few remaining stitches from his knife wound. She giggled, "Hush fi mi baby love, all dun" she replied, and I have to say despite his trauma, there was not a drop of Leroy's blood expelled. "Mmhm, not sure, I am happy to give it a go if everyone else wants to so it, Kite surfing I mean." "I will give it a miss, but will gladly watch, just in case of the shoulder wound." Leroy uttered, "Mi wud lakka tuh duh ah bit ah both Kite surfing an a mek out wid fi mi lover pan di sand he a such ah gud." Leroy kissed Goldie to quieten her before she went to far and said anything further that could embarrass or incriminate him, she was hopeless, far to open on the affairs of the heart!

We cleared away the debris leaving the place spick and span and hiding any evidence of us being there, just in case. We all then climbed into Tims car for the drive back to the remains of our burnt down villa and the shell of Leroy's truck.

Chapter 39

The smell of smoke was still heavy in the morning air, a strong stench that caught in your throat and felt like it was polluting your lungs. The villa was gone, even the walls that had remained last night were now flattened, it was just a pile of blackened ashes ready to be a new creation, the singed plants around would recover as would the blacked earth they were baked in. We had to move on now, there was no going back, but the memories of the great holiday we had will live within our hearts and souls forever and our burnt down villa will rise again just as Tim had promised.

Lourdes met us as we arrived, although devastated at the loss of one of her villas and the affect on her business, she was thankful that we were all safe. Tim had arranged for a team of people to arrive, they were already busying themselves with cleaning the other villas of smoke damage and a groundworks team were also clearing away the debris from the ashes. All those little details that Tim had sorted created expanding pockets of love and helpfulness gave me a certain sense of warmth, a fullness to share.

Tim took Lourdes by the arm, "How are you mum? Do you need anything? Everything is sorted, rebuilding will commence very soon and will be covered by the insurance, you will have a new villa within two months." Tim said smiling, pretty good going for the Caribbean, normally it would take longer than the UK, once they had deliberated, smoked and drank, nothing normally happened this fast, Tim was amazing at everything, well, except in the kitchen department, but I could work with that. "Thank you so much my darling, you are a superstar, I love you so much" Lourdes replied as she kissed him on the cheeks, "you are both very lucky to have found one another," she said glancing at me and winking. I was becoming increasing confused at the situation, had Tim told him we were dating, I want aware they were even related until recently when he called her mum. He certainly did not let on, when she delivered food to us before that. I looked at Goldie and whispered, "Does she know about us?" Goldie snorted, "Ah course silly Duh yuh nah tink ah son talks tuh feem mum."

We said our goodbyes once Tim had finalised a few further details with the works team and then drove to the other side of the Island for our kitesurfing. Tim knew the guy who owned the club, of course he did. As we stood beside the car, I grabbed Tim's arm, I couldn't help myself, I felt slightly angry that there were still secrets between us. "Tim have you told Lourdes about us? What have you told her?" The laughter that followed made me mellow a bit, "Jasmine, you are funny, where do you get your ideas from?" He asked, "Well," came my reply. He reached towards my face and touched my lips lightly with his, before the urge to kiss me took over, sending my mind into a sensual state of intoxication. "Of course I have, she's my mother, L have told her you are the girl of my dreams and will be by my side forever," he whispered. I stepped back stunned, staring into his eyes, at every turn there was a new surprise, is this is what my life was going to be like? "Oh my goodness," was all I could mutter, had he just said, we would be together forever? Nervous laughter broke free from both of us once more.

We strolled to the 'kite digs' as it was called and hired three, Leroy was adamant he would be fine watching. With that we collected everything we needed, changed into our wetsuits and headed to the beach. I had only had one lesson previously and as far as I was aware Goldie hadn't kite-surfed before, but after a few quick land lessons from Tim we were strapped into our harnesses and Goldie and I were as ready as we were ever going to be.

Taking our lead from the expert, we all headed off the beach, luckily there was only a gentle breeze today so it was not going to be too strenuous, I kept thinking of what Tim had taught us, "Catch the moment just right, if you have perfect timing, the wave will carry you on the ride of a lifetime." My kite caught the warm updrafts and I began to fly as if my kite had become my wings and I was a Manta Ray of the sky.

Bathed in the warm glow of the sun, a new sense of calm settled over me as I began to create a water-laced trail, riding on the top of the waves the sea offered up that day, it was so much fun, until I fell in. I repeated the action Tim had shown me and nearly managed it, but fell in more than I stayed on the board initially. It became quite difficult to get back up on the board and re-launch my kite the wetter and more tired I became, but I wanted to persevere.

Suddenly I caught a shout of alarm and looked towards the beach, now aware of Leroy waving his arms at Tim. I glanced over trying not to loose concentration and saw a person running towards Leroy on the beach. Tim flipped his kite around and headed for shore like something possessed, I hadn't realised these things could go so fast. I tried to follow in his wake with Goldie close behind me but at a slower speed.

As we arrived on the shoreline, the person was still running along the beach. It was Tilly and she had a knife in her hand, screaming like a banshee and running like the devil, "I'm going to twist your guts out." My heart began to quicken its beats, ready to explode and my mind became a scattered mess. I'm not particularly cool under pressure and could sense her malicious rage, I am sure she would take a twisted delight in my fear. "Get back in the water both of you, NOW," Tim shouted, we didn't argue, we didn't think, we just did as we were told, leaving our kite harness and kit on the sand and using the boards to paddle to a safe distance from which we could watch the drama unfold.

Tim reached Leroy before she got to him and together they tried to round her up, but she dropped the knife and veered into the ocean swimming like some crazed olympian swimmer towards us. "Git paddling Jaz." Goldie pushed my board and we both paddled into the surf, not our most elegant moves, but it would be more difficult for her to reach us in deeper water.

Just then a wave caught me and slightly tipped the board, I managed to correct it and stay on but was carried towards the beach. Then I felt a tug and looked behind me, oh my god, Tilly had reached me and had hold of the board, she started to grab at my feet, I screamed "Goldie, help me." Just as Goldie turned and was paddling towards me, something hit my board and I was pushed sideways still trying to cling on but failing miserably, I fell in. As my head bobbed up to the surface, a voice echoed in my ears, "Take my hand, one, two three, now," Tim scooped me up "put your arms around my neck and hold on for dear life," he uttered as the wind caught his parachute and we flew past Goldie, hitting something on the way. "Wah bout mi? Mi need help too," Goldie shouted. "Leroy is on his way, he will be with you…" before he could finish the sentence Leroy was there with Goldie, he seemed to have overcome his shoulder wound, but then faced with adversity, his training had kicked in and he had reacted to rescue his own damsel in distress.

Tim got me to the shoreline, "I have to go back for Tilly, Leroy will stay with you both," "Tim no please. Leave her, she will kill you, leave her." I begged him, but it fell on deaf ears and he was gone. As I watched him racing towards Tilly, I could see her bobbing up and down, her shouts echoed, "Help me, Jaz, help me" her voice was thin and distant. I screamed "Tim, Tilly," The three of us stood on the beach, "I'm going back to help Tim," Leroy shouted as he was in the water again, this time swimming, he was a strong swimmer, but the wind had got up and the waves were building on the tide.

Goldie and I could only watch, completely helpless. Just as Tim was about to reach her, the pull of the water became too strong. Her loud shouts and splashes ceased, her arms waved as she dipped below the waves and came up again in dramatic fashion, only to disappear completely as she slipped further from Tim's grasp. Tilly went under that final wave and never resurfaced despite the frantic search by our two heroes to find her, both diving again and again, she was gone. Gone to be with Ed.

As Tim and Leroy eventually swam back to us, I felt quite strange, melancholy, a sadness, a hopelessness but also a sense of freedom, Tilly has become a shadow of who she once was. In that cold stare as I looked out to sea, I bade her farewell, my face was passive, untroubled by her parting, she deserved it. "Criss riddance tuh rubbish." Goldie said, "You shouldn't speak ill of the dead, but this time I have to agree with you." I smiled back. Tim grabbed hold of me as he arrived back on the shore, there was something so heavenly about that tender moment as another burst of love is expressed, not caring that the water soaked through to chill my skin. It is a connection that shows the strength of the feeling, a mutual need, a rebellion against the elements.

We took ourselves back to the Ouch safe house, managed a quick supper and then disappeared into our respective rooms. "Passion a wah a did need now ah release ah all dat sexual tension." Goldie uttered, we all laughed but funnily enough no one disagreed.

Chapter 40

With our doors closed every pretence falls. The facade we showed the world melted away and all we wanted was to be intimate with each other. Tim's hand reached for mine and we interlocked as we kissed tentatively, passionately and tenderly. He pulled my top up over my head, little sparks of static danced and caressed my skin, his hands gently adding to a magical feeling that made me shiver with complete ecstasy. He gazed at me, unwavering and unabashed, my body held in anticipation of what was about to happen. I held my breath, I was floating on air into the clouds.

Every time he touched me, it was electric, all my knots became untied. I wanted this to never end, I wanted to be held for eternity in the arms I've grown so accustomed to. Then he kissed me, the world stopped, leaving just the two of us to wander the air together, his lips so passionate, so loving and the affection was off the scale as his warm hands roamed all over my now naked body leaving a trail of mischief in their wake. "Jaz, you are so beautiful" he whispered, his warm breath in my ear. I wrinkled my nose in protest. "Don't talk, just kiss me more." I whispered back. His lips gently brushed mine and I smelt his minty breath as our bodies pressed closer together. He slowly and gently massaged my breasts as we kissed, I arched my back and moaned softly into his mouth. I rolled my head to the side, my chest rose and fell dramatically under his influence. He smiled into the kiss as my fingers tugged at his short hair and my other hand smoothed his back. "Tim, I love you so much" I whispered as our eyes made contact. This is what falling in love was like, a story you never wanted to end, for so long I had yearned for this, and now I couldn't bare to lose it, I felt so complete.

He kissed me again, every kiss with a raw intensity, my breathing fastened along with my heart rate. Then before I could blink, our skin is moving softly together, I feel his hand searching below as our tongues entwined, and then he's inside me once again, changing my breathing with every thrust, he's licking and using his fingers all at once, watching my reaction, feeling how my body writhes. I had experienced this before as he tells me he's going to make me beg for it and I just let out a moan, unable to articulate a response. In seconds he's on me again, harder this time, just long enough to intoxicate my mind before stopping again. If it's begging he wants, he's going to have to stop long enough for my brain to catch up!

And then it was over as we lay back on the bed pulsing with a warm and happy numbness. I closed my eyes and drew in a lung full of air. In my quiet contemplation I thought about love, the people I cherished and all that was right with my life. I am definitely in love with Tim, he never leaves my mind mentally if not physically, it's just incomprehensible. He's my one stable force, my feelings for him are so strong it's overwhelming. I know we both feel the same, our love has no bounds nor length nor depth it's just absolute. I feels as though I'm in a dangerous fire, yet I'm completely safe at the same time.

My thinking was brought to an abrupt end as Tim hauled himself up off the bed and stood naked but serious before me."Jaz, I have something to say to you." I looked at him, oh dear I hope this wasn't the moment where my prince charming brings my fairytale to an abrupt end, the one that says I've had a great time, but your holiday is almost over and..etc. "Jaz, when I look into my heart, I see only you, if you can look into your heart and only see me, then we should spend the rest of our lives together, I want the story of our love to be only just beginning." I wobbled unceremoniously as I tried to stand up next to him. "Let's write our own happy ending, Jasmine Tormolis, will you marry me."

Before I could answer, he wrapped his arms around me and I let my head rest upon his chest, as he squeezed me tight. I arched backwards smiling at him,"Yes, yes, Timothy Meyers, I would love to marry you and spend the rest of my life by your side as your wife." With that he opened a small black box to reveal the most stunning engagement ring, a broad platinum band to the edges where it met a brilliant stripe of gold which housed the most magnificent sapphire, in all its celestial hues, accompanied by a dazzling diamond either side. Even in this darkness of the room, the ring had a sparkle to it, yet the sparkle it brought to my eyes was prettier still.

We were lost in paradise, he clutched his hands against my hips and pulled me in against his muscular body and I was weakened by his gentle seductive touch. I didn't care, nothing mattered, I was so happy. In the black of this Caribbean night there was more magic than a soul could ever realise it was possible to wish for.

My mobile beeped, damn, I thought I had turned it off, Tim picked it up and handed it to me. "How to kill the moment," he joked. I looked at it, "Jaz, sweetheart, what's wrong? Seriously I was only kidding." I showed him the text, it read, "I can't go on like this, you have to help me, come for me, please, Tilly." Tim was as stunned as I was, there was a moment of silence, you could see him thinking. "How can she possibly write this? She's dead, we watched her die, didn't we? You said she was dead, drowned, Tim, say something?"

Books by Vanessa Wrixon

Book Trilogy

Iberville
Book One
Iberville is the first of three in a murder mystery series, as small time English Journalist Jasmine Tormolis lands herself a new job in the Caribbean. From there on in, her life takes some twists and turns as she and some local fishermen discover a woman's body washed up on the beach. Despite the authorities best efforts to try and cover up, Jaz decides to do her own investigative work, which lands her in deep water and leads to a kidnapping and two further murders.

Temptation
Book Two
Continues to follow Jasmine Tormolis, but now as the boss of the Alise newspaper. Her and one of her reporters land themselves in hot water once more, when they are dealt a chance holiday to another Caribbean Island. Here they try to become helpful accomplishes to a couple of secret agents they meet. Once again they find themselves being hunted down for revenge until their killers are killed or are they?

Haunted
Book Three
Jasmine Meyers formally Tormolis, now resides at Iberville with her new husband. Her and her reporter Goldie remain inseparable and help each other renovating their new abodes. Both try their hand at detective work, but it's not as easy as it looks. Lady Amelie Wrexham, having once owned Iberville remains there as a ghost,

trying to perfect the art of haunting. However, failure to do this effectively gives her a chance opportunity to help Jaz catch and put her stalker behind bars for life. This is not without its problems when ghost tries to help.

Other Books by Vanessa Wrixon
Dark Nights
Camille Lavigne a French teacher at a secondary school, has arrived in England after a messy breakup. She finds her job frustrating to say the least. She becomes embroiled with a handsome man twelve years her junior, but despite a passionate steamy relationship, she is unaware of his dealings with the underworld and becomes the prime suspect in his murder, needing the help of her husband to bail her out.

Sowing the seed
Petra Defeu is on a stake out with her colleague. Having just moved into the area as a new detective, she hasn't quite got the measure of how things work and her colleagues can't yet get a measure of her. When she gets home from work one evening, her house has been burgled and there is a dead man in her kitchen. She then has to prove her innocence in a race against time before her colleagues or ruthless conspirators catch up with her.

Printed in Great Britain
by Amazon

11104333R00163